FOUR BLONDES

FOUR BLONDES

Candace Bushnell

Thorndike Press • Chivers Press
Waterville, Maine USA   Bath, England

This Large Print edition is published by Thorndike Press, USA and by Chivers Press, England.

Published in 2001 in the U.S. by arrangement with Grove Atlantic, Inc.

Published in 2001 in the U.K. by arrangement with Little, Brown & Company (UK).

U.S. Hardcover 0-7862-3151-3 (Basic Series Edition)
U.S. Softcover 0-7862-3152-1 (Basic Series Edition)
U.K. Hardcover 0-7540-1633-1 (Windsor Large Print)

The text of this Large Print edition is unabridged.
Other aspects of the book may vary from the original edition.

Set in 16 pt. Plantin by Susan Guthrie.

Printed in the United States on permanent paper.

British Library Cataloguing-in-Publication Data available

Library of Congress Cataloging-in-Publication Data
Bushnell, Candace.
    Four blondes / Candace Bushnell.
        p.   cm.
    ISBN 0-7862-3151-3 (lg. print : hc : alk. paper)
    ISBN 0-7862-3152-1 (lg. print : sc : alk. paper)
    1. Single women — Fiction.   2. Man-woman
relationships — Fiction.   3. Dating (Social customs) —
Fiction.   4. City and town life — Fiction.   5. New York
(N.Y.) — Fiction.   6. Sex customs — Fiction.   7. Large
type books.   I. Title.
PS3552.U8229 F68 2001
813'.54—dc21   00-066652

*For Anne Shearman Fell,
best friend and best blonde*

CONTENTS

NICE N'EASY

I

Janey Wilcox spent every summer for the last ten years in the Hamptons, and she'd never once rented a house or paid for anything, save for an occasional Jitney ticket. In the early nineties, Janey was enough of a model to become a sort of lukewarm celebrity, and the lukewarm celebrity got her a part ("thinking man's sex symbol") in one of those action movies. She never acted again, but her lukewarm celebrity was established and she figured out pretty quickly that it could get her things and keep on getting them, as long as she maintained her standards.

So every year around May, Janey went through the process of choosing a house for the summer. Or rather, choosing a man with a house for the summer. Janey had no money, but she'd found that was irrelevant as long as she had rich friends and could get rich men. The secret to getting rich men, which so many women never figured out, was that getting them was easy, as long as you didn't have any illusions about marrying them. There was no rich man in New York who would turn down regular blow jobs and entertaining company with no strings attached. Not that you'd want to marry any of these guys anyway. Every rich guy she'd been with had turned out to be weird — a freak or a pervert — so by the time Labor Day came around, she was usually pretty relieved to be able to end the relationship.

In exchange, Janey got a great house and, usually, the man's car to drive around. She liked sports cars the best, but if they were too sporty, like a Ferarri or a Porsche, that wasn't so good because the man usually had a fixation on his car and wouldn't let anyone drive it, especially a woman.

The guy she had been with last summer, Peter, was like that. Peter had golden-blond hair that he wore in a crew cut, and he was a famous entertainment lawyer, but he had a body that could rival any underwear model's. They were fixed up on a blind date, even though they'd actually met more than a dozen times at parties over the years, and he asked her to meet him at his town house in the West Village because he was too busy during the day to decide on a restaurant.

10

After she rang the buzzer, he left her waiting on the street for fifteen minutes. She didn't mind, because the friend who fixed them up, a socialite type who had gone to college with Peter, kept emphasizing what a great old house he had on Lily Pond Lane in East Hampton. After dinner, they went back to his town house, ostensibly because he had to walk his dog, Gumdrop, and when they were in the kitchen, she spotted a photograph of him, in his bathing suit on the beach, tacked to the refrigerator door. He had stomach muscles that looked like the underside of a turtle. She decided to have sex with him that night.

This was the Wednesday before Memorial Day, and the next morning, while he was noisily making cappuccino, he asked her if she wanted to come out to his house for the weekend. She had known he was going to ask her, even though the sex was among the worst she'd had in years (there was some awkward kissing, then he sat on the edge of the bed, rubbing himself until he was hard enough to put on a condom, and then he stuck it in), but she was grateful that he had asked her so quickly.

"You're a smart girl, you know," he said, pouring cappuccino into two enameled cups. He was wearing white French boxer shorts with buttons in the front.

"I know," she said.

"No, I mean it," he said. "Having sex with me last night."

"Much better to get it out of the way."

"Women don't understand that guys like me don't have time to chase them." He finished his cappuccino and carefully washed out the cup. "It's a fucking bore," he said. "You should do all of your friends a favor and tell them to quit playing those stupid girl games. If a girl doesn't put out by the second or third date, you know what I do?"

"No," Janey said.

He pointed his finger at her. "I never call her again. Fuck her."

"No. That's exactly what you don't do. Fuck her," Janey said.

He laughed. He came up to her and squeezed one of her breasts. "If everything goes well this weekend, maybe we'll spend the whole summer together. Know what I mean?" he said. He was still squeezing her breast.

"Ow," Janey said.

"Breast implants, huh?" he said. "I like 'em. They should make all women get them. All women should look like you. I'll call you."

Still, when he hadn't called by noon on

Friday, she began to have doubts. Maybe she'd read him wrong. Maybe he was totally full of shit. It was unlikely, though — they knew too many people in common. But how well did anybody really know anyone else in New York? She called up Lynelle, the socialite who had fixed them up. "Oh, I'm so glad you guys hit it off," Lynelle said.

"But he hasn't called. It's twelve-thirty," Janey said.

"He'll call. He's just a little . . . strange."

"Strange?"

"He's a great guy. We have this joke that if I weren't married to Richard, we'd be married. He calls me his non-future-ex-wife. Isn't that hysterical?"

"Hysterical," Janey said.

"Don't worry. You're just his type," Lynelle said. "Peter just has his own way of doing things."

At one-thirty, Janey called Peter's office. He was in a meeting. She called twice more, and at two-thirty, his secretary said he'd left for the day. She called the town house several times. His machine kept picking up. Finally, he called her at three-thirty. "Little anxious?" he asked. "You called eleven times. According to my caller ID."

They drove out to the Hamptons in his new Porsche Turbo. Gumdrop, a Bichon

13

Frise with blue bows in his topknot, had to sit on her lap, and kept trying to lick her face. All the way out, Peter kept making his hand into a gun shape, pretending to shoot at the other motorists. He called everyone "a fucking Polack." Janey tried to pretend that she thought it was funny.

In Southampton, they stopped for gas at the Hess station. That was a good sign. Janey always loved that gas station, with the attendants in their civilized white and green uniforms — it really made you feel like you were finally out of the city. There was a line of cars. Peter got out of the car and went to the bathroom, leaving the engine running. After a few minutes, the people behind her started honking. She slid into the driver's seat just as Peter came running out of the bathroom, waving his arms and screaming, "You fucking Polack, don't touch my car!"

"Huh?" she said, looking around in confusion.

He yanked open the car door. "Nobody drives my fucking car but me. Got that? Nobody touches my fucking car but me. It's my fucking car."

Janey slid gracefully out of the car. She was wearing tight jeans and high-heeled sandals that made her an inch taller than he was, and her long, nearly white, blond hair

14

hung straight down over a man's white but-ton-down shirt. Her hair was one of her most prized possessions: It was the kind of hair that made people look twice. She lifted her sunglasses, aware that everyone around them was now staring, recognizing her as Janey Wilcox, the model, and probably beginning to recognize Peter as well. "Listen, Buster," she said into his face. "Put a lid on it. Unless you want to see this little incident in the papers on Monday morning."

"Hey, where are you going?" he asked.

"Where do you think?" she said.

"Sorry about that," Peter said after she got back in the car. He rubbed her leg. "I've got a bad temper, baby. I explode. I can't help it. You should know that about me. It's probably because my mother beat me when I was a kid."

"Don't worry about it," Janey said. She adjusted her sunglasses.

Peter roared out of the gas station. "You are so hot, baby. So hot. You should have seen all those other men looking at you."

"Men always look at me," Janey said.

"This is going to be a great summer," Peter said.

Peter's house was everything Lynelle had promised. It was a converted farmhouse on three acres of manicured lawn, with six bed-

15

rooms and a decorator-perfect interior. As soon as they arrived, Peter got on his cell phone and started screaming at the gardener about his apple trees. Janey ignored him. She took off her clothes and walked naked out to the pool. She knew he was watching her through the sliding glass doors. When she got out of the water, he stuck his head out. "Hey baby, is the heat turned on in the pool? If it isn't, I'll call the guy and scream at him."

"It's on," she said. "I think we should figure out what parties we want to go to this weekend." She took out her own cell phone and, still naked, settled into a cushiony deck chair and started dialing.

In mid-May of the summer Janey was to turn thirty-one (her birthday was June first, and she always told everyone she was a "summer baby"), she went to the nightclub Moomba three times in one week. The first night was a party for the rap artist Toilet Paper. She stood in the middle of the room with one hip pushed out, letting photographers take her picture, then someone escorted her to a table in the corner. Joel Webb, the art collector, was there. Janey thought he was cute, even though everyone said he'd had a nose job and cheek implants and liposuction and wore lifts in his shoes because he was only five foot four. But that wasn't the problem. It was his house. For the past three years, he'd been building a big house in East Hampton; in the meantime, he'd been renting what Janey considered a shack — a rundown three-bedroom cottage.

"I need a girlfriend. Fix me up with one of your gorgeous friends, huh?" he said.

"How's your house coming?" Janey said.

"The contractors promised it would be done by July fourth. Come on," he said, "I know you can think of someone to fix me up with."

"I thought you had a girlfriend," Janey said.

"Only by default. We break up during the year, but by the time summer comes, I get so lonely I take her back."

Two nights later, Janey showed up at Moomba with Alan Mundy, whom everyone was calling the hottest comic in Hollywood. She'd met Alan years ago, when she was doing that film in Hollywood — he was a nobody then and had a tiny part in the movie, playing a lovesick busboy. They sort of became friends and sort of stayed in touch, talking on the phone about once a year, but Janey now told everyone he was a great friend of hers. Her booker at her modeling agency told her Alan was coming into New York on the sly, so Janie called his publicist and he called her right back. He'd just broken up with his girlfriend and was probably lonely. "Janey, Janey," he said. "I want to see all the hot places. Tear up the town."

"As long as we don't have to patch it back together when you're done," she said.

"God, I've missed you, Janey," he said.

He picked her up in a Rolls Royce limousine. His hair had been dyed red for his last movie role, and he had an inch of black roots. "Whatcha doing now, kid?" he asked. "Still acting?"

"I've been acting every day of my life," Janey said.

Inside the club, Alan drank three martinis in a row. Janey sat close to him and whispered in his ear and giggled a lot. She had no real interest in Alan, who in actuality was the kind of geeky guy who would work at a car wash, which was exactly what he used to do in between jobs before he became famous. But nobody else had to know that. It raised her status enormously to be seen with Alan, especially if it looked like they could potentially be an item.

Alan was drunk, sticking the plastic swords from his martinis into his frizzy hair. "What do you want, Janey?" he asked.

"What do you want out of life?"

"I want to have a good summer," Janey said.

She got up to go to the bathroom. She passed Redmon Richardly, the bad-boy southern writer. "Janey, Janey," he said. "I'm soooo glad to see you."

"Really?" Janey said. "You were never glad to see me before."

"I'm always glad to see you. You're one of my good friends," Redmon said. There was another man at the table. Short brown hair. Tanned. Slim. Too handsome. Just the way Janey liked them. "See? I always said Janey was a smart model," Redmon said to the man.

The man smiled. "Smart and a model. What could be better?"

"Dumb and a model. The way most men like them," Janey said. She smiled back, aware of the whiteness of her teeth.

"Zack Manners. Janey Wilcox," Redmon said. "Zack just arrived from England. He's looking for a house in the Hamptons. Maybe you can help him find one."

"Only if I get to live in it," Janey said.

"Interesting proposition," Zack said.

Janey went upstairs to the bathroom. Her heart was thumping. Zack Manners was the huge English record producer. She stood in line for the bathroom. Redmon Richardly came up behind her. "I want him," Janey said.

"Who? Zack?" He laughed. "You and a million other women all over the world."

"I don't care," Janey said. "I want him. And he's looking for a house in the Hamptons."

"Well . . . you . . . can't . . . have . . . him," Redmon said.

"Why not?" Janey stamped her foot.

Redmon put his arms around her like he was going to kiss her. He could do things like that and get away with it. "Come home with me tonight."

"Why?"

"Because it'd be fun."

"I'm not interested in fun."

"Ditch that geek you're with and come home with me. What are you doing with a geek like that, anyway? I don't care if he's famous. He's still a geek."

"Yeah, well, being with a geek like that makes men like you more interested in me."

"Oh, come on."

"I want to have a good summer," Janey said. "With Zack."

Janey and Alan left half an hour later, after Alan accidentally spilled two martinis. On their way out, they passed Redmon's table.

20

Janey casually slipped her hand into the back pocket of Alan's jeans. Then she looked over her shoulder at Zack.

"Call me later," Redmon said loudly.

II

Janey Wilcox heard about Harold Vane, the billionaire, in the bathroom of a club. That was two years ago, and even though Harold had turned out to be a little squeaker of a man, with his shiny round head and his ever-shiny shoes (he made the servants polish his Docksiders to a high sheen), he was one of the best summers. "I've got to find a man for the summer," Janey was complaining to her friend Allison when a voice from one of the stalls shouted out, "Harold Vane."

Harold had a stucco mansion on Gin Lane in Southampton. There was a long green lawn in front of the house, and a shorter green lawn in the back, edging down to the dunes and the beach. There was a sit-down lunch with wine and two courses on both Saturday and Sunday, a cook, and a man called Skaaden who mixed cocktails and discreetly served the food from silver platters. The grounds could be entered only through a wrought-iron gate with the letter

"H" on one side and "V" on the other. Harold had a security man who dressed like a gardener but carried a gun.

"Don't you worry that one of these guys is going to figure out what you're up to?" Allison asked. This was at the beginning of the Harold summer, when Janey had invited Allison (who had a share in a tiny house in Bridgehampton) over for the day.

"What do you mean?" Janey asked, thinking about the gardener.

"Using them. For their summer houses."

"I'm a feminist," Janey said. "It's about the redistribution of wealth." They were lying on chaises by the pool, and Skaaden kept bringing them glasses of iced tea.

"Where is Harold, anyway?" Allison asked. She had bulging gray eyes — no matter how you made her up, she would never be pretty, Janey thought. She had been waiting for Allison to ask the question. Allison was a sort of professional best friend to the rich and famous; as soon as she left, she'd probably call up everybody and tell them she'd been lunching at Harold Vane's house, and that they were now good friends. In fact, Janey expected that after she and Harold broke up at the end of the summer, Allison would continue to pursue his friendship. She'd invite him for drinks, and when she saw him at parties, she'd put her hand on his arm and whisper jokes in his ear to make him laugh.

"Harold's on the crapper," Janey said. She had a soft, girlish voice, and despite her stunning face and figure, she knew her voice was really her secret weapon — it allowed her to say anything and get away with it. "He spends an hour on the crapper every evening before he goes out, and on weekends, an hour in the morning and an hour in the late afternoon. It really cuts into the day. Last weekend we basically missed a book party because he wouldn't get off the can."

"What does he do in there?"

Janey shrugged. "I don't know. Shits. Reads. Although how it can take a person an hour to shit, I don't know. I keep telling him it's not good for his intestines."

"It's probably the only time he can get away from everything."

"Oh, no," Janey said. "He has a phone and e-mail in there." She looked at Allison. "Forget I said that, okay?" She could just imagine Allison going around to dinners telling people that Harold Vane spent an hour on the crapper while he talked on the phone and sent e-mails, and it made her feel guilty. After all, Harold had never done or said anything even remotely unpleasant to her, and she was actually a little bit in love with him.

That was the surprising thing about Harold. She couldn't bring herself to have sex with him at first — but after they'd finally done it, the second Saturday after Memorial Day, she'd wondered why she'd waited so long. Harold was commanding in bed. He told her what he wanted her to do and how to position herself (later on in the summer, he shaved off all her pubic hair and told her to sunbathe naked), and he had a huge penis.

His unmentionable was so large, in fact, that all during that summer, when other women came up to her to ask her if it was true she was really dating Harold (this seemed to happen most in the ladies' rooms at the various trendy Hamptons restaurants they frequented), Janey would roll up her lipstick and say confidentially that his willy was so enormous, the first time she saw it she told him there was no way he was going to put that thing in her. Then she would go back to lipsticking her open mouth. It might have been a little off color to talk about Harold's willy, but on the other hand, Janey felt she was doing him a favor — when she broke up with him, it would make it easier for him to get other women.

Not that he seemed to have any trouble. Harold was like everybody's Santa Claus. Old girlfriends were constantly calling, offering to fix him up with their friends, and Harold was always doling out advice, and sending these women little gifts to help them get through their crises — cell phones and computers and even paying for private nursery school for the child of a woman who'd had the kid out of wedlock. On Janey's first Hamptons weekend, he had pulled her by the hand out to his garage. "I want you to have your freedom this summer," he said. "I can tell that you're a girl who likes her freedom."

"You're right," Janey said.

"Otherwise, you'd be married by now," he said. He opened the side door to the garage and they went down three steps. He was behind her, and when she was at the bottom, he jerked her around and fastened his lips on hers and stuck his tongue in her mouth. It took Janey by surprise, and she sort of remembered flailing her arms around like a live insect impaled by a pin. But the kiss wasn't bad.

"Just a little something to get your motor running," he said. Then he pushed past her and turned on the light. "Pick the car you want to drive this summer," he said. There was a Range Rover and two Mercedeses, one a 550 coupe and the other an SL convertible. "There's only one rule. You can't change your mind in the middle of the summer. I don't want you coming to me and saying, 'I want to drive the Rover' when you've already chosen the Mercedes."

"What if I don't like any of them," Janey said. "What if I want a Maserati."

"I don't want you to get too spoiled," Harold said. "You'll end up hating me because no other guy is ever going to treat you as nice."

"That's probably true," she said, touching him affectionately on the nose with her index finger.

"Why don't you marry him," Allison kept hissing all summer.

"Oh no, I couldn't," Janey said. "I couldn't marry a man unless I was totally in love with him."

"I could be in love with him in two seconds," Allison said.

"Yes, you probably could," Janey said, not bothering to add that Allison wasn't anywhere near attractive enough to interest a man like Harold.

Harold took Janey a little bit seriously. "Be smart," he said. "Do something with your life. Let me help you."

27

Janey said she'd always wanted to do something important, like be a journalist or write a novel. So one Sunday, Harold invited a lady editor in chief to brunch. Harold always served cappuccino in oversized cups, and Janey remembered the lady editor, who was wearing a blue and white jacket in a swirly design, balancing the large cup on her thigh while they were sitting outside.

"Janey wants to be a writer," Harold said.

"Oh my," said the lady editor. She raised the cup to her lips. "Why is it that pretty girls always want to do something else?"

"Come on, Maeve," Harold roared. "You used to be pretty yourself. Before you got smart."

"And before you got rich," Maeve said. "What is it you want to do, dear?"

"I want your job," Janey said, in that soft voice that gave no offense.

When Janey and Harold broke up at the end of September, she actually cried on the street afterward. The breakup took place in his Park Avenue apartment — they arranged to meet there for a drink before going out to dinner. Harold was in the library. He was sipping a scotch, staring up at his prized Renoir. "Hello, crazy kid," he said. He took her hand and led her to a red silk couch. "Something's come up. I won't be able to make it to dinner tonight."

"I see," Janey said. She had an inkling of what was coming next.

"It was wonderful spending time with you this summer," he said. "But. . . ."

"It's over," Janey said.

"It's not you," said Harold. "It's me. I don't want to get married, and you should know that there's another woman I'd like to start seeing."

"Please," Janey said. She stood up. "I was going to break up with you tonight anyway. Isn't that funny?"

It was chilly, and she'd worn a lightweight blue silk coat. As Harold escorted her to the door, she saw Skaaden standing in the hallway with her coat over his arm. Harold had not only planned the breakup, he had discussed it with Skaaden beforehand. As Skaaden helped her into her coat, she imagined what Harold would have told him: "The young lady will be arriving for drinks, but leaving shortly thereafter. She may be upset, so be sure to have her coat ready," and she smiled. "Good-bye Harold," she said. She took his hand, but allowed him to kiss her on the cheek.

She made it as far as the corner, then she leaned over a garbage can and started crying. She had a dialogue with herself: "Come on," said one voice. "This has happened a million times before. You should be used to it."

"But it still hurts," said the other voice.

"Only a little. Harold was short and ugly and you never would have married him anyway. Besides, he spent an hour a day on the crapper."

"I loved him."

"Did not. You're only upset because he was going to take you to Bouley for dinner and you wanted the fois gras."

A cab stopped in front of Harold's building and a lanky blond girl got out. She was clutching a cheap leather bag. "My replacement," Janey thought. The cab's yellow light came on. Janey stuck out her hand and hailed it.

Two weeks later, Harold messengered an envelope to her apartment. Inside was a note that read, "If you ever need anything, please call," attached to a five-thousand-dollar gift certificate from Gucci.

The next summer, when Janey was with Peter, she ran into Harold at a big party in East Hampton, thrown on a beachfront estate. The summer was only half over, but she'd developed an unusual and alarming hatred for Peter. At the beach, he either talked on his cell phone to clients or criticized other women's bodies. His pet peeve was women over forty who'd had kids. "Look at her," he'd scream. "Look at that belly. Useless. Why doesn't she get off the beach?"

"Oh Peter," she'd say.

"Oh Peter what? It's in a man's nature to be attracted to beautiful young girls. It's instinctual. A man wants to sleep with as many beautiful young girls as possible. It's all about reproduction."

Driving on the back roads in his Porsche, he'd say, "I'm a little crazy, Janey," like he was proud of it. "Do you think I should go to a shrink?"

"I think it would be totally useless," Janey would say, and he'd laugh, taking it as a compliment, so by the time they arrived at the party, he'd have his hand on her leg. Then they'd walk, arms around each other, up somebody's lawn or gravel pathway, laughing, smiling over their shoulders at the other guests. All the PR people knew them, so they didn't even have to give their names at parties, and photographers took their picture. The summer was green and warm, and for those moments, anyway, it felt perfect.

The Monday after Janey and Peter ran

into Harold, Harold called.

"I'm worried about you, Janey," he said. "You're a nice girl. You shouldn't be with a guy like Peter."

"Why not?" she said.

"He's a creep."

"Oh Harold. You think every other guy is a creep."

"I'm serious, Janey," Harold said. "I want to give you some advice. Maybe it's not my place, but I'm going to give it to you anyway. Stop this running around and get married. You're not the kind of girl who's going to do something with her life, so marry a man you love and have his children."

"But I will do something, Harold."

"What?"

"I don't know."

"Take my advice, Janey. You're young now, and you're beautiful. This is the time to find a real guy."

"Who?" Janey asked.

"A nice young guy. A good-looking guy. I don't know. I'll fix you up with my architect. He's thirty-three and wants to get married."

"No thanks," Janey said, and laughed softly.

The relationship with Peter went from bad to worse. It was partly the sex. Peter didn't want to be touched, and could barely bring himself to touch her. They had sex once every three weeks. "Do you think maybe you're gay?" Janey asked. She'd developed a habit of baiting him. "I'm going to find some hot young guy to have sex with. Men over forty really can't perform, you know." Then they'd get into a screaming argument in his house. One morning, Janey burned some toast, and he stormed into the kitchen and fished the burnt toast out of the garbage, scraped it off, and tried to make her eat it. She fed it to Gumdrop instead, who promptly threw up. Janey had fantasies of killing Peter, and wondered if she accidentally threw his cell-phone recharger into the pool, he'd be electrocuted.

They'd make up because they always had parties to go to, and eventually, the summer passed.

Moomba again. Janey sat by herself, sipping a martini at the bar. The bartender was young. He said, "I remember you in that movie. I'm embarrassed about this, but I used to masturbate to your picture."

"Good," Janey said. "Then I guess I don't need to give you a tip."

"This is on me," he said, nodding at the martini. He leaned over the bar. "What are you doing now?"

"Waiting for a friend," she said, and turned away.

She was willing Zack Manners to show up. She'd found she had this uncanny knack: If she willed something hard enough, it would happen. Instead, Redmon Richardly, the novelist, came in. He nodded at her, then walked all around the club to see who else was there. Then he came over.

"Where's Zack?" she asked.

"How the hell should I know."

"I'm hoping he'll show up."

"Forget about Zack," Redmon said. "I'm the best you're going to do tonight."

"I want Zack."

"Zack is a weirdo," Redmon said. He ordered a scotch.

"So are you."

"No, really a weirdo," Redmon said. "I've spent a lot of time with him in London. I know girls who have slept with him. You don't want to get involved in that shit. It's that weird Euro sex shit. It's gross. It's not American."

Then, sure enough, Zack did turn up. "Zack!" Redmon said. "We were just talking about you."

Zack was with some other people. "Come to the table," he mouthed.

After Zack's group was seated, Janey went

34

over and wedged a chair in next to Zack. "You again," he said. "You look like one of those girls who's everywhere. Are you a socialite?"

Janey just smiled and sipped her drink. She knew she didn't have to say anything. Eventually her looks would begin to affect him. She turned to the man on her other side. He was a little English fellow, eager to talk.

"Are you going to the Hamptons too, this summer?" she asked.

"No, but I'm fascinated by it. We don't have anything like it in England. It sounds marvelous. All those movie stars fighting the traffic."

"I go every summer," Janey said. "It's wonderful."

"Will you be there this summer?"

"Oh yes. I'm looking forward to having a really good summer this year."

Zack leaned over. "What is it with you and this 'good summer' business?" he asked. "Are you mentally impaired in some way that I should know about?"

"Probably," Janey said. She put down her drink. "I have to go," she said. "Call me."

"I don't call girls. I get in touch," said Zack.

"Then I'll look forward to your 'getting in touch,' " Janey said.

Two days letter, Zack messengered an envelope to her apartment. Written on an engraved card was this brief missive: *Janey, would you like to meet for a drink? Please ring my secretary, who will give you the time and place. Regards, Zack.*

III

Every five minutes during the Jitney ride out to the Hamptons on Memorial Day weekend, Janey wanted to stand up and scream, "I'm Janey Wilcox, the model, and I'm spending the weekend with Zack Manners, the English billionaire record producer. So fuck you. All of you," just to make herself feel better. She was sitting in the front of the bus, wearing a baseball cap and sunglasses with her hair pulled back in a ponytail, trying to read *The Sheltering Sky*. But a niggling thought kept inserting itself into her brain, like a pencil point being pushed into Silly Putty: Zack Manners was not exactly there. He was not, as Janey liked to say, completely "in." His invitation had been vague — he had left instructions with his secretary to inform Janey that they should meet "sixish" for drinks at The Palm in East Hampton on Friday evening. Janey wasn't sure if the invitation extended to the weekend, and the uncertainty made her more excited about Zack than she had been about any man in a long time. The night before, she had gone to Moomba, and as the various men came by her table to pay their doting respects, Janey had said boldly, "Oh, yes, I'm wonderful. I've finally met a man I could fall madly in love with. He's brilliant and funny and sexy." And she said it in such a way as to imply that, while Zack was all those things, these other men decidedly were not.

The amazing thing was that this didn't seem to turn any of the men off. They clustered around the table, ordering drinks and smoking cigarettes. Janey had recently developed a theory that the worse you treated men, the more they wanted you. Peter, from three summers ago, came over, swinging a chair around to sit with his arms draped over the back. "You've changed, Janey. You seem so confident," he said.

"I'm not the same girl I was two years ago, Peter," she said, and smiled viciously. "I would never put up with your shit today."

"I never gave you any shit."

"The ultimate was Labor Day weekend. Driving back from the Hamptons in the pouring rain. Remember? You dropped me off just outside the midtown tunnel. On Thirty-fifth Street and Third Avenue. 'Get a cab,' you said."

"It was over," Peter said, and grinned. "And you lived all the way uptown. Why should I drive a girl all the way uptown if I'm not even going to get laid?"

Janey expected Zack to be at the bar in The Palm when she arrived at six-fifteen. He wasn't. When he still hadn't turned up ten minutes later, she took up two guys on their offer to buy her a drink. She ordered a margarita. At six-forty-five, there was a slight commotion outside. A green 1954 250 GT Ellena Body Ferrari pulled into the circular driveway. Right-hand drive. Zack got out. He wore old tennis shoes and walked with his hands in the front pockets of his khaki trousers. Janey became very animated, talking to the two men. Zack came up behind her. Whispered in her ear, "Hello there."

She jumped a little. "Oh. Hi," she said. She looked at her watch. "I was going to scold you for being late, but the car makes up for it."

"The car is priceless," Zack said. He slid onto the bar stool next to her. He took her hand. "If you want to be with me, Janey, never, ever scold me. Unless I ask you to."

"That sounds promising."

"It is. If you play your cards right." He leaned toward her. "Do you have a dark side, Janey? You look like a girl who has a dark side."

Janey laughed, and so did Zack. She flipped her hair over her shoulder. Zack lit a cigarette. Filterless. In the daylight, he was not quite as attractive as she remembered. He had bad English teeth, ranging in color from sickly yellow to light gray. His fingers were stained with nicotine and his nails were dirty. But there was the car. And his money. And the whole summer and hopefully even longer ahead of her. "Let's take things one step at a time, okay?" she said.

"I guess that means you want to see my house before you decide whether or not you want to fuck me," Zack said.

"Come on," Janey said. "I'm interested in you. Everyone says you're fascinating."

"Everyone is a fool," Zack said. And then: "You're going to love the house. It's perfect." He stood up and pulled her off the bar stool. He put his arm around her, walking her to the door. He was taller than she, the perfect size, she thought. "I got the house just for you," he said.

"Of course you did," Janey said. She believed him, not thinking for a moment that it was unusual for a complete stranger to rent a house in the Hamptons in the hope that she would be with him. She nodded at the

40

valet, who held open the car door. She slid into the front seat. The car was in perfect condition. She took off her baseball cap and shook out her hair. She laughed. "It's beautiful," she said, feeling generous. Zack started the engine. "Ah yes," he said, pulling out of the driveway. "I suppose that's where I'm supposed to say, 'No, you're beautiful, Janey.' " He looked at her. "Feel like you're in a movie?"

"Yes."

"You're a very silly girl. Don't you know that it's dangerous to be so silly?"

"Maybe I'm not silly," Janey said. "Maybe it's just an act."

"Maybe it's all just an act," Zack said. "But then where does that leave you?"

He turned the car onto Further Lane. "I told the rental agent I wanted a house on the best road in the best town in the Hamptons. I hope she hasn't done me wrong, Janey." He growled a bit on the word "wrong" and Janey thought he was adorable all over again. They turned in to a long gravel driveway. "I know the house," Janey said. "It's one of my favorites."

"Really?"

"A friend of mine rented it five years ago. It's the perfect summer house. Pool, tennis courts . . ."

41

"Did you play tennis without your knickers on?"

"Oh please, Zack."

"That's how I imagine you, all in white, without your knickers . . ."

The house was situated well back from the road, fronted by a long green lawn that was always set up for croquet. It was a classic, shingled-style manse, built in the 1920s for a rich family with a pack of kids and servants. Zack pulled up to the front. "Come along, come along my lovely, and we shall see . . ." he said, jumping out of the car and taking her hand. There was a wide porch and a balcony that ran around the second floor. He opened the door. "A veritable fun house," he said, turning around. "Now, I expect you to play lots of naughty games."

"Like what?"

Zack rustled through a paper sack. "Provisions," he said, holding up a bottle of vodka and a plastic container of tonicwater.

Janey laughed a little nervously.

Zack went to the kitchen and returned with two cocktails. "Chin-chin," he said, holding up his glass. "Cheers," Janey said. "To a great summer."

Zack came up behind her. He put his arm around her waist and pressed her to him.

"What's behind all this great summer non-sense?"

Janey turned and slipped out of his grasp. "Nothing," she said.

"There must be something. I've never heard of anyone so obsessed with summer. I spent my summers working in a factory."

"Of course you did," Janey said softly.

He pointed his finger at her and shook it. "You have to answer my questions. That's one of the rules. I get bored very easily. Right now I'm interested. In hearing all about you. About all of the men who have had you before me."

"What?" Janey said.

"This is going to be fun," Zack said. "Do you take coke?"

"Coca-Cola?"

"Cocaine," Zack said with mock patience. Then: "You're not very bright, are you? When I first met you, I didn't think you were, but then I thought perhaps I'd made a mistake." He sat down on the couch in front of a coffee table, looked up at her, and smiled. "But then, one doesn't really need intelligence in these situations. Just a sense of adventure."

"I don't do cocaine," Janey said coldly.

"What a shame," Zack said. "I figured you for a player." He tapped some cocaine out

43

on the coffee table, rolled up a bill, and snorted it up. He tipped his head back, inhaling deeply, the bill still in his nostril. Janey stared, and he caught her eye. "Stop playing the good little American girl, will you," he said.

"How do you know I'm not?"

"Oh, come off it," Zack said. He stood up. Walked to her. Touched her hair. "I didn't invite you here to be my girlfriend," he said.

"Then why did you invite me?"

"I didn't. You invited yourself. Remember?"

"Fuck off," Janey said softly.

"Come here," he said. "Sit down. My dear, you're as transparent as that shirt you're wearing. Everyone knows what your game is. You're available. For the summer. Providing the man is rich enough. At least I want to know why."

"Because I just want to have a good summer," Janey screamed. "Is there anything wrong with that?"

"But you don't do anything," Zack said. He snorted some more cocaine.

"I don't do anything because I don't want to. I don't have to."

"You don't feel much of anything, do you, Janey?"

"No," she said. She shrugged. "Even if the

44

sex is great, it doesn't mean anything. Because the guy isn't going to stick around. So why not beat men at their own game. Use them. I'm a feminist, Zack," she said, which somehow made her feel better.

"Oh, the modern woman speaks," Zack said. "How old are you?"

"Twenty-eight," Janey said, casually lying. She'd been fibbing about her age for professional reasons for so long that she actually believed it.

"You look older," he said, and laughed. "You use men, but you yourself are totally useless. You think your views are revolutionary, but they're not. They're just annoying and immature."

"And yours aren't?"

"As a matter of fact, they're not," Zack said. "I'm what you Yanks would call a self-made man. Everything I have, I got myself." He lit up a cigarette. "But along the way, I noticed something curious. I lost my emotions. My ability to feel. It comes from having to fuck people over all the time to get what you think you want." He smiled. Those teeth! Janey thought. "So you see, you and I are really quite alike."

"I have my reasons," Janey said.

"No doubt you do. But they're probably very mundane," he said. Janey reached

45

across the couch and slapped him. He grabbed her wrist. "Very good," he said. "You're getting the idea."

"I'm not mundane," Janey hissed.

"Oh, but you are," he said. He pushed her back against the couch. She didn't struggle too much. "Degradation," he said into her face. She could smell his breath. "That's all that's left for people like us. Degradation. It's the only way we can feel."

"You're nuts," Janey said.

"Come upstairs. Quickly!" he said. He grabbed her hand. He hopped up the stairs two at a time. He pulled her into the bedroom. "I've been looking forward to this all week." He pulled off his shirt and pants. Underneath, he was wearing tatty stained briefs that were frayed in the leg holes. He turned around and pulled down his underpants. His bottom was splattered with pimples. "Hit me, Mum!" he shouted.

"I'm not your mum," Janey said.

"Hit me, Mum! Please!"

Janey didn't know what to do, so she started screaming. She backed toward the window. It was open. She backed out of it, onto the balcony. Then she ran to the edge and jumped over, onto the roof. She scrambled across that and jumped to the ground. "Owwww," she screamed.

For a few minutes, she just lay there. Then she heard footsteps coming down the stairs and the front door banged open. Zack, still naked, and smoking a cigarette, walked toward her. "Get up, you silly cow. You're not hurt."

"Fuck off," Janey said.

"I'd appreciate it if you'd leave the premises as quickly and expediently as possible," Zack said. Then he went back in the house and snorted more cocaine.

Janey limped into the house. She passed Zack. He didn't look up. She went into the kitchen to make a phone call. "Please, please be home," she said, then, "Thank God." She started sobbing. "It's me. Something terrible has happened. I was with this English guy and he went crazy. I'm scared. Yes. Yes," she said, sniveling, and gave the address. Then she went out onto the porch to wait.

Twenty minutes later, a Range Rover came roaring up Further Lane. The driver bypassed the driveway, and drove across the lawn, scattering bits of the croquet set. The Rover stopped in front of the house and Harold got out. He kept the car door open. "Your ride is here," he said.

Zack ran out of the house with a towel around his waist. "You really fucked it up," he said to Janey. "You had a chance. We

47

could have spent the whole summer together. You blew it."

"Get away from her," Harold said.

Zack ignored him, following Janey as she limped to the car. "Go back to your little Jew boys. Where you feel safe."

Harold took a step forward. "Hey. Listen here, asshole. Take it easy. This is America. You can't talk like that."

"Oh yeah?" Zack laughed. He took a drag on his cigarette. "I'll say whatever I damn please."

"When my lawyers get finished with you, you won't be out of court for years," Harold said calmly. He got into the car and slammed the door.

"Yeah, yeah, 'course you will," Zack shouted. "You Yanks. Take all the fun out of everything with your damn lawyers." He hiked the towel up around his waist and walked back into the house.

Harold backed the car across the lawn. "Jesus Christ, Janey," he said.

"Harold," Janey said. She put her hands over her eyes. "I can't really take any lectures right now, okay?"

"I'm not going to lecture you, baby. I just want to make sure you're all right. He didn't . . ."

"No," she said.

"Who is that creep?"

"Zack Manners," Janey said. "The English record producer."

"Goddamn Brits," Harold said. "Why don't they go back to England where they belong? Don't worry," he said, patting Janey's hand, "I'll see to it that he's persona non grata on the East End. He won't be able to get a reservation anywhere."

"You're wonderful, Harold. You really are," Janey said.

"I know," Harold said.

"I just wanted to have a good summer," Janey said an hour later, lying in a bed in a private room in Southampton Hospital. "Like when I was sixteen."

"Shhhh," said the nurse. "Everyone wants to be sixteen again. Count backwards from a hundred and go to sleep."

Sixteen. That was the summer when Janey had gone from ugly to beautiful. Until then, she'd been the pudgy, funny-faced kid in a family of beauties. Her father was six foot two, all-American, the town's local doctor. He wanted Janey to be a nurse, so she'd find a decent husband. Her mother was French and perfect. Janey was the middle child, sandwiched between a boy and a girl who could do no wrong. While the rest of the family ate veal with a mushroom cream sauce, Janey's mother served her half a head of iceberg lettuce. "If you don't lose weight, you won't find a man. Then you'll have to work. There is nothing more unattractive than a woman who works," she'd say.

"I want to be a vet," Janey said.

Every summer, spent at the country club, was agony. Janey's mother, thin, tanned, in a Pucci bathing suit, was constantly drinking iced tea and flirting with the lifeguards, and later, with her son's friends, who adored her. Janey's brother and sister, both on the swim team, were state champs. Janey, who had a fat belly and fat thighs, was never able to distinguish herself. At fourteen, when she got her period, her mother said, "Janey, you must be very careful with boys. Boys like to take advantage of girls who are not pretty because the boys know the girl is, how you say, desperate. For attention."

Then Janey turned sixteen. She grew four inches. When she walked into the country club that summer, no one recognized her. She took to wearing her mother's Pucci bathing suits. She stole her lipstick. She smoked cigarettes behind the clubhouse. Boys flocked around. Her mother caught her kissing a boy under a picnic table. She slapped Janey across the face. That was when Janey knew she'd won. "I'll show you," Janey said. "I'll do better than you."

"You cannot do better than me," said her mother.

"Oh yes I can," Janey said.

The Saturday after Janey jumped from Zack's roof, she showed up at Media Beach in Sagaponic with Redmon Richardly. Her foot was in a cast, and Redmon helped her, limping, across the sand. He settled her on a beach towel, then he went to take a swim. Allison came running over. "Is it true?" she asked breathlessly.

"Which part?" Janey asked. She leaned back on her elbows, in order to better display her magnificent body. "You mean about Redmon and me being together?"

"No. About last night."

"Don't say anything to Redmon. Especially don't mention Zack's name," Janey said.

The night before, Janey and Redmon had stopped at the club Twenty-Seven on their way out to the Hamptons. Zack was there. He walked by Redmon and said, "Another sucker born every minute. Isn't that what you Yanks say?" and Redmon had taken a swing at him. Since then, Redmon had told everyone that Zack had been in love with

51

Janey, but she'd left Zack for him, and that's why Zack was flipping out.

It was a small misperception that Janey had no intention of ever correcting.

IV

The next year, Janey determined to get her own house for the summer. This would probably entail a certain amount of hardship, since the kind of houses she was used to staying in probably cost their occupants upward of a hundred thousand dollars for the season. Nevertheless, she had a strong feeling that it would be a much better "look" for her to be independent, even if it meant doing without a pool, a gardener, a cook, a car, and maybe even a dishwasher.

But even this would be preferable to what she'd had to endure the summer before with Redmon and Zack. Something Zack had said kept repeating itself in her head like an annoying pop tune: "You're available. For the summer. Providing the man is rich enough." It was one thing to date rich men, but another to have people thinking you were a whore. Someday (maybe soon), Janey would likely have to make one of these rich men her husband. She would have to be madly in love with him, but even so, it wouldn't do if this rich man heard that his future wife had a reputation for being a prostitute. Janey had learned that while most rich men thought women were whores deep down anyway, they didn't actually want you to be one.

And so, around about February, when it was time to start thinking about summer houses, Janey began putting the word out.

"I'm looking for my own house this summer," she said, flipping her long hair over her shoulder and standing with her hip pushed out, to the various rich men she ran into at restaurants and parties. "I've decided it's time to grow up." The rich men laughed and made suggestive comments like "Don't grow up too much," but not one of them took the bait. Janey was hoping that someone would say they had a carriage house where Janey could stay for free, but the only one who offered anything was Allison.

"You could share my house," Allison said eagerly. They had just arrived at a dinner for a European fashion designer who was trying to stage a comeback in New York.

"That's not the point," Janey said, moving forward to allow the photographers to take her picture while Allison moved to the side;

54

luckily, Allison had been on the scene long enough to understand that her presence in a photograph would likely render it unpublishable.

"I just don't know what kind of summer I want to have," Janey explained. "I might want to spend the whole summer reading books."

Allison made a completely unnecessary gesture of choking on her cocktail. "Books? You? Janey Wilcox?"

"I do read books, Allison. Maybe you should try it sometime."

Allison changed her tack. "Oh, I get it," she said, sounding hurt. "Why didn't you tell me you wanted to share with Aleeka Norton."

"I'm not sharing a house with Aleeka," Janey said. Aleeka Norton was a beautiful black model whom Janey considered a "friend" even though she only saw her a couple of times a year at the fashion shows. Aleeka, who was Janey's age, was writing a novel, and when people asked her what she did, she always said, "I'm a *writer*," like they were really stupid to think that she might be anything less, like a model. This approach seemed to get Aleeka a lot more respect from men. Joel Webb, the art collector, had actually lent Aleeka his little three-bedroom house for the summer so she would have a quiet place to work. And he didn't even want to have sex with her. True, the house was basically a shack, but the one thing Janey had learned after the Redmon summer was if you had to be in a shack, you were better off being in your own shack.

"Allison," Janey hissed, moving through the crowd. "Haven't you noticed? Something happens when you get into your thirties. People catch on to your shit. Especially men. It's important to look like you're doing something, even if you're not."

"But Redmon wasn't like that," Allison said.

Janey looked at her. Poor Allison. She had a huge crush on Redmon, having read all his books and fantasized that deep down, Redmon was like the men he put into his novels: sensitive, misunderstood, and looking for the love of one good woman.

"Redmon lives in a dream world," Janey said.

"He was nice to you. Really nice," Allison said.

Janey smiled. She sipped her martini. "He was a loser," she said.

The Redmon summer, which was supposed to be the Zack summer, spent in Zack's amazing house, Janey thought bitterly, was one of the worst summers in years.

"Well, at least Redmon was better than Zack. You have to admit that," Allison said.

Janey took another sip of her martini. She kept her face impassive. Zack! Every time she heard his name, she wanted to scream. But it wouldn't do for Allison to know that.

"Zack Manners," Janey said. She smiled and waved at someone across the room. "I haven't thought about him for months."

The very first thing Zack had done last summer, after Janey dumped him and went with Redmon, was to immediately begin dating some Russian model whose name no one could remember, but whom Zack insisted on practically fucking every time they were in public. Janey had consoled herself with the fact that everybody knew that the Russian "model" was really a prostitute. But then she screwed things up when she bumped into Zack coming out of the bathroom at a club. She was a little drunk, and she sneered, "I see you're with your whore."

Zack laughed. "Yeah," he said, "But she's honest about it. She admits to what she is. Why don't you?" Janey had taken a step forward and raised her hand as if to slap him, but she stumbled a little and had to steady herself against the wall. Zack had laughed

57

again and lit a cigarette. "Why don't you get a life, baby?" he said.

The summer went steadily downhill from there.

It was all Zack's fault. She and Redmon went to a beach party on Flying Point Road, and as they walked across the sand, they spotted Zack Manners sitting on the wooden steps leading up to the house. It was the fifth time they'd gone to a party and run into Zack. "That's it," Redmon said on the drive back home. "I'm not going to any more parties. They're all filled with assholes like Zack Manners. The Hamptons," he said dramatically, "are over." After that, he swore he wouldn't leave the house, except to go to the supermarket, the beach, and his friends' houses for dinner.

This might have been bearable, if it weren't for Redmon's own house.

Even calling it a house was pushing it. Despite being a mere thousand yards from the beach, there was no getting around the fact that the "house" was nothing more than a dirty shack. But the weirdest thing about it was how Redmon didn't have a clue. "I think this house is as nice as any house I've ever been to in the Hamptons," he said one afternoon, when Allison had stopped by for a "chat." "It's certainly as nice as the Westacotts', don't you think?" he said.

"It's soooo charming," Allison gushed. "It's so hard to find these antique houses that haven't been completely ruined."

Janey was mystified. The shack couldn't have been more than four hundred square feet (about the size of the master bedrooms in the houses she normally stayed in) and the roof looked like it was caving in. There was a broken window in the bedroom, which Redmon had taped over with a piece of newspaper from *The New York Times* — from August 1995. The galley kitchen contained stained appliances (the first time Janey opened the refrigerator, she had screamed), and the furnishings were sparse and uncomfortable — like the couch, which was one of those flat wooden-legged affairs that appeared to have been purchased at a tag sale. The bathroom was so tiny, there was no room for towels: When they came back from the beach, they had to throw their towels on the bushes outside the house to dry.

"Actually, Redmon," Janey said. "I would have thought you could do better than this."

"Better?" Redmon said. "I love this house. I've been renting it for fifteen years. This house is like my home. What's wrong with this house?" he demanded.

"Are you insane?" Janey asked.

"Redmon is so cool," Allison said when Redmon went back into the house. They were sitting in the tiny backyard at the picnic table; Redmon's only other concession to lawn furniture was two moldy, ripped folding chairs.

"Please," Janey said. She put her hand over her eyes. "All he talks about is how the Hamptons are filled with assholes and he wants to have a real life and be with real people. He doesn't understand that those assholes *are* real people. I keep telling him if he doesn't like it, he should move to Des Moines."

That was the problem with Redmon. His perceptions about life were totally off. One evening, when he was cooking pasta (his specialties were pasta primavera and blackened redfish — he had learned to cook in the eighties and had never progressed), he said to her, "You know, Janey, I'm a millionaire."

Janey was flipping through a fashion magazine. "That's nice," she said.

"Hell," he said, pouring the pasta into a strainer that was missing one of its legs, causing the pasta to spill all over the sink, "I think it's pretty amazing. How many writers do you know who are millionaires?"

"Well," she said, "I actually know a lot of people who are billionaires."

"Yeah, but they're all . . . *business people,*" he said, implying that business people were lower than cockroaches.

"So?" Janey said.

"So who gives a shit how much money you have if you don't have a soul?"

The next day, on the beach, Redmon brought up his financial situation again.

"I figure that in another year or so, I'll have two million dollars," he said. "I'll be able to retire. With two million, I could buy a seven-hundred-and-fifty-thousand-dollar apartment in New York."

Janey was rubbing herself was suntan lotion, and then, she couldn't help it, she snorted. "You can't buy an apartment in New York City for a *million* dollars," she said.

"What the hell are you talking about?" he said, opening a beer.

"Okay, you could buy an apartment, but it would be, like, a really small two-bedroom. Maybe with no doorman."

"So?" Redmon said, taking a chug. "What the hell's wrong with that?"

"Nothing," Janey said, "If you don't mind being poor."

For the rest of the afternoon, he would only give yes or no answers every time she tried to make conversation. Then, when they were back in the shack, making nachos, he slammed the oven door. "I'd hardly call two million dollars being poor," he said.

I would, Janey thought, but she said nothing.

"I mean, Jesus Christ, Janey," he said. "What the hell is your problem? Isn't two million dollars good enough for you?"

"Oh, Redmon. It's not that," she said.

"Well, what the hell is it?" he asked, handing her a plate of nachos. "I mean, I don't see you bringing in a lot of dough. What is it you want? You hardly work and you don't take care of a husband and children. . . . Even Helen Westacott takes care of her kids, no matter what you might think about her. . . ."

Janey spread a tiny paper napkin on her lap. He was right. What was it she wanted? Why wasn't he good enough? She took a bite of nacho and burned her mouth on the cheese. Her eyes filled with tears.

"Oh, geez, Janey," Redmon said. "I didn't mean to upset you. I'm sorry I yelled. Come here," he said. "Let me give you a hug."

"I'm okay," she said, wiping the tears away. She didn't want Redmon to know that what she was crying about was the prospect of spending every summer for the rest of her life in this shack.

"Hey," he said. "I've got an idea. Why don't we go by the Westacotts' for a drink? I'm sure they're still up. It's only ten o'clock."

"Whatever," Janey said.

It was still the beginning of the summer then.

Bill and Helen Westacott were Redmon's very best friends. Redmon insisted on seeing them practically every weekend, which made, as far as Janey was concerned, what ended up happening, really his fault. She had tried her best to avoid it. Had, in fact, refused to see them again after the first time they had dinner together. But it was no good. The next weekend, Redmon had simply gone to dinner without her, leaving her behind in the shack, where she swatted at mosquitoes all night and wondered if spending the summer in the city would really be that bad. But when she'd gone back to the city on Monday, her apartment wasn't air-conditioned and cockroaches had taken over the kitchen. She decided it was easier to give in.

Bill Westacott was a famous screenwriter

who had written five hit movies in the past seven years. Unlike Redmon, he truly was a rich writer, and he and his wife, Helen, and their two sons lived on a fifteen-acre "farm" off of Route 27. They'd been living in the Hamptons for about five years, being part of a trend of married couples with children who had chucked city life and moved full-time to the country. They had horses and servants as well as a pool and tennis court, and being able to hang out at their house for part of the weekends would have almost salvaged the summer. There was only one problem: the Westacotts themselves.

Bill Westacott was arrogant and angry and immature, while Helen Westacott was . . . well, there was only one word for Helen: crazy.

Janey wished Redmon had warned her about Helen's insanity before they went to their house for dinner the first time, but he hadn't. Instead, in his typical clueless Redmon manner, he banged on and on about what he perceived to be their amazing attributes: Helen was from "one of the best" families in Washington and her father had been a senator; Bill's mother had been an actress who was now married to a famous actor; Bill had gone to Harvard (he himself, he reminded her, had gone to Yale — he and

Bill met in a bar after a famous Harvard-Yale football game and had taken swings at each other); Helen had won a literary prize for her first novel, which she wrote when she was twenty-five. Janey was going to love them. They were one of the coolest couples in the world.

About the very first thing that happened when they pulled up to the Westacotts' house in Redmon's rented Dodge Charger, was that Bill Westacott was standing in the freshly graveled driveway, smoking a cigar with his arms folded across his chest.

Redmon rolled down his window. "Hey Bi . . ." he started to say, but before he could finish, Bill had charged up to the car and stuck his head in the window. He was a large, good-looking man with a full head of gorgeous, curly blond hair. "Shit, man. I'm glad you're here. Or I think I am. I can't decide if it's a good thing or a bad thing."

"What's the problem?" Redmon asked.

"The Gorgon is in one of her moods," Bill said.

Janey got out of the car. She was wearing a tight-fitting Lycra top, which had cost about five hundred dollars and was slit halfway down to her navel, no bra, and tight-fitting orange capri pants.

"Hello," she said, holding out her hand. "I'm Janey."

"Oh shit, man," Bill said, swiveling his head around as if he were looking for a place to hide. "This is not good."

"Helloooo . . ." Janey said.

Bill took a few steps back. "I know who you are, okay?" he said. "You're that dangerous woman."

"What's wrong with me?" Janey said.

"What's wrong with her?" Bill said, turning to Redmon. "You bring this chick who stands here asking what's wrong with her? For starters, what's wrong with you is you're a woman, okay? Which means that you are genetically insane, inane, and will probably be up my ass in about thirty seconds over some kind of bullshit I have no control over and can't do anything about. Should I go on?"

"Are you on drugs?" Janey asked.

Redmon laughed and put his arm around her. "That's Bill's way of saying he likes you. He's terrified of beautiful women."

"Well, Bill," Janey said, unable to help herself, "you sure have a funny way of showing it."

"Don't get smart with me," Bill said, pointing his cigar at her. "I know what you're up to. I know all your tricks. I work in Hollywood, remember?"

66

"Janey's not really an actress," Redmon said, taking her hand and squeezing it.

Janey leaned a little bit against him. "I'm a . . . *personality*," she said.

They went into the house. "Hey Helen," Bill bellowed. "Come and meet Redmon's . . . *personality*."

Helen Westacott was small and dark and skinny with tiny, even features — you could see that she'd probably once been beautiful. "Oh," she said despondently, looking at Janey. "Oh." She went over to Redmon and gave him a kiss. She patted his chest. "Oh Redmon," she said. "When are you going to find a nice girl and get married? Nothing against *you*, " she said to Janey. "I don't even know you, and my husband is always telling me that I shouldn't say things about people that aren't nice who I don't know, but guess what? I do it anyway. And you don't look like a nice girl. You look like a girl who would steal one of my friend's husbands."

There was silence. Janey looked around the living room, which was really quite beautiful with its large white couches and oriental rugs, and French doors that opened out onto a patio, beyond which you could see a horse pasture. It was really a shame, Janey thought. Why was it always people like this that had these kinds of beautiful summer houses?

"C'mon, Helen," Redmon said, as if he were dealing with a small, confused child. "Janey is a nice girl."

"No she isn't," Helen said stubbornly.

"Hey Hel," Bill said, puffing on his cigar. "What do you care who Redmon fucks?"

At first, Janey figured that she could have almost gotten used to Helen (it wasn't her fault she was insane, Redmon explained, and Bill would have divorced her except that he'd promised her family he wouldn't), but she couldn't deal with Bill.

He seemed to have a deep, unexplained hatred for her. Or for women like her, anyway. Every time Janey saw him, he would invariably launch into some kind of diatribe that was apropos of nothing. "All of your type think they know more than they do," he'd say, "and you berate men, and berate men, and use your tits and your pussy" — there was something about the way he said "pussy" that made Janey wince with excitement — "to get what you want and then you put the man down for having used you."

"Excuse me," Janey would say, "but have I ever met you before?"

"Probably," he'd say. "But you wouldn't remember, would you?" And Janey would turn away and sip some red wine and look over her glass at Redmon, who would look over at her and wink, thinking this was all great fun and wasn't everyone having a terrific time?

And then the inevitable happened.

It must have been well into July that first night that Bill followed her into the bathroom. She must have known that he was going to follow her, because she'd left the door unlocked and had peed quickly and was leaning over the sink, applying lipstick, when the door handle turned. Bill slipped in and quickly shut the door behind him.

"Hello," Janey said nonchalantly.

"Janey," he said. "You're driving me insane."

Janey rolled up her lipstick and smiled. "God, Bill. You're always so dramatic. I think you've been writing too many screenplays."

"Screenplays, fuck it," he said, taking a step toward her. "I know Redmon's in love with you, goddammit, but so am I."

"I thought you hated me," Janey said.

"I do," he said. "I hate you because I fell in love with you the minute I saw you. And you're with Redmon. What the hell are you doing with him anyway?"

Men are so disloyal, Janey thought.

He raked his fingers through his hair. "Jesus Christ, Janey," he said. "Just tell me what you want. I could get you a part in a movie . . ."

"Oh Bill," Janey said. "Don't be ridiculous."

He came toward her and put his arm around her neck. He kissed her and put his tongue in her mouth. She kissed him back and put her hand on his penis. It wasn't quite as large as she hoped it would be, but it would do. He tried to put his hand down her pants, but they were too tight.

"Stop it," she said. "What if someone comes?"

"What if they do?" he said, raising his eyebrows.

"Get out of here," she said, pushing him out the door.

She reapplied her lipstick and went back to the table. "Everything okay?" Redmon asked.

"Oh yes," she said. "Everything's fine."

Janey began fucking Bill whenever she could. They did it in one of the stalls in his barn. In the bathrooms at restaurants. Even in Redmon's bed during the day, when Redmon was grocery shopping at the King Kullen. When Redmon returned, swinging white plastic bags, she and Bill would be sitting in the living room, pretending he had just stopped by. It was terrible and she knew it, but dammit, she reasoned. It wasn't fair. Why did he have to be married? He was the kind of guy she could marry. Why was it that guys like Bill always ended up being caught by insane women like Helen? The world made no sense. And that house. She could be happy in a house like that for a long time.

"Redmon," she would say innocently, when they were buying lettuce and strawberries at the produce stand up the street, "are you sure Bill will never divorce Helen?"

"I'm sure he wants to," Redmon would say. "But he can't."

"Why not?"

"Because she's insane. And you can't divorce an insane woman." Redmon picked up a peach and squeezed it. "Christ, Janey. Haven't you ever heard of Zelda Fitzgerald? F. Scott Fitzgerald?" he asked. "Bill and Helen are the same. They have to stay together."

Redmon found out about it, of course. He probably wouldn't have, but Bill told him.

It was the middle of August. The weekend. Redmon kept looking at her, watching her. It was the first weekend they didn't go to the Westacotts'.

"What's wrong?" Janey asked.

"Why don't you tell me?" he said.

71

"Don't you want to go to the Westacotts'?"

"Do you?"

"I don't care," Janey said. "Why should I care?"

And later: "Maybe the Westacotts want to come over here?" she said.

"Do you want them to?"

"It might be fun," she said, "considering you're in such a bad mood."

"I'm not in a bad mood," he said.

"Could have fooled me," she said.

"Besides, I don't think Helen would like to."

"She's come over here before," Janey said.

"That's not what I mean," he said.

"Are you going to cook pasta for dinner?" she asked.

On Sunday morning, they got into an argument about the messy kitchen.

"Fuck it!" he screamed.

Janey came running out of the bedroom. "What's wrong?" she said.

"Look at this mess!" he shouted. He was holding a roll of paper towels in his hand.

"So?" Janey said.

"So don't you ever clean up?"

"Redmon," Janey said coolly. "You know what I am. I don't clean."

"That's right," he screamed. "How could I have been so stupid? You're a modern woman. You don't cook, you don't clean, you don't take care of a husband and children, and you don't *work*. You just expect some rich guy to take care of you because you're . . . a . . . a . . . *woman!* And the whole world *owes you*," he finished, throwing a damp sponge at her.

"Golly, Redmon," Janey said calmly. "You sound just like Bill Westacott."

"Oh yeah?" he said. "Well maybe there's a *reason* for that. Since you've been *fucking him*."

"I have not," Janey said, injured.

"That's what he said. He told me."

"He only told you because he's jealous. He wanted to fuck me and I wouldn't."

"Oh Christ," Redmon said. "Do I need this?" He put his head down in his arms. "I always knew I should never have gotten involved with a girl who can't even read a newspaper."

"I can read a newspaper," she said. "But I choose not to. They're boring, okay? Like you and all of your friends."

Redmon said nothing. Janey drummed her fingernails on the counter. "What else did Bill say?"

"He said you were a whore." He picked up his head and looked at Janey. "He said you have no money . . . you're just looking for a rich guy . . . you'd never stick around."

Janey said nothing for a moment. And then she screamed; "Fuck you! How dare you! You have some nerve, laying this crap on me. You're not in love with me and I'm not in love with you. So stop being such a baby."

"But that's the problem," he said. "I was in love with you."

He drove her to the Jitney stop in Bridgehampton. They didn't speak during the ride. Janey got out of the car with her bag. Redmon drove off. She looked down the street to see if the Jitney was coming. It wasn't. She sat on a bench in the bright sunshine. A man walked by with a dog and she asked him when the Jitney was coming and he said not for another hour. She went across the street to the Candy Kitchen and bought an ice cream cone. She went back to the bench. She wanted to call Bill Westacott, but she didn't think it would be a good idea.

She probably shouldn't have done what she did, but was it really her fault? This was something that men just couldn't seem to understand. It was okay for them to fuck around and to do it in the name of biology ("I have to spread my seed around"), but when a woman behaved the same way, they were horrified. Didn't they know that the door swung both ways? There was Redmon, who had some money and was sort of okay when it came to status, with his tiny little shack, and there was Bill, who was rich and successful, with his big house. What did Redmon think was going to happen? That she was going to waste herself on him? Why should she, when she knew she could do better? It was *biology*.

Halfway back to the city, her cell phone rang. Redmon. "Listen," he said. "I just want you to know. Helen was here. She was hysterical. Bill told her too. The thing you probably didn't get about Bill is that he's a big, big baby. He can't live without Helen, even if she is insane. She supported him when he started writing screenplays."

"So?" Janey said.

"So you have basically messed up three people's lives. For no reason. Not to mention their kids. Bill had to come and get Helen and take her to the hospital."

"I'm sure Bill's had lots of affairs," Janey said. "It's not my fault if he can't keep his pecker in his pants."

"But I'm their friend," Redmon said. "I was the one who brought you around, and I thought you were my friend too. What did you think was going to happen, Janey? Did you think Bill was going to leave his wife for you?"

"Exactly what are you trying to say, Redmon? That I'm not good enough?"

"That's exactly what I'm saying."

"Then I don't think we need to continue this conversation," Janey said.

"Just think about this," he said. "Where do you think you're going to end up, Janey? What do you think's going to happen to you if you keep messing up people's lives like this?"

"What about *my* life, Redmon? Why don't you assholes ever think about how *I* feel?" she said. She hung up the phone.

There were two weeks left of summer, but Janey didn't go to the Hamptons again. She sat in her sweltering apartment for the rest of August, taking a couple of hours of refuge a day in the coolness of her air-conditioned gym. As she banged away on the treadmill, she thought over and over again, "I'll show you. I'll show you all."

Next year, she would get her own house for the summer.

V

"Janey!" Joel Webb said.

"Hi!" Janey said. She waved and moved toward him, pushing through the crowd. Her martini sloshed out of its glass. She licked the rim.

"I haven't seen you for ages," Joel said.

They were at yet another party for an Internet site, held in another smoky, over-heated club. It was February, and everyone was sweating. Janey bent over to allow Joel to kiss her on the cheek.

"Whew," he said. "Who are all these people?"

"I have no idea," Janey said, and laughed. "It seems like none of the old crowd goes out anymore."

"But you ought to be able to find a rich guy here," Joel said. "Aren't all these Internet guys billionaires?"

"They're boring," Janey shouted above the crowd noise. "Besides, I'm getting my own house this summer."

"Well, this is one of my last nights out," he said. "I'm having a baby. Or rather, my girlfriend's having a baby."

"That's terrific."

"No, it isn't. I was trying to break up with her. I've been trying to break up with her for years. And then she got pregnant. I still won't marry her though. I told her, 'I'll live with you, I'll pay the bills, but it's your responsibility.' "

"That's so kind," Janey said sarcastically.

He didn't catch the sarcasm. "Yeah, I think it is. Hey," he said. "Why didn't you tell me you had a gorgeous little sister?"

"What are you talking about?"

"Your sister. Patty. You could have fixed me up with her and saved me all this trouble."

"I think she already has a boyfriend," Janey said. She moved away. Patty! Everywhere she went, it was Patty and her boyfriend, Digger. Janey hadn't even thought about Patty for years. But Patty had suddenly materialized. She'd actually been living in New York for five years, but Janey never paid any attention to her and saw her only on holidays at home, and even then it was like they lived in separate cities.

But this year was different.

Janey had never thought that Patty, who

78

was the darling of the family but who had ended up not being a beauty (she was prone to being twenty pounds overweight), would amount to anything, but mysteriously she had. Patty, five years younger than Janey, had moved to New York right after college and started working for VH1 as some kind of assistant. Which, Janey figured, was where she would stay.

But suddenly Patty blossomed. She was now some hot-shit TV producer (*New York* magazine had put her in a story about up-and-coming young talents), she lost weight, and she had a serious boyfriend — a pallid, sickly looking guy named Digger who everyone was convinced was the next Mick Jagger.

And now Patty and Digger were everywhere — or at least at all of the places Janey seemed to go. She'd walk into a club, and some PR girl would say, "Oh, Janey, your sister is here!" and then lead her up a narrow staircase and lift a velvet rope, and there would be her sister with Digger, lounging in a banquette, smoking cigarettes, and as likely as not wearing sunglasses and the latest East Village fashion; like pants made out of silver foil. "Your sister is waaaaay cool," the PR girl would whisper.

"Hey," Patty would say, stubbing out her cigarette.

"Hello," Janey said. The hello always came out with a slightly hostile edge. It wasn't that she didn't like Patty, it was simply that she and Patty never had anything to say to each other. They'd sort of sit there, looking away from each other, and then Janey would blurt out, "Um, how's Mom?"

"Mom's a pain in my fucking ass," Patty would say eagerly, relieved to have something to talk about. "She still calls me once a week and asks me when I'm getting married."

"She's given up on me," Janey would say. The truth was her mother rarely called. She didn't care about her enough to even bug her about marriage.

And now here was her little sister, Patty, the toast of the town. For the first time in her life, Janey felt old. After all, Patty really was twenty-seven. Her skin was better, but it wasn't just her outside that was younger: Patty had a freshness about her. Her world was new, and she was enthusiastic about everything. "Guess what?" she said to Janey one night, nearly knocking over her drink in excitement. "I'm going to be in a fashion spread in *Vogue*! And someone's asked me — *me* — to star in this movie they're making about downtown New York. Isn't that great?"

Janey didn't have the heart to tell her it was unlikely that any of it would happen, but she found herself involuntarily pursing her lips in disapproval like an old lady. But if it really was all pie in the sky, then why did Janey feel like she and Patty were on two different planets? And everyone was on Patty's planet, and not hers?

For months, Janey tried to avoid mentioning Patty's name, as if she didn't talk about her maybe she would go away. But she didn't. Janey spilled it all out to Harold.

"I can't figure out how it . . . happened," Janey said, in a tone of voice that was much lighter than what she really felt. "I don't want to be mean, Harold," she said, intending to be just that, "but no one paid any attention to Patty after she was sixteen. It was like she was just another adolescent lump."

"Maybe she didn't want to compete with you," Harold said. They were at the gala dinner for the opening of the ballet. The theme was Midwinter Night's Dream and the floor was awash in sparkle and fake snow.

"She couldn't compete with me," Janey said. She reached out and lightly touched the centerpiece, a miniature pine tree spray-painted white and studded with pink roses.

"And besides," she said. "Why would she want to?"

"I think you're suffering from a case of good old garden-variety jealousy," Harold said. "You feel like she's doing something with her life and you're not. If you would just do *something* . . ."

"But I have, Harold," Janey said. "I've done a lot . . ."

"Real estate," Harold said. "Become a realtor. That's the ticket."

Janey rolled her eyes. In the last six months, she and Harold had become great friends, which was wonderful because he took her to black-tie dinners, gave her money to pay her rent, and didn't ask for anything in return. Unfortunately, after Janey told him about Zack and Redmon and Bill, he became determined to help Janey find a new career. This might have been tolerable, but his ideas about what Janey should do for a living were so painfully mundane that she could hardly bear to discuss it.

Two weeks ago, he'd been convinced she should become a paralegal ("You've got a good mind, Janey, you should use it."), and the week before that, a tutor for underprivileged kids ("It'll take your mind off your own problems." "Yes, but then *I* couldn't afford to eat."). This week, it was real estate.

"Can we please discuss Patty?" Janey asked. "I feel like she's secretly trying to be me."

"Patty isn't your problem," Harold said. "You need to find something rewarding to do. Patty will take care of herself."

"I'm sure she will," Janey said softly. "But I couldn't be a real estate agent either." She sipped her champagne and looked around the room. They were seated at one of the best tables. A real estate agent! She knew girls who had done that. It was pathetic. It was one thing to be Janey Wilcox, the model, and quite another to be Janey Wilcox, the real estate agent.

"Why not? It's the perfect profession for you," Harold said, picking up his fork. "Who wouldn't buy a house from you? You could do it in the Hamptons. You know every house out there worth knowing anyway."

"I've certainly stayed in them . . ."

"All you'd have to do is apply yourself a bit and — well, I'd pay for the course. My treat."

The room swirled around them. Someone stopped and said hello; there were pictures taken.

"Oh Harold, how could I be a real estate agent?" she said impatiently, throwing down her napkin. She was wearing her hair in ringlets that she'd swept back from her face; her breasts spilled out of a beaded ivory bustier. Her skin was dazzlingly white, and she knew the whole effect was what she had come to think of as an "Elizabethan fairy princess." She was certainly one of the most beautiful women in the room, if not the most beautiful.

"Janey," Harold said patiently. "Look at the facts. You live in a lousy one-bedroom apartment on the East Side. You don't even have a doorman. You're broke. You're not interested in dating anyone who's remotely sensible for you . . ."

"By sensible, you mean boring," Janey said.

"I mean a regular guy who stays home and watches football on Sunday. A guy who really loves you."

"But I could never love a guy like that," Janey said. "Don't you understand?"

"Have you ever loved anyone, Janey?" he asked.

"As a matter of fact, I have."

"Who?" Harold demanded.

"Just some guy," Janey said. "When I was younger. Twenty-three."

"You see," Harold said. "Just some guy. You said it yourself."

Janey pushed her salad around her plate and said nothing. It was ridiculous to call Charlie "just some guy" because he was anything but, but there was no point in explaining to Harold. She'd met Charlie at a fashion shoot when she was twenty-three and he was twenty-one (he was modeling as a joke, to piss off his father), and they had instantly fallen in love. Charlie was the scion of a wealthy oil family from Denver; it was rumored that he'd inherited sixty million dollars when he turned eighteen. But it wasn't his money that made him attractive. There was the time he bought Rollerblades and skated down Fifth Avenue in a tux. The Valentine's Day that he drove her around in the back of a flower van filled with roses. And the birthday when he gave her a pug named Popeye that they dressed up like a baby and snuck into their friends' apartment buildings. He called her Willie (short for Wilcox, he said) and was the only man who ever thought she was funny.

They lived together for a year and a half, and then he bought a five-thousand-acre ranch in Montana. He wanted to get married and live there and raise cattle. He wanted to be a cowboy. Janey thought it was another joke. She told him he was the only twenty-three-year-old in the world who was dying to get married and have kids. But he was serious.

"I can't move to Montana and live on a ranch," she screamed. Her career was starting to take off. She'd just gotten the part in that movie.

She was convinced if she moved to Montana, her life would be over. Everything she had would be wasted.

At first, he used to call her on the set. "I got up at four A.M. I had my lunch at nine!" he would shout excitedly. "We rounded up four hundred head of cattle." But by the time she'd finished shooting the movie and it was a hit and she thought she was going to have a career as an actress and then realized she wasn't, he had married his old girlfriend from high school.

"Janey! Smile!" a photographer said. Janey complied, leaning her head on Harold's shoulder. Harold patted her hand. "Why don't you get married?" she said.

Harold shook his head. "You know I don't want to get married until I'm at least sixty."

"You'll be nearly dead by then."

"My father didn't marry my mother until he was sixty. And she was twenty-five. They were very happy together."

Janey nodded. She'd heard this story before, and what Harold didn't point out was that his father had died at seventy, and Harold had grown up a frightened little boy raised by his mother and two aunts in a crabbed Fifth Avenue apartment: the result being that Harold was an anal retentive who spent an hour a day on the crapper and still saw his old mother every Sunday. It was so stupid. If only men like Harold would do their part and behave sensibly — i.e., get married and have children — then women like Janey wouldn't have to worry about how they were supposed to support themselves and — ugh — make a living. Didn't Harold realize that there really wasn't any profession in which she could make as much money as he did, short of becoming a famous movie star, no matter how hard she tried?

"We could be married and have children by now," Janey said. "Do you ever think about that?"

"Children!" Harold said. "I'm still a child myself. But think about what I've said, won't you?"

Janey nodded.

"I won't be able to lend you money forever," he said quietly.

"No. Of course not," Janey said. She picked up her fork and concentrated on her lobster quadrilles. Rich people were always like that, weren't they? They'd help you out a couple of times and then, no matter how much money they had and how meaningless the amount would have meant to them, they cut you off. They didn't want to be *used*.

And then there was the Swish Daily incident.

Janey was in the designer showroom, getting fitted for his runway show, when suddenly he came in, looked at her, and screamed, "Oh my dear! Those hips!"

The fitter, a nondescript woman of about fifty, looked at Janey and shrugged. Janey tried to laugh, but the fact was that she had gained about ten pounds in the last year and hadn't been able to lose it.

"What are you talking about?" Janey said, turning sideways in the mirror to hide her discomfort, but it was no use. Swish came rushing up, knelt down, and put his hands on either side of her thighs.

"This is going to be a prob-lem," he said.

At that moment, Aleeka Norton arrived in the showroom. She threw down a Louis Vuitton handbag and called across the floor, "Hey, Swish, leave her alone about her hips, huh? She's a woman, for Christ's sake. That's the problem with you fags. You don't know women."

"Hello, darling," Swish said. "I hope you're not getting fat on me too."

"Oh shut up, Swish," Aleeka said. "Why don't you try eating pussy sometime? Then we'll talk about hips."

Swish giggled and the fitting continued as if nothing had happened, but Janey was scared. She'd been pudgy as a child, and she'd heard stories about girls who got into their early thirties and suddenly put on weight and couldn't take it off, even if they'd never had children. Afterward she found Swish in his office, where he was pretending to study fabric swatches.

"I'm not over, am I?" she asked. She was usually never this frank, but on the other hand, she usually didn't have to be.

"Oh my dear," Swish said sadly. "Of course you're not over. But your type of figure . . . that nineties, fake-titted thing . . ."

"I could take out the implants," Janey said.

"But can you take out everything else?" Swish said. He put down the fabric samples and regarded her frankly. "You know what it's like, Janey. You've seen these new girls. They've got hips the size of swizzle sticks. I think Ghisele is a size two. And she's five-eleven."

"I get it," Janey said.

"Oh listen, Janey." Swish came out from behind the desk and took her hands in his. "We've known each other a long time. You were in my first fashion show. Remember?"

Janey nodded. The show had been held in an art gallery in SoHo. "It was so hot," she said. "And we were late. We kept the audience waiting an hour and a half. And then they loved it."

"They went mad," he said. "And the funny thing was, none of us knew what we were doing then." He let go of her hands and lit a cigarette, turning toward the large window that overlooked Prince Street. A bus had pulled up outside and was unloading tourists.

"You know, in some ways I really miss those days," he said. "There was everything to look forward to. It was like a big amusement ride, wasn't it, Janey?" He stubbed out his cigarette. "We didn't know then how nasty people could be."

"No," Janey said. "We didn't."

"I always wonder if it's the times that change, or just us getting older. Do you know?"

"No."

He began moving things around on his desk. Janey shifted from one foot to the other. "You're not over, Janey," he said.

"Not one of us can ever be over unless we decide to be. But take my advice. I tell all the girls this. Go to London."

"London?" Janey said.

"London," Swish said, nodding. "You get married."

"Well. Really —" Janey said.

Swish held up his hand. "But not to just anyone. You marry . . . a titled Englishman. You know, a lord, a duke, a marquis . . . Rupert and I were just over there in October and it was fantastic."

Janey nodded patiently.

"Lady . . . Janey," Swish said. "You have the stately home, the title, money, hounds . . ." The phone rang, but Swish didn't answer it. "Oh darling, hounds are just fantastic, aren't they? You've got to do it. I could do the most fantastic trousseau for you. I could design my whole fall line around it. Lady Janey's Trousseau. What do you think?"

"Fantastic," Janey said. "But I don't know anyone in England."

"Darling, you don't need to know anyone," Swish said. He laughed, caught up in his own fantasy. "A beautiful girl like you? English girls look like crap. There's no competition. You show up in London, and within minutes, you'll be everywhere."

Janey smiled coldly but said nothing. Why

91

was it, she thought, everyone assumed that if you were beautiful, things just fell in your lap? Ever since she was sixteen, she'd been promised this big fucking prize for being beautiful and (later) having tits, but where was it? Where was this fantastic life her beauty was supposed to bring her?

And now she had to move to another country? "I don't think so," she said.

"You could go this summer. I hear the summer season is very hot in London. Ascot and all that. I'll make you a hat."

"I always go to the Hamptons for the summer," Janey said.

"The Hamptons?" Swish said. "You're not still caught up in that, are you? Darling," he said, "the Hamptons are over."

"I'm looking for my own house this year," Janey said. She kissed him on the cheek and went out the door and got into the freight elevator. It was already early April. She was fat. And she still didn't have a house for the summer.

When she came out onto the street, she banged her hand against the building in frustration.

Her nail broke painfully below the quick. She stuck her finger in her mouth. A couple of tourists wandered by. "Are you a model?" one of them asked. They were foreign, maybe from Denmark.

"Yes," Janey said.

"Do you mind if we take your picture?"

"I don't give a shit what you do," Janey said.

Two days later, she met Comstock Dibble.

His first words to her were: "They used to make fun of me in school. What did they do to you?"

"They stole my bicycle," Janey said.

He was smoking a cigar. He took a puff and held out his hand, clenching the cigar between his teeth. "Comstock Dibble," he said.

"The man who's going to save the movies," Janey said.

"Oh. So you read that shit, huh?" he said.

"Who didn't?" Janey said. "It was only on the cover of the Sunday *Times Magazine.*"

They were standing in the middle of the VIP room in the nightclub Float, at the premiere for Comstock Dibble's new movie, *Watches.* It was crowded and smoky and loud. He shifted the cigar from one side of his mouth to the other.

"I like you," he said. "I want to get to know you better. Do you want to get to know me?"

Janey leaned toward him and put her

hand on his shoulder. "Yes," she whispered.

The next day, a brand-new bicycle arrived at her apartment.

Janey ripped open the attached card with glee. It read:

Dear Janey:
If anyone tries to steal this bicycle, they'll have to deal with me.
Regards, Comstock Dibble.

VI

Memorial Day weekend again. The grass and trees were beginning to turn a deep green, reminding Janey of every summer she'd had in the Hamptons and, she thought happily, was going to have again. The cottage she'd rented was only a converted carriage house in the back of a Victorian house in the town of Bridgehampton, but it was hers. It had a tiny kitchen, a living room with built-in cupboards that contained mismatched glassware, and two attic bedrooms that were furnished with old photographs and down comforters and feather pillows. It was charming. A steal, the real estate agent said, adding that the only reason it had been available was that the couple who usually rented it had decided to get divorced the week before, and couldn't agree on which one should get the house.

"My luck," Janey said, as her cell phone rang.

"Is it great?" the male voice asked.

"It is great." Janey giggled. She walked toward a little garden framed by hedges that contained white wicker tables and chairs, where she imagined she would hostess small but important dinners that summer. . . . She'd invite Comstock, and Harold Vane . . . hell, she might even invite Redmon. After all, Redmon was a best-selling author no matter what you thought about the rest of him.

"I told you it would happen, didn't I?"

"Yes," Janey said happily.

"I told you it would happen, and what happened?"

"It happened," Janey said.

"Who can make your dreams come true?"

"Oh, Comstock," Janey said.

"I'll see you later," he said. "You'll be home? Or will you be out trying to pick up my replacement?"

"Never," Janey said

"I'm losing you," he said, and rang off.

Janey smiled and snapped the cell phone shut. It was tiny and violet and brand-new, the smallest model available. Comstock had given it to her two weeks before (he was paying the phone bill, which went directly to his office), along with a Macintosh laptop and a twenty-thousand-dollar check with which to rent the cottage.

The cottage had actually only cost fifteen grand, but Janey thought she'd keep that information to herself. After all, she'd need the five grand for expenses and car rentals. And besides, Comstock wouldn't care. He was the most generous man she'd ever been with — not just monetarily but spiritually and emotionally as well.

"I'm in love," she said to Allison, who was sworn to secrecy as to the identity of her swain. If the press got wind of the affair, they'd be all over them in two seconds. They probably wouldn't be able to walk down the street.

"He's not a movie star," Allison commented. "Don't you think you're exaggerating? Just a little?"

And later: "Oh Janey. How *can* you be in love with Comstock Dibble? How can you have sex with him?"

"This is big," Janey said warningly. "I might even marry him."

"But think about your kids," Allison said helplessly. "What if they looked like him?"

"Don't be so old-fashioned," Janey said.

She did have to admit, however, that at first her feelings for Comstock were as much a surprise to her as they were to Allison. Never in a million years did she think that she would fall in love with a man like Comstock Dibble (or, correction, a man who looked like Comstock Dibble). But when you thought about it, it made sense. That first night they'd gone out together, he had taken her back to her apartment in his chauffeured Mercedes and then casually invited himself upstairs for a "nightcap." Janey liked the sound of the old-fashioned word, and she liked the way he shyly took her hand in the elevator. He was wearing a tweedy gray overcoat, which he took off and held folded over his arm when they walked into her apartment. "Should I put this down, or are you going to ask me to leave right away?" he asked.

"Why would I want you to leave?" Janey asked. "You just got here."

"Janey," he said. He took her hand and pulled her to the large, gilt-framed mirror that hung on the wall in her tiny living room. "Look at you," he said. "And look at me. You're a beauty, Janey, and I'm an ugly, ugly man. My whole life I've had to deal with this . . . this creature."

He was right. He was ugly. But, like everything else about his life, his ugliness had a sort of legendary quality to it that became (in Janey's mind, anyway) a badge of honor. His face and body were riddled with deep pockmarks — the result of the kind of uncontrollable acne in which it seems the skin is trying to destroy the body — and his red hair was sparse and curly. His one good feature was his nose, which was small, but was unfortunately set off by a large gap between his front teeth. He had a receding chin.

But spend ten minutes in his company and you forgot about how he looked. Which was what she kept telling Allison. "I don't think so, Janey," Allison said, shaking her head. "I couldn't sleep with him no matter how much time I spent with him." She paused. "Now that you mention it, I don't think I would want to spend any time with him, either."

"Allison," Janey said patiently. "He's a great man. He's succeeded against all odds."

"Oh yes, I know," Allison said. "I read that story in *The New York Times*, too. Don't forget the part about him being a bully and a fraud, and being sued for sexual harassment and arrested for possession of cocaine."

"He was framed," Janey said. "The cops framed him because they didn't like that movie he made about the ten-year-old cop killers."

"That was a horrible movie," Allison said.

Janey didn't care. As far as she was concerned (and as far as a lot of other people were concerned as well), Comstock was a genuis. People said he was the most important producer in the business. Movie stars worshiped him. Gossip columnists vied for his attention at parties. Powerful men in Hollywood were afraid of him. He was rich, and he'd earned every penny himself.

Janey had laughed that first evening and pulled him down to the couch. "Oh Comstock," she said. "Don't you realize that, really, we're the same? We're like twins. My whole life I've had to deal with this creature too. This creature who looks a certain way, who makes people think I am a certain way. All my life, people have told me that I'm stupid." She turned her head away so that he could see the beauty of her profile. "I'm beginning to think that they're right. That I am . . . stupid. I mean, if I weren't stupid, I guess my life would have turned out better."

"You're not stupid, Janey," he said gently.

"I don't know," she said.

"You just haven't been given a chance," he said. His hand snaked out and intertwined with hers again. "I'm going to help you, Janey. I help people all the time. If you could do anything, and we're talking wish list here, what would it be?"

"I don't know," Janey said slowly. "I guess

I've always wanted to . . . write. Aleeka's writing a novel. . . ."

"Why do you want to write?" he asked carefully.

"I don't know," she said. "I feel like . . . I've got so much inside me — so many things that nobody knows about — I observe people all the time, you know. They don't know that I'm observing them, but I am."

"Forget novels," he said. "You should write a screenplay."

After that, it was easy to fall into bed with him.

All during that first month of summer, Janey felt like calling up everyone she knew and announcing, "Hi, it's Janey Wilcox. I've got my own house this summer and I'm writing a screenplay." Indeed, when people did call her during the day at her little cottage in Bridgehampton, with the split-rail fence and espaliered roses, she often as not said, "D'you mind if I call you back? I'm right in the middle of a scene."

Comstock told her that she had "vision." He said he'd make her movie a hit. That he could promote the hell out of anything, that, hell, he could strong-arm an Oscar if he had to.

"I can do anything, Janey," he said. "You've got to remember, I'm from Jersey and my father was a plumber." He was lying in her bed naked, smoking a cigar. He wasn't a big man, and he had (rather disconcertingly) skinny little legs, but he had a barrel chest and his voice was deep and impressive. It was a voice that Janey could listen to forever. "Being a successful movie producer is better than being president," he said, twirling the tip of the cigar in his lips. "You have more impact on the lives of the people, and you — hey hey — have a hell of a lot more fun." He winked at her leeringly.

"You naughty man!" Janey squealed, throwing herself on him. He grabbed her and twisted her around, kissing her face. "Who's naughty?" he asked. "Who's the naughty one?" His cigar fell to the floor as he spanked her bottom.

Mostly, though, they had serious discussions about life, with a capital "L." Janey loved those evenings when he'd turn up at her house around midnight, after he'd been out at some business dinner. During the evening, Janey would usually be at some stupid party at a store, and she'd get a message from him: "Chicken, Chicken Little. It's the Big Bad Wolf calling to huff and puff

102

down your door — hey hey — your back door! See you later?" And Janey would make her excuses and rush home to greet him in lingerie. "Am I the luckiest guy in the world or what?" he said.

"You don't know a thing about fairy tales." Janey giggled. "It was the three little pigs who had their door huffed down."

They almost always got around to sex, but not before they talked for a couple of hours. They would sit around her glass coffee table, snorting tiny amounts of cocaine and drinking neat vodka. It was not at all like Janey to snort cocaine, but then again, since she'd met Comstock, she felt like she was discovering parts of herself that she didn't know existed. He was opening her up. To life. To sex. To the realities of her own possibilities.

It was dizzying.

They talked about his movies. "What did you think of that one?" he asked her again and again. "What's your opinion?"

"I like the way you don't think you're too smart or too good to talk to anybody," Janey said.

He told her about his success — how he'd imagined it, struggled for it, finally won it — and how it was important to do something that had meaning, not just for yourself but for others as well.

"You're the only person who understands me," Janey said. "Who doesn't put me down for what I'm about and what I think."

"It's important for people to feel free even if they're not free," he said.

Then he'd lean over and put his hand under her shirt, pinching her nipples until she thought she would scream in agony.

He would watch her, his breathing getting heavier and heavier.

And then he would come at her from behind, spreading her cheeks and ramming her asshole with his penis.

"Fuck you, fuck you, fuck you," he'd say.

Luckily, it was small, so it didn't hurt too much.

Even her sister was impressed.

"Why didn't you tell me you knew Comstock Dibble," she squealed into the phone one morning at the beginning of summer.

"Why didn't you ask?" Janey said. A light rain was falling, slowly darkening the dirt in the flower beds outside her door.

"Gosh, Janey. He's only the man I want to meet most in the world."

Janey couldn't help rubbing it in a little. "Why?" she asked.

"Because I'm a producer? Because I want

to make movies for him?"

Janey moved around her little house, plumping up the cushions on the couch. "But I thought you were a *television* producer," she said. "Isn't it . . . I mean, it's my understanding that those two things are completely different animals."

"Goddammit, Janey. You've only known that I wanted to be a movie producer since I was eight!" Patty screamed.

Janey smiled, picturing Patty gritting her teeth in frustration, the way she had when she and Janey were kids and they would fight, which was basically every minute they were in a room together.

"Oh, really?" Janey said. "As a matter of fact, I didn't know that."

"Christ, Janey. I've only been working my butt off for five years. I need a break. I've been trying to meet Comstock Dibble for-*ever* . . . Janey," she pleaded, "If you told him I was your *sister* . . ."

Janey went into her tiny bathroom and looked at herself in the mirror. "I don't mind introducing you, but as a matter of fact, he's already helping me."

"He is?"

"I'm writing a screenplay for him."

There was silence.

"You're not the only smart one in the

family," Janey said viciously.

"I think that's . . . awesome," Patty said. She spoke to someone else in the room. "Hey Digger," she said. "Janey's writing a screenplay for Comstock Dibble."

Digger got on the phone. "Janey?" he said. "That's way cool."

"Thank you," Janey said primly.

"Hey," he said. "Why don't you come over to our house for dinner."

"I'm in the Hamptons," Janey said patiently.

"So are we. We've got a house here. Where's that place we have a house?" he called to Patty.

"Sagaponack," Patty yelled back.

"Sagaponack," Digger said. "Shit, who can keep up with these Indian names?"

Janey winced. Sagaponack was only her favorite area in the Hamptons. How had Patty gotten a house in Sagaponic?

"Come this Saturday," he said. "I've got the guys from the band staying here. Oh, and, hey, if you do this thing with Comstock, you should think about making Patty a producer. And bring Comstock on Saturday night too."

"I'll try," Janey said. She should have been pissed off, but she was actually pleased.

Janey wrote twenty-five pages, then thirty,

then thirty-three. She wrote in the morning, and in the afternoon, around one o'clock, she would hop on her bicycle and pedal to the beach. She knew she made a pretty picture cycling down the tree-lined streets with her blond hair flying out behind her and her bicycle basket filled with books and suntan lotion. One afternoon she ran into Bill Westacott. He was standing in the middle of the beach, looking troubled, but then again, that was probably his normal state. Janey tried to avoid him, but he spotted her anyway.

"Janey!" he called. She stopped and turned. Christ, he *was* good-looking. He was wearing a wet suit, tied around his waist; he certainly kept his body in good shape. He'd behaved stupidly the summer before, but on the other hand, he was a screenwriter. A successful one. He might be useful down the road.

"Hello," Janey said.

He marched over, looking sheepish. "I should have called you. After last summer. But I didn't have your number, and I didn't want to ask Redmon for it — I called information and you weren't listed —"

"How *is* Redmon?" Janey asked.

"He hardly talks to me, but that's okay. We've had these things before. Over women.

He'll get over it." He moved closer and Janey felt the heat between them.

"How's your wife?" she asked, swinging her hair over her shoulder. "Will she get over it?"

"She hasn't gotten over it for fifteen fucking years. And I suspect she won't get over it anytime in the future. I could be a fucking monk and she wouldn't get over it."

"That's too bad," she said.

"Janey," he said.

"Yes?"

"I . . . I haven't stopped thinking about you, you know?"

"Oh Bill." Janey laughed. "I've definitely stopped thinking about you." She began to turn away, but he grabbed her arm.

"Janey, don't. Don't do this, okay? I'm pouring my heart out to you and you're stomping all over it. What is it with you women? You want us to fall in love with you and then we do and then you kick us in the teeth and won't stop kicking."

"Bill," Janey said patiently. "I am not kicking you in the teeth. You're married. Remember? Your wife is insane?"

"Don't torture me," he growled. "Where are you staying?"

"I have my own house. In Bridgehampton."

"I have to see you. In your house."

"Don't be ridiculous," Janey said, laughing and pulling away. "You can't come over. I have a boyfriend."

"Who?"

"Someone famous."

"I hate you, Janey," he said.

She finally agreed to meet him later, at the bar in Bridgehampton. When she turned up, he was there, waiting. He was freshly showered, wearing a worn yellow oxford-cloth shirt and khakis. Damn, he looked good. He was talking to the bartender. Janey slipped onto the barstool next to him.

"Hiya." He kissed her quickly on the mouth. He lit up a cigar and introduced her to the bartender.

"So. What do you do?" the bartender asked.

"I'm a writer," she said.

"Puh! A writer," Bill said, choking on his drink.

"I am," Janey said, turning to him accusingly. "I'm writing a screenplay."

"For whom?"

Janey smiled. She'd been waiting for this moment. "Oh, just for Comstock Dibble."

Bill looked relieved. "Comstock Dibble? He'll hire anyone to write a screenplay."

"Will not," Janey said playfully.

"Will too," he said. "I heard he once hired

his doorman. It didn't work out, though. It never does with amateurs."

"You're jealous," Janey squealed. She loved the way Bill made her feel like a little girl. "You probably thought I was just a dumb model. I've written thirty-three pages!"

"Is he paying you?"

"What do you think?" Janey said.

"I'll bet he's your lover too," Bill said slyly, poking her in the ribs.

"He is not my lover."

"He isn't?"

"Well . . ." Janey said. "Let me put it this way. If he were my lover, he'd be my boyfriend."

"No, he wouldn't," Bill said.

"Why not?" Janey said.

"Because he's married," Bill said.

"Is not!"

"Is so!"

"He is *not* married," Janey said. "I would know."

"Hey, Jake," Bill said to the bartender. "Isn't Comstock Dibble married?"

"I dunno."

"You ever see him in here with anyone?"

"Only that socialite. Whasername. The one with the face like a horse."

"See?" Janey said.

"He *is* married," Bill said. "To the horsey

110

socialite. He keeps her in a barn and only lets her out on special occasions when she has to race other horsey socialites. And the grand prize is . . . one million dollars for charity! Whe-e-e-e-e-e."

"Oh Bill," she said.

She let him walk her home, and she let him kiss her on the stoop. She hoped that Comstock wouldn't drive up at that moment, but it was unlikely, as he only came to the Hamptons on weekends. "Go away," she said after a while.

"Janey," he said, smearing kisses over her face. "Why can't I be your lover again? If you can sleep with Comstock Dibble, surely you can sleep with me."

"Who said I'm sleeping with Comstock Dibble?"

"He's so ugly."

"As a matter of fact, he's the sexiest man I've ever met in my life, but you don't need to know that."

"I'll never understand you women," Bill said.

"Good-bye, Bill," Janey said.

"I want to see you again," he whined.

She poked him in the chest with her index finger. "Only if you help me with my screenplay."

"What's it about?"

She turned to go back into the house. "What do you think it's about?" she called over her shoulder.

"I don't know."

"Me!"

She closed the screen door and flopped onto the couch. She laughed. She picked up the phone and left Comstock a sexy message.

This was going to be the best summer ever.

VII

On July Fourth weekend, Patty announced that she and Digger were getting married. The papers were full of the news. Over on Parsonage Lane, where Patty's house was, Janey sat in Patty's antique-style kitchen, poring over the clippings and trying not to be jealous. Patty and Digger had immediately been proclaimed "The New New Couple" of the Millennium. They were good-looking (that was really pushing it on Digger's part, Janey thought), creative, successful and rich. They weren't from conventional "society" backgrounds. And they were under thirty.

"Look at this," Janey said, turning over the pages of *The New York Times* style section, which featured a two-page story (with color pictures) about Patty and Digger, their careers, lifestyle, and who they hung out with and where. "You'd think they'd never heard of anyone getting married before."

"It's crazy, isn't it," Patty said. "Especially considering that Digger's such a goof." She looked out the window affectionately at Digger, who was pacing around the pool, wearing black sunglasses and what appeared to be a dish towel wrapped around his waist. As usual, he was talking on his cell phone and smoking unfiltered cigarettes. He looked, Janey thought, like he had cold sores, although she had never actually seen one. He usually had bits of tobacco in his teeth, however. "I mean," Patty said, "he can't even swim."

"He can't?" Janey said, thinking, what a waste. In fact, she couldn't help thinking the whole house was wasted on Digger, who, she'd found out, had grown up in a tiny ranch house in Des Moines, Iowa. Every time she pedaled up to the house, she felt nearly dizzy with envy. How had Patty managed to get it right, while she was still struggling? Patty's house was one of the nicest in Sagaponack — a big, lazy shingled farmhouse with charming outbuildings, a long gunnite pool, and a huge green lawn that opened out into a field of wildflowers.

"Oh yes," Patty said. "You know his best friend drowned in a quarry when he was a kid. He named his first album after him. You remember? *Dead Blue Best Friend?*"

"Hey!" Digger said, coming into the

114

kitchen. He leaned over and wrapped his skinny arms around Patty; he stuck his tongue in her ear. "Don't I have the most beautiful chick in the world?" he asked Janey, and Patty giggled and pushed him away. He pointed a long, bony index finger at her. "Just wait till our wedding night, ba-a-a-a-by," he said.

"Haven't you had sex yet?" Janey asked primly. This prompted Digger to make a humping motion with his hips, which was disgusting since he had one of those stomachs that looks like it contains a small melon, like a starving child's in Africa. Then he got a beer out of the fridge.

"Don't you think it's kind of . . . weird . . . the way you and Digger come from such different backgrounds?" Janey asked after he'd left.

"No," Patty said. "We don't, anyway. We're both middle-class."

"Patty," Janey said patiently. "Digger is white trash. I mean, just that name: *Digger.*"

"He made it up," Patty said.

"Why would anyone *make up* a name like Digger?"

Patty looked up from her list-making. "He used to dig a lot in the dirt when he was a kid." She chewed on the end of her pen. "Anyway, who cares? He's a genius and the voice of his generation."

"Patty," Janey asked. "Has anything bad ever happened to you?"

"Well," she said, "there was that time you went to the Mick Jagger concert when you were sixteen and didn't come home all night and Mom and Dad interrogated me for three hours, but other than that, no."

"That's what I thought," Janey said.

"I thought you were so cool back then," Patty said. "I wanted to be just like you."

Janey had taken up with Bill Westacott again. She had promised herself she wouldn't, but it was a meaningless protest. She wondered how could she be with Bill when she was in love with Comstock, and justified it by telling herself that both men flattered her in different ways. Comstock believed that she could do anything, while Bill seemed surprised that she could do anything at all — which was, in itself, a sort of triumph. Comstock would ask her how many pages she had written and encourage her to write more; with Bill, she would tell him how many pages she'd written to rub it in. He had been so lofty when she'd met him, she loved pulling him down and pointing out that really, he was no better (if not worse) than she was.

"You see, Bill," she said. "I'm just like you. I'm going to make a million dollars and buy a big house."

"You damn women!" Bill said grumpily, sitting on her couch in his boxer shorts, smoking a joint, and leaning back to display his still nearly-washboard stomach. "You all think you're just as good as men. You think you deserve everything that men have but that you should get it without working for it. Christ, Janey. Do you know how long I've been writing?"

"Twenty years?"

"That's fucking right. Twenty years of hard fucking labor. And after fifteen years they maybe stop jerking you around and start taking you seriously."

"You're saying that I shouldn't even try just because I haven't been doing it for fifteen years."

"No. I'm not saying that. Why don't you fucking listen? I'm saying that if you think you're going to do this and you think it's going to be a success, you're out of your fucking mind."

"You're jealous," she said. "You can't stand the fact that I could do this and it could be a success, because then where does that leave you, Bill?"

They would banter like this almost every

time they saw each other, but one day it got out of hand.

"Janey," Bill said. "Why the fuck do you want to write a screenplay? It's an impossible business, and even if you do succeed, you'll end up making a lot less money than you thought you would, because it'll be spread out over five years."

"I don't need to hear this," Janey said.

"Yeah? Well, you do. Because you've been hearing a lot of drivel from Comstock Dibble. Jesus, Janey. The guy wants to fuck you. You're a smart girl, or at least you pretend you are. You know men will say anything to get laid."

"He doesn't need to."

"Oh. So you'd just fuck him anyway? Who are you kidding, Janey? We both know how you are. Did he pay for this house?"

"He's in love with me."

Bill pulled deeply on the joint. "Janey," he said, holding the smoke in his lungs and then exhaling. "Comstock Dibble is one of the most ruthless men in the movie business. He's incredibly charming until he gets what he wants. When he's finished with you, he'll drop you so fast you won't know what hit you. You'll turn around and every door will be locked and bolted behind you. Get it?"

"I don't believe you," Janey said. "I'm so sick of hearing this kind of shit from people. You're just jealous because he's more successful than you are —"

"I know actresses who have slept with him. Beautiful actresses. Do you think you're the only one who wants to sleep with him? Do you think you're doing him a favor because he's ugly? Get a clue. Does he fuck you up the butt? And only fuck you up the butt? Because that's what he does. So there's no risk of anyone getting pregnant."

Janey was silent.

"Considerate, ain't he?" Bill said. "If there's one thing an old Hollywood hand knows, it's how to avoid those messy situations called life."

"Get out," Janey said quietly.

"I'm going," he said, standing up and pulling on his shirt. "I've said my piece."

"I knew I shouldn't have talked to you on the beach that day."

"That's right. You probably shouldn't have."

"You want to destroy everyone else's dreams just because your own have been destroyed."

"Oh Janey," he said sadly. "Where do you pick up that kind of sentimental crap?"

119

"I'm just trying to do something with my life!"

"So do something with it. But at least be honest about it. Put in an honest day's work and take your lumps like everybody else." He went out and banged the screen door behind him. Then he came back. "You're right about one thing," he shouted through the screen. "We are alike. We're both pathetic!"

They didn't speak for a week, but then they ran into each other on the beach again. They pretended that nothing had happened, but it seemed like a pall had been cast over the summer. Every day was ninety degrees. The little cottage was stifling, and the attic bedrooms were unbearable at night, so Janey had taken to sleeping fitfully on the couch. She tried to write in the mornings, but found, after thirty-eight pages, she couldn't go on. She had gotten to the part where "the girl" (as Janey had come to think of the main character) is on the movie set for the first day, and the director comes into her trailer and guilts her into giving him a blow job. The story was supposed to be about her life as a model and actress and the struggles she'd gone through to be taken seriously as a person, but it seemed to have no point. Where would it end? Everybody said you had to have sex in Hollywood to get ahead. Why had she believed it? It hadn't helped her. But once you did it a couple of times, it got you over the shame of having to do it again.

Or so you thought.

A strange incident happened. She was in the King Kullen supermarket when she spotted Helen Westacott in the condiment aisle. Janey hurried past with her head down, hoping that Helen wouldn't see her, but when she looked back, Helen was staring at her with a strange, conniving expression on her little face. Janey kept thinking that she saw Helen out of the corner of her eye — in front of the soft drinks, by the meat counter, near the toothpaste; but every time she looked up, Helen wasn't there. Janey did her shopping quickly, picking up the few items she'd come in for, and when she was checking out, her cart was bumped softly from behind.

Janey looked up. Helen was behind her, her hands on a cart, her two sons next to her. Helen said nothing, just stared. The two boys, who were beautiful and dark-haired with large brown eyes, gazed at her curiously. Janey gave Helen a half smile and noticed with horror that her cart was empty.

Helen followed her out through the

parking lot. Janey wanted to run, but realized this would give Helen too much satisfaction. Then Helen veered off and got into her car.

Janey went to parties, but the people at the parties were always the same, and everybody had run out of things to say to one another. They asked her about her screenplay. "I wrote five more pages," she'd lie. She got drunk a lot.

Comstock left to stay on some movie star's yacht in the Greek Islands. Janey was hoping he'd ask her to go with him, but when she mentioned it, all he said was "I already got you a house." This was not a good sign. Then she asked him if they could have sex the regular way, and he said he wouldn't be able to get a hard-on. This was not a good sign, either. He promised he'd be back in three weeks, in time for Patty's wedding on Labor Day weekend.

"I'm just trying to be your friend," Bill said. "Do you know what a big deal that is for me?"

It seemed like the summer would never end.

VIII

"Okay, everybody! Remember, at the end of the day, it's just another party." The wedding planner, a slim young man with floppy dark hair, clapped his hands. "Do we all know our places? Patty, I know you know what to do. Any other questions?"

Janey's mother, Monique, raised her hand.

"Yes, Mrs. Wilcox?" the young man said faux-patiently.

"I do not weesh to walk barefoot. I weesh to wear my shoes."

"Mrs. Wilcox," the young man said, as if he were explaining to a small child, "we all decided that no one is going to wear shoes. It's a barefoot wedding. It said so on the invitation."

"But the feet. They are so ugly."

"I'm sure your feet are very beautiful, Mrs. Wilcox, just like the rest of you." The young man paused for a moment, looking around the room. "This is the social event of the season, folks. So let's make it *dazzle!*"

There was a round of applause. Janey looked over at her mother. She was just as bossy and self-centered as ever. Almost since the moment Monique had arrived for the wedding two days ago, she'd been nothing but trouble, questioning the caterers, flirting with the cameraman (someone was making a documentary of the wedding for Lifetime), and terrorizing Digger's mother, Pammy, to the point where Pammy, a small gray-haired woman with a perm, a flat midwestern accent, and a Samsonite suitcase full of Keds sneakers, now refused to come out of her room.

"Janey," her mother had said within an hour of her arrival, "what is this nonsense I hear about you writing something? Patty is the smart one. You must work on your modeling and on finding a husband. In two years it will be too late for the children and then you will not be able to find a man. A man does not want a wife who cannot bear his children."

"Maman, I don't want a husband," Janey said between clenched teeth.

"You girls are so foolish," her mother said, lighting up a cigarette (she chain-smoked Virginia Slims). "This business of living without a man is nonsense. In five years you will be very, very sorry. Look at Patty. She is the smart one to marry this Deegar. He is young and he is reech. You don't even have a boyfriend."

"Well, Patty always was the perfect one, Maman," Janey said bitterly.

"No, she is not perfect. But she is smart. She knows she has to work at life. You are very beautiful, Janey. But even if you are very beautiful, you must work at life."

"Maman, I do work at life," Janey said. "That's why I'm writing."

Her mother rolled her eyes and blew smoke out her nostrils. Her hair was perfectly coiffed into a blond helmet, and she still wore frosted pink lipstick. It was so typical of her, Janey thought. She was always right and always dismissive of how she, Janey, might really feel; Janey's feelings were completely irrelevant unless they dovetailed perfectly with hers.

"Your mother is soooo fantastic!" Swish Daily kept saying. He'd designed Patty's and Janey's dresses (Janey was the only bridesmaid), and had cut short his vacation on the Italian Riviera to be there.

"My mother is very old-fashioned," Janey said dryly.

"Oh no. Quite the opposite. She's absolutely modern," Swish said. "So chic. And soooo seventies. Every time I look at her I want to start singing 'Mrs. Robinson.' "

The wedding planner held up his arm and tapped his wristwatch. "Fifteen minutes until the guests start arriving," he said. "Places, everyone."

It seemed like everyone had been waiting weeks for Patty's wedding. The guest list included four hundred people and was A-list, meaning the people on it were either famous, or had a recognizable tag line after their name, such as "editor in chief of fashion magazine" or "architect to the famous." Janey didn't know whether to laugh or cry. For the past ten years she'd been climbing the Hamptons' social ladder, trying to stay in the best houses and going to the best parties, and in one season Patty had arrived on the scene and floated effortlessly to the highest rung. She and Digger had a genuine nonchalance about it, as though they really hadn't noticed, which was coupled with an attitude of careless entitlement, as if it were completely natural — even inevitable — that they should find themselves in this position. And meanwhile, Janey felt like she was begging for scraps: allowing herself to become the secret lover of a powerful man who fucked her up the ass so she couldn't get pregnant, and attempting to enter a new career in which even she, despite her arrogance, could see that she had no aptitude for.

How had this happened, she wondered, as she smiled and greeted the guests, delicately holding a glass of champagne between her thumb and forefinger. She had obviously made a wrong turn somewhere, but where? Why hadn't anyone ever told her?

"Janey!" Peter called, sweeping her into his arms and lifting her off her feet. "I haven't seen you all summer. You look fantastic, as always." Peter! Well, of course he was invited, he was Digger's lawyer. "I've been thinking about you. We should get together."

"We should," Janey said, noncommitally.

"Hey, you know Gumdrop died."

"Oh Peter. I'm so sorry," she said.

"Yeah, well, dogs are like women. They can always be replaced." He moved on with a half smile. How sad he was. In ten years, he'd be fifty-five. What would happen to him then?

"Hello, Janey," Redmon said.

"Oh Redmon," Janey said. She kissed him on both cheeks. "I'm sorry about . . . about last summer . . ."

"What about last summer?" Redmon said. "All I remember is that *I* had a *great* time."

"Well, then. So did I," Janey said.

"Well, well, sister of the bride. I hope it's not always a bridesmaid, never a bride."

"Zack!"

"Had your good summer, luv?"

"Oh yes. And I didn't even have to spank anyone."

"Harold my darling." She bent over and gave him a hug.

"I so wish this was your day, crazy kid. Maybe next year, huh?"

"Maybe," Janey said. She looked up past the crowd. A large chauffeured Mercedes was pulling into the driveway. The driver hopped out and opened the door. Comstock got out, stretched, and looked around. Then the driver went around to the other side. He must have brought the movie star with him, Janey thought, but instead, a tall, dark-haired woman got out. She came happily around the back of the car. Comstock took her hand.

"Janey! You look so pretty!" Allison said. She leaned in. "Did you see Zack Manners? He looks terrible. You must be so happy you're not with him. I heard he was pulled over for drunk driving and got caught stuffing a vial of cocaine into his sock. Socks! In the summer! When is your house over?"

"Tomorrow," Janey said. "But my land-lord said I could have it for an extra day."

"Goodie. I'll come and visit you," Allison said.

"Sure," Janey said. She watched Comstock approaching out of the corner of her eye. She knew that woman he was with . . . why was he holding her hand and whispering in her ear . . . he looked so pleased with himself, and so did she . . . oh God . . . she was that socialite — the one who'd been married to that Hollywood guy and then that guy who ran for president — but she was so ugly! She had a face like a horse, you could tell even though she was wearing huge black sunglasses like she was afraid of being recognized. . . . She was supposed to be really scary and really rich: What was he doing with *her?*

"Hello, Janey," he said.

"Comstock," she faltered.

"I'd like to present my fiancée. Morgan Binchely."

"Hello," Janey said. She couldn't take her eyes off his face. She hadn't seen him for three weeks, and for the first time she saw that beneath the ugliness was cruelty. His eyes were cruel. Without those cruel eyes, he could have never overcome his ugliness. People would have dismissed him or taken advantage. He smiled, his pink lips parting slightly to reveal the gap in his teeth. His expression seemed to sneer *Show me.*

She'd show him, all right.

"This is happy news," she said. "When did you get engaged?"

"In Greece," Morgan said. The accent in her voice hinted at finishing schools and horseback riding in Connecticut. "It was quite a surprise, I must say." She tightened her hold on his arm. "We'd only been seeing each other for — what? — six months?"

"That's right," Comstock said.

"*Mon dieu!* Mr. Comstock Dibble?" Janey's mother said, suddenly appearing at her side. "But I should curtsy. You are a king. A king of the movies!"

"This is my mother, Monique," Janey said.

"I know all your films," her mother said, dramatically placing her hand on her heart.

"You're very kind," Comstock said.

"You are a friend of Janey's?" her mother inquired, linking her arm through hers.

"Janey is writing something for me."

"I see," her mother said curiously.

"Excuse me," Janey said.

"Janey!" Comstock said

Janey turned. She looked at Comstock and shook her head.

"Tch! Let her go," her mother said. "She is always — how you call it — *martyr.*"

They all laughed.

IX

"What I'd like to do now is to go around the room and have everybody introduce themselves. And please say a few words about why you're here." The instructor, a fifty-year-old man with a mustache and an ill-fitting suit that looked like it had been dry-cleaned too many times, nodded at a woman in the front row. "Why don't we start with you," he said.

"Well," the woman said. "I'm Susan Fazzino and I'm forty-three . . ."

"We don't need ages," the instructor said.

"Okay . . . I'm married and I've got two kids, a boy and a girl, and I was a teacher and I'm looking for a way to make more money. With flexible hours."

"Very good," the instructor said. "But if your career in real estate takes off, you'll be working twelve hours a day."

"Oh! I didn't know that."

Janey sat back in her chair and tapped her pencil on her notebook. God, this was boring. She'd only been in the course for ten minutes, but already her mind was wandering.

"I'm Nelson Pavlak . . ."

Well, she supposed she was lucky to have gotten off as easily as she did. "Janey," Comstock had said. He actually had the nerve to stop by her house the next afternoon on his way back to the city as she was packing up her things. "Nothing has to change just because I'm getting married. We can continue. Morgan knows me. She knows that I'm not going to be faithful to her. She just doesn't want it in her face."

"Why would anyone marry a man who they knew was going to cheat?" Janey said viciously. "She must be pretty desperate."

"She's European," he said, unwrapping a cigar. And then: "Christ, Janey. Don't be so conventional. It's such a bore."

"Do you fuck her up the butt too?" Janey asked, folding towels.

"Actually, I don't. We're trying to get pregnant . . ."

". . . I'm Nancy McKnight. And I've always wanted to be a real estate agent . . . !"

". . . Everybody knows why he's marrying her," Allison had said. "And it's not love. She's got money. And status. I'll give her that. But doesn't she understand that he's using her? Someone should warn her.

133

Christ on a cross. She must be forty-five. She's already been married twice. You'd think by now she'd know better."

"She's what he wants," Janey had said. She was surprised at how little she felt, considering she'd thought she was madly in love with him.

"Of course," Allison said, pouring herself the last of Janey's wine. "Think about it. No matter how much money he has, or success, or power — I mean, who cares if he *is* the head of a movie company and hangs out with actors — the one thing he couldn't get was Fifth Avenue. What co-op board," she asked, "would let him in?"

"Now they all will," Janey said. She imagined Comstock in the lobby of a glossy Fifth Avenue apartment building. His suit would be wrinkled and he'd be sweating, handing out twenty-dollar tips to the doormen. . . .

". . . And what about you?" the instructor said, nodding at Janey.

Janey jumped.

"I'm . . . Janey Wilcox. The model," she said. "Or anyway, I used to be a model. I'm . . . trying to change my life. So I thought I should probably change my career as well . . ."

"We have lots of people who change from another career into real estate. But how

134

much education do you have? There's a lot of math involved in real estate."

"Well," Janey said. "I have a year and a half of college . . . and I think I used to be good at math when I was a kid."

Everyone laughed.

"Very good, Janey," the instructor said, pulling at his mustache. "If you need any extra help, I'm available."

Oh God.

Janey walked home. It was September, still warm and still light. She swung her books in a Gucci satchel Harold had bought her. He was trying to make it as enticing as possible, but in the end, she knew it wouldn't make any difference. Her days would stretch before her. There would be a certain blandness to them, but after all, wasn't that what most people's lives were like? Most people got up every morning and went to a job. They dated ordinary people and went to the movies. They didn't go to black-tie events. They didn't model in fashion shows. They didn't date best-selling authors or billionaires or movie moguls. They didn't have their names in the gossip columns, good or bad, and they especially didn't have summer houses in the Hamptons. And they survived.

Hell, they were probably happy.

She would never be happy that way. She knew she wouldn't, just as she knew she would never finish the screenplay. She would never turn up in Comstock's office and throw the finished manuscript down on his desk and say, "Read that, you asshole!" Write what you know, everybody said. And maybe it was stupid and maybe she was a loser, but that was what she knew. She could still remember the first time she'd come to New York, when she was sixteen, to become a model. Her mother had actually let her take the Amtrak train from Springfield to New York City with her brother, and had actually paid for them to stay overnight in a hotel. Which was such a weird thing for her mother to do, because she never did anything for Janey. Before or after. But that one time she had said yes, and Janey and her brother, Pete, had taken the train to Penn Station, passing the grungy little towns and cities along the way, the scenery becoming browner and more crowded and more industrial and more frightening (but Janey had loved it), until they passed through a long tunnel and arrived in New York City. It smelled of urine back then. It wasn't safe. They stayed at the Howard Johnson's on Eighth Avenue, and the horns and the clatter and the cars and the shouts kept them up all night, but Janey didn't mind a bit.

The next morning, she had taken her first taxi to the Ford Models Agency. It was on East Sixtieth Street then, in a narrow red town house. She walked up the steps. She pushed open the door. The room had industrial gray carpeting and posters of magazine covers on the wall.

She waited.

Then Eileen Ford herself came out. She was a small woman with curly gray hair, but Janey knew she was Eileen Ford by the commanding way she held herself. She was wearing brown shoes with a one-inch heel.

She scanned the room. There were four other girls. She looked at Janey. "You," she said. "Come with me."

Janey followed her to her office.

"How tall are you?" Eileen Ford asked.

"Five-ten," she said.

"Age?"

"Sixteen," Janey whispered.

"I want you to come back on Monday at noon. Can you do that?"

"Yes," Janey said breathlessly.

"Give me your phone number. I'll need to get your parents' permission."

"Am I going to be a model?"

"Yes," Eileen Ford nodded. "I think you are."

Janey walked out of the office. She was shaking. "I'm going to be a model," she wanted to shout. She wanted to run and skip and jump. "A model! A model! A model!" And then, as she was leaving, a beautiful girl walked in, a girl whose face Janey recognized from the cover of magazines and glossy advertisements. Janey sucked in her breath, watching her. The girl was wearing an ornately beaded jacket with jeans. She had on suede Gucci loafers and was carrying a Louis Vuitton valise. Janey had never seen such a glamorous creature.

"Hello, Bea," the girl said to the receptionist. She had long blond hair that fell in perfect waves down her back. "I've come to pick up my check."

It was Friday.

"Going away this weekend?" Bea, the receptionist asked, handing her an envelope.

"The Hamptons. I'm catching the eleven-fifteen Jitney."

"Have a good one," Bea said.

"You too," the girl said. She waved.

The Hamptons! Janey said the words over and over again in her head. She'd never heard of them. But surely, they must be the most magical place in the world.

When she got home from the class, her

phone was ringing. It was probably Harold. He'd promised to call, to find out how "school" went. She picked it up.

"Janey!" It was her booker at the modeling agency. "I've been trying to get you all evening. This just came in. Victoria's Secret. They called. Asked specifically for you. They've got a new campaign. They want you to audition to be one of their girls."

"That's nice," Janey said.

"Get this. They want women. They said women. No skinny little girls. So act your age. And Janey," he said warningly. "Don't blow it. Blow this, and I promise you, your career is over."

Janey laughed.

"Janey Wilcox?" the woman asked, holding out her hand. "I'm Mariah. I'm the head of corporate for Victoria's Secret."

"Nice to meet you," Janey said. They shook hands. Mariah had long dark hair. She was pretty, about thirty-five. Her handshake was firm. There were hundreds of women like this in the industry. They weren't quite attractive enough to be models themselves, but they wanted to do something "glamorous," and they took themselves a little too seriously.

"We all loved your book," Mariah said.

"We wanted to meet you."

"Thank you," Janey said. She followed Mariah into a large, open studio. There were other people there. Desks. Layouts. A man with a video camera.

"We're looking for a few special girls," Mariah said, the emphasis on "special." "It's not enough to be beautiful. We want girls who have personality. Who have lived a little. We want," she said, taking a breath for emphasis, "girls who can be role models for our customers."

In other words, Janey thought, smart models. Now there's a new one. She nodded.

The other people came around.

"Do you mind putting on some lingerie?" they whispered. They always treated you with kid gloves at these auditions, so they couldn't be accused of sexual harassment.

"Do you mind lying on that couch?"

"Do you mind if we videotape you?"

"I don't mind," Janey said. "I'll go naked if you want."

Mariah laughed. "Luckily, this isn't *Playboy*," she said.

Oh, but it practically is, Janey thought.

She lay down on the couch. She arranged her magnificent body, resting her head on her hand.

"Tell us a little bit about yourself, Janey."

"Well," Janey began, in that soft voice that gave no offense, "I'm thirty-two. I've been a model for . . . sixteen years now, I guess, and an actress too, although I like to say I've been acting every day of my life. I'm pretty independent. I've never been married. I guess I like to take care of myself. But it's hard, you know? I'm a model, but more than that, I'm a single woman, trying to make my way through life. I have my ups and downs like every other woman." She smiled and turned onto her back.

"I have days when I feel ugly. And days when I feel fat . . . like right now . . . and days when I think, 'Am I ever going to find a guy I really like?' I try pretty hard. Last summer I worked on a screenplay about my life."

"And what do you want out of life, Janey?"

"I don't know what I want, but I know I want something."

"And what about your goals?"

Janey smiled and pushed her hair back. She turned onto her stomach, swinging one leg up. She put her head in both hands. Her expression was serious, but not too serious. She looked directly at the camera.

"I guess you could say . . . I don't know where I'm going." She paused a second for effect. "But I know I'm going somewhere."

"Brilliant," they said.

Eight months later.

Janey pulled into the driveway of the house on Daniel's Lane in Sagaponack in her new Porsche Boxster convertible. The car was pure flash: silver paint with a red leather interior, a special order. It was a bonus from the Victoria's Secret people, not that they had to give her one, since she had a two-million-dollar contract for four years. It called for a maximum of fifty days of work a year, which meant, as her new agent pointed out, she'd have plenty of time to go on auditions and even do a television series or a movie. She'd already gone on three auditions for an action film with a big movie star, and they were "seriously interested."

Janey closed the car door carefully. It wouldn't do to scratch the paint. Already her sister had asked if she could drive the car, and Janey had said no. "You've got plenty of money, Patty. Get your own car," she said.

"But I want to drive *your* car," Patty whined. She looked so plaintive, they'd both cracked up.

Janey walked toward the house, twirling the keys around her finger. It was an unusual house, with the kitchen and living room (with fireplace) on the second floor, with a large deck from which you could see the ocean. There were five big bedrooms downstairs, and outside, a charming antique shack that could be used as a separate guest cottage or an office.

"Do you plan to have lots of company?" the real estate agent had asked.

"No," Janey said. "I'll probably use it to do some writing. I'm working on a screenplay, you know."

"Really?" the real estate agent said. "I know you're in that Victoria's Secret ad. But I didn't know you were a writer. Beautiful and smart. What a lucky girl."

"Thank you," Janey said.

"I just love that line you say in the ad. . . . How does it go again?"

"I don't know where I'm going, but I know I'm going somewhere," Janey said.

"That's it," the real estate agent said. "Don't we all feel that way, though."

Janey opened the door to the house. Her house, she thought. Her house alone. It smelled a little musty, but all summer houses smelled musty the first day you opened them up. In an hour, it would pass. In the meantime, she'd take a swim.

She went into the master bedroom and stripped off her clothes. The room was at least six hundred square feet, with a California king bed and a marble bathroom that contained a Jacuzzi and sauna. The house was terribly expensive, but what the hell? She could afford it.

Not bad for a single woman.

She opened the sliding glass door and walked out to the pool. It was unusually long. Sixty feet. She stood at the edge by the deep end. She paused. For a moment, she wished that Bill would show up. Walk up her flagstone path, up the steps and through the white picket gate to the pool. "Janey," he'd say. He'd fold her naked body into his arms, kissing her hair, her face . . . "I love you," he'd say. "I'm going to leave my wife and marry you."

It was never going to happen.

Janey stuck her toe in the water. It was ninety degrees.

Perfect.

She dove in.

HIGHLIGHTS
(FOR ADULTS)

I

THE DIEKES

This is a story about two people with jobs. Two people with very, very important jobs. Two very very important people with two very, very important jobs who are married to each other and have one child.

Meet James and Winnie Dieke (pronounced "deek," not "dyke"). The perfect couple. (Or, in their minds anyway, the perfect couple.) They live in a five-room apartment on the Upper West Side. They graduated (from?) Ivy League colleges (he Harvard and she Smith). Winnie is thirty-seven. James is forty-two (in their minds, the perfect age difference for a man and a woman). They've been married nearly seven years. Their lives revolve around their work (and their child). They love to work. Their work keeps them busy and neurotic. Their work separates them from other people. Their work (in their minds anyway) actually makes them superior to other people.

They are journalists. Serious journalists.

Winnie writes a political/style column ("Is that an oxymoron?" James asked her when she first told him about the job) for a major news magazine. James is a well known and highly respected journalist — he writes five-to-ten-thousand-word pieces for publications like the Sunday *Times Magazine*, *The New Republic*, and *The New Yorker*.

James and Winnie agree on just about everything. They have definite opinions. "There is something wrong with people who don't have intelligent, informed opinions about things," Winnie said to James when they met for the first time, at a party in an apartment on the Upper West Side. Everyone at the party was "in publishing" and under thirty-five. Most of the women (like Winnie) were working at women's magazines (something Winnie never talks about now). James had just won an ASME award for a story on fly-fishing. Everyone knew who he was. He was tall and skinny, with floppy, curly blond hair and glasses (he's still tall and skinny, but he's lost most of his hair). There were girls all around him.

Here are a few of the things they agree on: They hate anyone who isn't like them. They hate anyone who is wealthy and successful and gets press (especially Donald Trump). They hate trendy people and things (although James did just buy a pair of Dolce & Gabbanna sunglasses). They hate TV; big-budget movies; all commercial, poorly written books on *The New York Times* best-seller list (and the people who read them); fast-food restaurants; guns; Republicans; neo-Nazi youth groups; the religious right wing anti-abortion groups; fashion models (fashion editors); fat on red meat; small, yappy dogs and the people who own them.

They hate people who do drugs. They hate people who drink too much (unless it's one of their friends, and then they complain bitterly about the person afterward). They hate the Hamptons (but rent a house there anyway, on Shelter Island, which, they remind themselves, isn't *really* the Hamptons). They believe in the poor (they do not know anyone who is poor, except their Jamaican nanny, who is not exactly poor). They believe in black writers (they know two, and Winnie is working on becoming friends with a third, whom she met at a convention). They hate music and especially MTV (but Winnie sometimes watches "Where Are They Now?" on VH1, especially if the artist in question is now a drug addict or alcoholic). They think fashion is silly (but secretly identify with the people in Dewar's ads). They think the stock market is a scam (but James invests ten thousand dollars a year anyway, and checks his stocks every morning on the Internet). They hate Internet entrepreneurs who are suddenly worth hundreds of millions of dollars (but Winnie secretly wishes James would go on the Internet and somehow make hundreds of millions of dollars. She wishes he were more successful. Much more successful). They hate what is happening to the world. They don't believe in a free lunch.

They do believe in women writers (as long as the women do not become too successful or get too much attention or write about things the Diekes don't approve of — like sex — unless it's lesbian sex). James, who is secretly afraid of homosexuals (he's afraid he might be one, because he's secretly fascinated with both his and Winnie's assholes), says he is a feminist, but always puts down women who are not like Winnie (including her sister). Who are not serious. Who do not have children. Who are not married. Winnie gets physically ill at the sight of a woman she considers a slut. Or worse, a whore.

The Diekes don't know people who go to clubs or stay out late, or have sex (except

Winnie's sister). People who stay up late can't, by their definition, be "serious." It takes the Diekes all day (and often well into the evenings) to get their jobs done. By then, they are so exhausted, they can only go home and eat dinner (prepared by the Jamaican nanny) and go to sleep. (Winnie has to get up at six to be with her child and go running. The child is four. Winnie hopes that the child will soon be able to run with her.) At home, they are cozy and superior, and sometimes (when they're not working) sit around in fuzzy flannel pajamas with their child. Winnie and the child wear slippers in the shape of stuffed animals, and Winnie makes their slippered, stuffed-animal feet talk to one another. The child is a sweet and happy and beautiful child who never complains. (He crawls into bed with Winnie as often as he can. He says, "Mommy, I love you.") He is learning to read. (Winnie and James know he is a genuis.) "But he's a real boy," Winnie always says to her friends, who, like her, are well adjusted and earning incomes over a hundred and fifty thousand a year, who also have one or two children. It always shocks Winnie when she says this. It makes her a little afraid, because she does not like to admit that men and women are different. (If men and women are different, where does that leave her?)

Winnie believes (no, knows) that she is as smart as James (even though she's not sure that he will ever admit it) and as good a journalist as he is and as good a writer. She often thinks that she is actually better than he (in every way, not just journalism), but he (being a man) has gotten more breaks. James's style of writing and her style of writing (which she picked up from James, who picked it up from other writers of his ilk) was not hard to figure out how to do, once she understood the motivation. Ditto for their conversational style: pseudo-intellectual and desperately clever at the same time — "cl-intellectual." (Tell me I'm smart — or I'll wound you.)

Winnie is deeply bitter and James is deeply bitter but they never talk about it.

JAMES IS SCARED

James is scared about his work. Every time he finishes a piece, he's scared he won't get another one. When he gets another assignment (he always does, but it doesn't make any difference), he's scared he won't make the deadline. When he makes the deadline, he's scared his editor (or editors

— there are always faceless editors lurking around in dark little offices at magazines), won't like the piece. When they like the piece, he's scared that it won't get published. When it does get published, he's scared that no one will read it or talk about it and all his hard work will have been for nothing. If people do talk about it (and they don't always, in which case he's scared that he's not a great journalist), he's scared that he won't be able to pull it off again.

James is scared of the Internet. (He secretly wishes it had never been invented. It scares him that it wasn't, ten years ago). Every time he sends an e-mail (and he seems to be spending more and more time sending e-mails these days, and less time doing actual work, but isn't everybody?), he's frightened it will go to the wrong people. When the right people get it, he's frightened they'll send it to the wrong people. James knows he should send short, to-the-point e-mails, but something happens when he logs on. He feels angry and superior (he feels frustrated. He knows he's smarter than most people on the Internet. He wants them to know it, and is afraid they don't). He's convinced that Internet spies are watching him. He knows his credit card number is going to be stolen. (He knows that someday, probably soon, all real books and magazines will be replaced with Internet books and magazines. He pretends, along with his friends, that this won't happen. That Internet books and magazines will only add to what already exists. He knows they will not. He knows they will probably mean that he'll be out of a job.)

But most of all, James is scared of his wife. Winnie. Winnie doesn't seem to be scared of anything, and that scares him. When Winnie should be scared — when she has an impossible deadline, or can't get people to cooperate on interviews, or doesn't think she's getting the assignments she wants — she gets angry. She calls people and screams. She sends e-mails. (She spends most of her time on her computer. She prides herself on her e-mails. They are pithy and clever, unlike James's, which are rambling, vicious, and too introspective. Winnie sometimes accuses him now of overwriting.) She marches into her editors' offices and has hissy fits. "I hope you're not implying that my work isn't good enough," she says threateningly. "Because I've already done a kazillion" (that's one of her favorite words, kazillion) "pieces for you, and *they* were good enough. So if you don't want to give me the assignment. . . ." She lets her voice trail off. She never says the words: "sexual discrimination." Everyone is just a tiny bit scared of Winnie, and James is scared that one of these days she won't get the assignment, or she'll get fired.

But she always does get the assignment. Then, at the potluck suppers ("our salon," they call it) Winnie and James host at their apartment every other Tuesday night (they invite other serious journalists and discuss the political implications of everything from cell-phone shields to celebrities with bodyguards, to what's happened to the journalists who have left real magazines and gone to the Internet — "Anybody can be a writer now. That's the problem. What's the point of being a writer if everybody can be one?" James says), Winnie will usually bring up whatever new story she is working on. Everyone will be sitting around the living room, with Limoges plates (Winnie believes in serving guests on only the best china) on their laps, and they will be eating iceberg lettuce with fat-free salad dressing and skinless chicken breasts, and maybe some rice (none of the women in this group are good cooks or care much about food). They will drink a little bit of wine. No one they know drinks hard alcohol anymore.

And then Winnie will say something like

"I want to know what everyone thinks about youth violence. I'm writing about it this week." When she started doing this a couple of years ago, James thought it was sort of cute. But now he gets annoyed (although he never shows it). Why is she always asking everyone else what they think? Doesn't she have her own thoughts? And he looks around the room to see if any of the other men (husbands) are sharing the same sentiment.

He can't tell. He can never tell. He often wants to ask these other husbands what they think of their wives. Are they scared of them too? Do they hate them? Do they ever have fantasies of pushing their wives down on the bed and ripping off their underpants and giving it to them in the butt? (James sort of tried something like that at the beginning with Winnie, but she slapped him and wouldn't talk to him for three days afterward.)

Sometimes James thinks Winnie is scared that *he's* going to leave *her.* But she never says she's scared. Instead, she says something like "We've been married for seven years and have a child. I'd get half of everything, you know, if we ever got divorced. It'd be awfully hard for you to live on half of what we own and only your income minus child support." (What Winnie doesn't know is that James is more afraid that she'll leave *him*, because she's right: It would be impossible for him to live without her income. And he wouldn't want to leave his boy.)

James tries not to think about this too much, because when he does think about it, he doesn't feel like the man in the relationship. When he doesn't feel like the man, he asks himself what Winnie would ask him if she knew he were feeling that way. Specifically: What does it mean to "feel like a man," anyway? What does "a man" feel like? And since he never can answer those questions, he has to agree with Winnie — even thinking that way is passé.

Winnie told James this story on their second date: In the seventies, she smoked marijuana (age fourteen), let boys feel her up (and down) at sixteen, and lost her virginity the summer she was seventeen, to a neighborhood boy who was eighteen and very good-looking (she'd had a crush on him for years, but he never paid any attention to her until the night he sensed she would let him have sex with her. Winnie didn't tell James that part). After he came, he drove her the half mile to her house (they did it in the basement of his parents' house, where he had a cot set up). He wasn't impressed that she was going to Smith in the fall, and he didn't care that she was number three in her high school class (tolerable only because the two students above her were boys). She learned that in certain situations, achievement and intelligence were not a guarantee against being treated badly, and she vowed never to be in that situation again.

Winnie's birthday is coming, and James is scared.

"EVIL"

Winnie has a sister and a brother. Everybody loves Winnie's brother. He graduated (from?) UCLA film school and just finished an important documentary about adolescent sex slaves in China. (He sold it to The Learning Channel. Nobody is worried about him.) Everybody is worried about Winnie's sister, Evie ("Evil," Winnie calls her sometimes), who is two years younger than Winnie. Eight summers ago, Evie had to go to rehab. Hazelden. Since then, she changes her mind about what she wants to do every six months. Actress. Landscape architect. Singer. Real estate agent. Novelist. Movie director. Fashion designer. Now she wants to be a journalist. Like Winnie.

The week before, Evie showed up at a very important, very serious party for a journalist who had just written a book about a right-wing politician. (He was a *New York Times* journalist who wrote a book about every five years. His books are always favorably reviewed in *The New York Times Book Review*. This is what Winnie wants for James.) Evie's blouse was unbuttoned too low and she was showing off her breasts. (She used to be fairly flat-chested, like Winnie, but a couple of years ago, her breasts mysteriously grew. Winnie thinks she had breast implants, but they never talk about it.) Evie walked right up to the important journalist and kept him engaged in conversation so no one else could talk to him. The other women were fuming. They stood around the crudité platter chomping on carrot sticks. They rolled their eyes and gave Evie dirty looks. But they couldn't "take care of" Evie the way they normally would have, because Evie was Winnie's sister.

The next day, Winnie got a phone call from a female colleague who found out that Evie had gone to the important journalist's hotel room and spent the night with him. "Winnie, I just want you to know that I'm not going to judge you by your sister's behavior," she said. Then Evie herself called.

"I think I'm going to get an assignment from *The New York Times*," she squealed.

"Stay out of my life," Winnie warned her (quietly). Then she added (cleverly), "Why don't you get a job at a fashion magazine, if you want to be a journalist so much?"

"Oh no," Evie said. She swallowed loudly. She was drinking a Diet Coke. She drank five Diet Cokes a day. (Just another thing to be addicted to, Winnie thought.) "I'm going to change my life. I'm going to be really successful. Just like my big sis."

Evie is a mess, and sometimes James wonders if he should have married her instead.

James sees Evie as little as possible, but every year he asks her to help him pick out Winnie's birthday present. At first he did it "as a treat for Evie" (it was good for Evie to spend time around a man who wasn't a user, an asshole, or a scumbag — and Winnie agreed). But then he realized that she was attracted to him.

He calls her up. "Evie," he says.

"Hey, bro," Evie says. "Did you hear about my night with . . . ," she says, naming the serious important journalist. "And I might get my first assignment. With *The New York Times*. I think that's pretty great, don't you?" Evie is always chipper, and always acts as though her behavior is that of a

160

normal, decent person. (She is in denial, James thinks.)

"It's Winnie's birthday," James says (staying in control by getting right to the point).

"I know," she says.

"Any suggestions?" he asks. "I think I want to get her something from Barneys. Jewelry."

"No, Jimmy," Evie says. "You can't afford jewelry worth giving anyone."

(This is why everyone hates you, he thinks.) "So what, then?" he says.

"Shoes," she says. "Winnie needs a great pair of high-heeled sexy shoes."

"Okay," he says, knowing that high-heeled sexy shoes are the last thing that Winnie would want (or need). He agrees to meet Evie in the shoe department at Bloomingdale's. He hangs up the phone and feels scared.

Then he realizes he has a hard-on.

WINNIE IS WORRIED

On the day of Winnie Dieke's thirty-eighth birthday, James Dieke wakes up and is scared. Winnie Dieke wakes up and is depressed. Not that she has anything to be depressed about. She has, after all, hit all her life landmarks in style: first job at twenty-two, first major assignment for a prestigious magazine at twenty-seven, met future husband at twenty-eight, married at thirty, established herself as a "serious journalist" at thirty-one, co-op apartment at thirty-one, pregnant at thirty-two, own column at thirty-four. For the past few weeks, Winnie has been spending a lot of time (too much time, which she knows should be spent thinking about other things, like ideas) reminding herself of everything she's achieved. Reminding herself how clever she is not to be one of those desperate single women (like Evie). But something is wrong.

Winnie doesn't want to admit it (she never wants to admit that there possibly could be anything wrong with her life), but that something might be James. Lately, she's been worried about James. (Irritated, actually, but worried is such a better way to look at it.) James hasn't been holding up his end of the bargain. He should have written a major, important work by now (preferably about politics: so easy, considering the political climate), which would have elevated her status in the journalistic world as his wife (she didn't take his last name for no reason). If James had written an important, influential book by now, they would have access to more important, influential people. They would *be* more important, influential people. But instead, James keeps writing the same kind of pieces. And agonizing over them. Half the time now, James calls her up during the day and says, "I can't write. I'm stuck. I'm blocked."

"Oh please, James," she'll say. "I've got a kazillion things going on. I've got the CEO of a major corporation on the other line. If you're blocked, go to the supermarket and pick up something for dinner. And make sure it doesn't have any fat in it." Then she'll hang up. She wishes he would just get on with it.

James is frustrated and Winnie is frustrated but they can't talk about it.

When Winnie tries, when she gently suggests (the way shrinks are always telling you to do it, picking the "right" moment, when you're both relaxed) that maybe he should really get to work on a book proposal, he sulks. He turns on the TV and watches some idiotic, mindless show like *Hercules*. Sometimes Winnie freaks out and unplugs the TV. Sometimes she just screams. But the argument always ends with Winnie shouting, "Do I have to do everything? Do I have to work and take care of our child" (even though she doesn't really take care of the child — the nanny does most of the caretaking, and Winnie only spends an hour with him in the morning and two hours in the evening) "and keep our careers on track? Do I have to make us famous?"

"We're already famous," James shouts back (thinking, You make me sick and why did I marry you? but never having the nerve to say it, because Winnie would probably leave and people would find out). "We're as famous as we're going to get, Winnie. What else do you want me to do?"

"I'm doing more," Winnie says, calmer now, because she doesn't have the stamina to go on screaming forever (but she does, James thinks, have the stamina to do enough screaming). "Why don't we move to Washington?"

"I don't want to move to Washington. All my editors are here," James says. And then he plugs in the TV or retrieves the remote control from where it has been flung under a chair, and goes back to watching *Hercules*.

Winnie and James never tell their friends about these arguments. On the weekends, when they're hiking or gardening or antiquing with their friends (everybody piles into somebody's car and they go to a nursery and buy plants or go "poking around" in western Connecticut), they present a united front: They respect and admire each other and each other's work and they are best friends. Even when they had that horrendous discussion with their friends one Saturday evening (they all agreed the next morning that maybe a little too much red wine had been consumed — four bottles between the eight of them — and vowed never to let it happen again) about what social class they were from and what social class they now belonged to, they all remained good friends. And they might not have. While Winnie's class background was established beyond a doubt ("textbook, practically," James had said) — she came from a well-to-do Irish family and grew up in a ten-room colonial house on twenty acres in Pennsylvania, where her father was a judge — James's was not. His father owned three dry-cleaning stores on Long Island. Dry cleaning was definitely blue-collar, but no one could agree on whether or not the fact that he "owned three stores" elevated him to white-collar.

James knows what is wrong with his life. With his writing. He's been losing his drive at about the same rate that he's been losing his hard-on.

On the morning of Winnie's birthday,

James Dieke wakes up and is afraid. He's going to do something to Winnie. Something she won't like. And he's excited.

At noon, James goes to Bloomingdale's to meet Winnie's sister. As he walks toward the shoe department, he realizes his worst fear has taken place — Evie is not there.

He stands in the middle of the shoe department, not knowing what to do. Everybody is watching him. He is on display (like a shoe). He picks up a shoe and puts it down. A salesman comes over. What kind of a man is a salesman in a women's shoe department? The man asks if he can help him. James says, "No, I'm waiting for someone. My wife. It's her birthday." Why has he lied to the salesman? Why has he told him anything? What if the man (a stranger) finds out that Evie is not his wife? He will think Evie is his mistress. What if Evie were his mistress? What if he were secretly fucking his wife's sister? (It could happen. Evie fucks everyone, has a new boyfriend every two weeks, sleeps with married men, sleeps with men she meets in classes at the Learning Annex, at AA, at the snack bar in the Met.) When Winnie is feeling charitable, she says that they shouldn't judge Evie, that Evie can't help herself because she's a sex addict.

James walks around the shoe department. He thinks about leaving, about teaching Evie a lesson. (He can think of lots of lessons he'd like to teach Evie.) But she might show up any minute. He sits down.

He tries to look comfortable. (He's getting angry.) When he was four, he once got separated from his mother while she was shopping at Bloomingdale's. He had wandered into the lingerie department. It was full of pointy bras and girdles hanging from racks above his head. It was like a forest, and he had circled around and around, thinking he was going to see his mother around the next clump of Lycra (was it Lycra they used then, or something else?). He didn't. He sat down. He cried. (He wanted to scream.) He was scared, more scared than he'd ever been in his life, before or since. And angry. He thought his mother had abandoned him. On purpose. He didn't know what to do. (He was just a little boy.)

"Hello, Jimmy." Evie comes up behind him and puts her hands over his eyes. He doesn't move. (He must not reward her inappropriate behavior. But he feels silly sitting in the shoe department at Bloomingdale's with a sexy woman's hands over his eyes.)

"Dammit, Evie," he says. "I don't have

much time." (Reminding her of whom she is dealing with.)

"Deadline?" Evie says (smartly, he thinks).

"I'm always on deadline," he says. "It's about responsibility. Something you're not familiar with."

"Gee, thanks," Evie says. She is a little bit crushed, he can tell. But he has to crush her. (He can't let her flirt with him. Evie must learn about boundaries. Then maybe she'll be able to find a man, keep him, and get married. Become a healthy member of society.)

"Let's make this quick, then," Evie says. She turns and smiles. "I've got a deadline too. I wanted it to be a surprise, a wonderful surprise for you and Winnie. I got that assignment from *The New York Times*! Oh Jimmy," she says. "You're going to have to help me. I'm going to be calling you every day, asking for advice. You don't mind, do you?"

"How'd you do that?" James asks. He wants to be happy for her, but he can't. Evie doesn't deserve to get an assignment from *The New York Times*. She's never written a piece before in her life. He wants to scream (as he so often wants to scream these days), *What is the world coming to?* "Well, good for you," he says.

Evie picks out some shoes. All high-heeled sandals. Fuck-me shoes, Winnie would call them. He watches as Evie's foot slides into the sandal. She has good legs. Great legs, actually. She models the shoes, turning this way and that. "Jimmy," she says, "I really want you to be happy for me. I'm trying. Trying to make something out of my life. Why can't you and Winnie be supportive? For a change."

"We are," James says.

Evie puts her hand on his shoulder for balance as she leans down to take off the shoe. He doesn't brush her hand away. She looks at him suggestively, and for once, he looks at her suggestively back. If she can break the rules, he thinks, maybe he can too.

He spends four hours shoe-shopping with Evie. They go to Barneys. Bergdorf's. Saks. They go to lunch (Gino's). Evie drinks wine and he does too (he objects at first, ordering bottled mineral water, but then, after Evie has nearly consumed her first glass, he quietly orders a glass for himself, over his shoulder, as if she might not notice). Finally, they decide on the perfect pair of shoes for Winnie. Manolo Blahniks. Sandals. The shoes cost five hundred dollars. He pays gleefully. He and Evie part on the street corner. "I'm going to call you tomorrow," she says. "So we can discuss my article."

"It's a piece, Evie, a piece. Not an article," he says.

He walks away. The little bit of alcohol (and it really was only a little bit, one glass only) is wearing off and he feels slightly queasy, like a thing that's been left out in the elements for too long. What has he done (has he done anything)? He hails a cab. For the first time in his marriage, he wishes he didn't have to go home. (But he can't think of where he'd like to go instead.)

WINNIE LOOKS AROUND

Winnie still considers it her job to be the good-looking one in the relationship. Being good-looking is part of mastering the world. It is part of being perfect. (It is not about being beautiful. Beautiful women are self-indulgent. Beautiful women are stupid because they don't have to try.) She is five-seven and weighs 125 pounds. If she let herself go, let her body reach its natural weight, she'd probably weigh between 130 and 135 pounds. But she won't let herself go. (It's about control.)

Winnie thinks about weight a lot (probably too much. She should be thinking about more important things, like ideas. But who can help it?). She is very, very against women's magazines using skinny young models. It's one of her pet peeves. (She wrote a two-part series about the topic, called "Skin and Bones is Not Sexy," and afterward, she went on two newsmagazine programs on TV, where she destroyed her opponent, a fashion editor from a women's magazine.) But she would never want to be "fat" herself. (She feels bad when she sees friends who have gained weight. She feels superior. But only because she knows they are unhappy.) She keeps her weight under control by running around the reservoir in Central Park every weekday morning at seven A.M. (she knows it could be dangerous, but it would be more dangerous to gain weight). She weighs herself afterward. Examines her naked body in the mirror. Turns sideways to make sure her stomach isn't bulging and her breasts aren't sagging. But they both are. A little bit. (It's frustrating. It makes her hate herself. She reminds herself that she's had a child, which doesn't help much.) If she is two pounds overweight, she takes care of it. Taking care of herself is part of being a nice girl.

Sometimes, when Winnie looks around (meaning her office or the sites she goes to on the Internet), she feels like she's the only nice girl left in the world. (Sometimes she feels like it's a crime.) When Winnie was growing up, everyone was from a "nice" family. (They might not have been that nice behind closed doors, but no one talked about it.) Winnie's mother was always perfectly dressed. Her house was beautifully decorated (with antiques and silk draperies). She cooked and cleaned. Winnie didn't. And her mother didn't make her. They both knew that Winnie would have "a career" and "a cleaning lady." (They would never call anyone "a maid" or "a servant.") Her father was remote but not unpleasant. He was just a father, like everybody else's father. He wasn't that important. He paid the bills. Her parents are still married.

Sometimes, when Winnie looks around, at the young women who now work in her office, she wonders what happened to the nice girl. (She knows what her assistant would say: "The nice girl is s-o-o-o-o-o over." Then she would look at Winnie. She wouldn't say anything. She wouldn't have to. Winnie would know what she was thinking: that Winnie was over.) None of the young women are nice girls anymore (and they don't care). They wear black and flaunt their (ample, sometimes already sagging) bosoms. They wear short skirts. Dresses that look like lingerie. They have tattoos. And piercings. They live downtown in dirty little apartments and have sex a lot and talk to one another about it the next day. No one can say anything to them. Everyone is afraid of sexual harassment.

Sometimes (and Winnie can't believe this) Winnie is afraid of *them*. She can't believe she is already ten years older than they are. She has nothing in common with them. Even when she was ten years younger, she wasn't like them. She was more ambitious. And more focused. She didn't use sex to get ahead. (Although she did marry James, which, she has to admit, didn't exactly hurt her career.) She didn't come to the office hungover, and she didn't take drugs. (Last year, one of these young women was caught shooting up heroin in the ladies' room. She was found nodding out in a stall. By a cleaning lady. The girl was sent to rehab. She wasn't fired. She couldn't be. She came back two months later.

Eventually, she was gently moved to another magazine.)

These young women aren't scared of anything. (They're hungry. And arrogant. They'll do anything to get ahead.) Last year, two young women were caught plagiarizing.

One of them plagiarized two paragraphs from a piece Winnie had written three years before. When Winnie read it, she felt sick. (She felt violated. By another woman. She couldn't believe another woman would do this to her. She thought women were supposed to stick together.)

Nothing happened. (Winnie complained. The management said she should be flattered the young woman plagiarized her. It was a compliment.) Eventually the young woman was promoted.

Winnie would like to try to be friends with these young women. But she's afraid the gulf is too wide. She would like to say, "Hey, when I was young, I was a rebel too." But she knows they would look at her blankly. (That's what they always do. To gain control. Stare blankly.) She would like to tell them that when she was a teenager, wanting to move to New York City and do "great things" was considered daring. As was having seven lovers before she met James. (One was a one-night stand. And one was an affair with a professor. Who was twenty years older. He was the first man to perform oral sex on her.) But she won't tell them. She knows they would laugh. She knows that, by the time they've gotten to twenty-five, these young girls have already had a hundred lovers. (And probably a veneral disease. Or an infection. From a piercing or a tattoo.)

On the day of Winnie Dieke's thirty-eighth birthday, she wakes up and feels depressed.

That afternoon, Winnie does what she has been doing on the afternoon of her birthday for the past ten years: She goes to Elizabeth Arden.

She pampers.

She has her hair highlighted and blown dry. She has a manicure and a facial. She has a bikini wax. (She would never shave down there. Shaving reminds her of what happened when she had the baby. She's not sure she wants to do that again.)

The bikini wax hurts. She hates it, but she has one every two months. It gives her ingrown hairs, which she sometimes picks at absently with a pair of old tweezers before she gets into bed. (James ignores this. He has gross habits too, like picking his nose while he's reading and rolling the snot into a little ball and examining it before he flicks it away onto the carpet.) During the bikini wax, Winnie wears paper panties. She has to spread her legs a little (but only a little, she tells herself), and the woman (the facialist) has to touch her a little down there. They both pretend that she isn't, just as Winnie desperately tries to pretend that she isn't thinking about sex. But she always does. She tries not to. She tries not to think about the young women in her office and how they've probably had sex with other women as well as men. Tries not to imagine that women know what other women want. They want someone to spread their legs. Instead, Winnie wonders what will happen when she gets gray hairs. Down there. It's going to happen someday. What will James think?

Does she care?

She and James don't have sex much anymore. When they do, it's always the same. He performs oral sex on her. She has an orgasm. They have intercourse. He comes. Winnie has never had an orgasm from "just fucking." (She doesn't believe it's possible. She secretly thinks that women who say they can are faking it.)

After the bikini wax, when the woman leaves the room and Winnie puts on her own underpants (practical black cotton bikinis), she always wants to touch herself down there, but she doesn't. There are limits to how far she will go. Especially when it comes to being "sexy." She will not wear lingerie. Overly short skirts. See-through blouses. Or ridiculous shoes.

"What are these, James?" she asks later, standing in the bedroom. The strappy sandal, so delicate it looks like it might break from simply walking across a room, dangles from her finger.

"It's your birthday present," James says.

"Why?" Winnie asks.

"You don't like them," James says in a hurt voice (knowing it's the only way he might possibly get out of this horrendous situation he's created, which he is beginning to enjoy).

"You know I don't wear shoes like this. I don't approve of shoes like this," Winnie says.

"Evie got that assignment from *The New York Times*," he says.

"Did Evie pick out these shoes?" Winnie asks.

"It's disgusting. She got it by sleeping with . . . ," he says, naming the famous journalist Evie picked up at the book party a couple of weeks before. "She says she's still seeing him."

Winnie looks at James. When she first met him, she wanted to be him. (Everybody wanted to be James then. He was going to have a big career. The kind of career that Winnie wanted. James was the next best thing.)

"Do you think people still want to be you, James?" she asks. Casually. (He knows that when Winnie asks these questions out of left field she is laying a trap for him. But he's too weary, and a little hungover, to figure this one out.)

"Why would anybody want to be me?" James asks.

"That's just what I was wondering," Winnie says. She carefully packs the sandals back into their box. "This is really a pain, you know," she says. "I want to return these, but I don't know when I'm going to have the time."

"Do it on your lunch hour."

"I don't have a lunch hour," Winnie says. "Not anymore. The magazine is expanding my column. To two pages. So I'm going to be twice as busy."

"Well, good for you."

"Can't you sound a little more excited? I'm a big deal now."

"I am excited," James says. "Can't you tell?"

"Why don't you get dressed now, James," Winnie says.

He and Winnie are going out. He changes his shirt and puts on a tie. He feels angry. (He can never do anything right.) He taught Winnie everything she knows (or thinks he did). When they first met, Winnie would sit for hours, listening to him and asking him questions about his work. When she got drunk (they used to get drunk quite a bit at the beginning and have easy, passionate sex), she would sometimes say that she wanted to be a serious journalist too. That she had ambitions and aspirations. That she was smart. James never really paid attention. He wouldn't have cared if she was dumb. (And now he sometimes wishes that she were. Dumb.)

At first, James saw Winnie as one-dimensional. And only in relation to him. She was the high school girl he could never get in high school. Then he saw that she had other qualities. With Winnie, situations that felt awkward before (parties, socializing) felt natural. After a year, everyone started asking when they were going to get married. Suddenly, he found himself asking the same question. (He wasn't sure where it came from. Inside? Or was he just repeating what everyone else was saying?) She wasn't perfect (he couldn't put his finger on why), but he didn't think he'd meet anyone better. Plus, all his friends were getting married. Buying co-ops. Having kids (or talking about it). He would be the odd man out again, like in high school.

And he's still the odd man out. (He wishes he were still with Evie. He wishes he were getting a blow job from her right now.)

"Come on, James," Winnie says.

They go to Bouley for Winnie's birthday, where, as usual, they pretend (and it really is just pretending now, James thinks) to get along. When the bill comes, they each put down their credit cards and take their receipts, which they will turn into their magazines as a business expense.

EVIE'S "PIECE"

"Have you read it?" James asks. It's a few days later. Sunday morning. Early. The Sunday morning Evie's piece is scheduled to appear in *The New York Times*.

"Read what?" Winnie asks. She's in the kitchen, cooking breakfast. It's really the only time she cooks (if you can call it that, James thinks), cutting grapefruit and putting out slices of smoked salmon and smearing cream cheese on bagels.

"Evie's piece," James says.

"Oh. Is it in this weekend?"

"She says it is."

"Really?" Winnie says. "I haven't talked to her."

"She calls me," James says.

"I hope you don't talk to her either."

"She's still seeing . . . ," he says, naming the famous important journalist.

"That's nice," Winnie says. She puts the platters out on the dining room table. She unfolds a paper napkin. She begins eating.

"Aren't you curious?" James asks.

"I'll get to it later," Winnie says. "In the meantime, I'm thinking that maybe we should run our salon more efficiently. Maybe we should e-mail people a question the day before, so everyone has time to think about their answers. I think we'll get better responses that way."

"I thought we were" (*you* were, James thinks) "getting good responses."

"We can always do better, can't we, James?"

Winnie eats two bagels stuffed with cream cheese and salmon. "Be right back," she says. "Have to brush my teeth. Onions."

She goes into the bathroom, and, as she has been doing after almost every meal lately, sticks her finger down her throat and throws up.

When she returns, James is reading the paper.

"You're disgusting," she says.

"What? I'm not supposed to read the *Times* just because Evie has a piece in it?"

"Oh come on, James," Winnie says. She snatches up half of the paper. She begins turning the pages (she can't help herself, James thinks, she can never help herself). Finally, she gets to the Styles section. There, under the heading "Thing" is a tiny box with a story on meat loaf. At the bottom is Evie's byline.

"Did you know about this?" Winnie asks.

"What?"

"Evie's 'piece.' " Winnie tosses the paper to him. She stands up. "Are there any more bagels left? I'm still hungry."

In the afternoon, Winnie calls Evie. "Congratulations," she says.

"Hey!" Evie says. "Thanks."

"So how does it feel to be a journalist?"

"Great," Evie says. "I'm working on another piece for them next week. See? I got the lingo right. I said 'piece,' not 'article.' " There is the sound of shuffling in the background. Evie laughs. "Can you hold on?"

"Is someone there?" Winnie asks. (God, Evie is so rude, she thinks.)

"Mmmm, yeah . . ." Evie says, naming the famous important journalist.

"That's perfect," Winnie says. "Because James and I wanted to know if you and . . ." she says, naming the serious important journalist, "wanted to come to dinner next week. Our treat. We'll work it around his schedule. Oh, and Evie?"

"Yes?" Evie says, somewhat suspiciously.

"Just remember one thing," Winnie says.

"What's that?" Evie says.

"You're one of us now," Winnie says (smoothly, so that Evie won't suspect how difficult it is for her to choke out those words). "And we *are* the media."

II

WINNIE'S BAD HABIT

Winnie has developed a bad habit and she can't help herself.

Every morning now, when she enters her office — a large black building on Sixth Avenue that screams "I'm important" — she hurries through the lobby and into the elevator (she once calculated that she spends an hour a day waiting for elevators and riding in them, and wishes someone would invent a faster one), walks quickly along the beige-carpeted hallway and enters her office — a small, bland white room with a window, three sickly spider plants, and a small blue couch — and flips on her computer.

She types in her password. Takes off her coat. Types in "www.ama" and hits enter, at which point the computer goes immediately to Amazon.com. And then (she can't help herself, she can never help herself) she types in the name of the serious, important journalist.

She has been doing this every morning for the past two weeks.

She checks his book's sales ranking, then she scrolls down over the reader reviews.

Her favorite one is this:

Boring and Utterly Pointless

"Imagine if your most boring poly-sci professor wrote a book and forced everyone in the class to read it? You (sic) want to kill the guy, right? Read the ingredients on your cereal box instead. It's more interesting."

As always, Winnie feels thrilled and terrified at the same time.

Ever since she discovered the site (she'd known about it before but didn't acknowledge it, as people like her still bought their books from actual bookstores), she hasn't known what to think. Part of her is outraged. These people shouldn't be buying books. They're too stupid to read. They have no imagination. No ability to read and comprehend. If a book doesn't conform to what they believe about the world in their own narrow, unsophisticated minds, they pan it. They're like the dumb kids in class who never understood what the teacher was talking about and got angry instead of understanding what everyone else in the class understood — that they were too dumb to understand. But part of her is (not even secretly) afraid that they might be right. The book is a little boring. Winnie read two chapters and skipped to the end and didn't pick it up again. But it's an important book. Why does some git in Seattle who's probably never written more than an e-mail have the right to pan it? To tell other people not to buy it?

Winnie is disturbed.

The world is not right. (Or is it right, and she's not? Maybe she's like the dumb kid in the class. But she knows she isn't. Dumb. Sometimes she thinks there should be a test for dumbness while a baby is still in the womb, and all the dumb fetuses should be aborted. She knows what the argument against it would be: "Who will decide what dumb is?" She has the answer: She would. She'd be happy to decide.)

Then she checks the sites of the ten or so other writers she and James know who have published books in the last year. She checks their sales ratings. If the ratings are very bad, like around 286,000, she can't help it. She feels good.

She has to stop doing this. But she can't. It's research. What will happen if James writes a book? She wants to be prepared. She will have to numb herself against the inevitable bad reader reviews. She knows she can't take them personally, but she will. She takes everything personally. Especially herself.

Maybe it would be better if James didn't write a book. (Maybe it would be better if they moved to Vermont and worked for a small local newspaper. After two months, it would be like they were dead — everyone they knew would forget about them, and Winnie isn't ready to do that. Yet.)

The phone rings. She picks it up.

"Yes," she says.

"It's me." (It's James.)

"Hi," she says. She suddenly remembers that she has all these things to do. Like work.

"Are you okay?" he asks.

"I'm stressed. I've got a kazillion things to do."

You've always got a kazillion things to do, and I wish you'd shut up about it, James thinks. Wondering: Why don't you pay attention to me? Why don't you make me feel good? Why is it always about you? Aloud, he says, "I got a call this morning. From Clay. Tanner's coming to town."

"Is he?" Winnie says. She isn't sure how she feels about this information yet.

"He has a movie premiere. On Thursday."

"Ugh," Winnie says. For the first time in days, she knows that James is thinking the same thing she is. "Another —"

"Yup. Bang-'em-up, shoot-'em-up, big-budget movie, courtesy of Paramount Pictures."

"I suppose we have to go," Winnie says, emitting a long sigh.

"You don't have to," James says. "But I'm going to."

"If you're going, I'm going," Winnie says.

"Fine," James says in a small voice.

"Don't you want me to go?" Winnie says. Threatening.

(Why does she always become immediately threatening? James thinks. Even wasps let you swat them away before they sting you.)

"I do want you to go," James says. "But you hate things like that."

"I don't."

"You do."

"I don't hate them. I think they're boring. You know how I feel about celebrity worship."

"Tanner wants me to be there," James says.

"I'm sure he wants us both to be there. But that doesn't mean we have to do whatever Tanner wants."

"He's only in town twice a year," James says. "I want to go."

(I'm sure you do, Winnie thinks. So you can ogle dumb blondes.) "Fine," she says. She hangs up the phone.

Now she has to be "concerned" (a much better word, more accurate than "worried") about James for a week. Specifically about what he's going to do (how he's going to behave) when Tanner is in town. She will spend hours (time that should be spent doing something important, like thinking of ideas) reacting to James's as yet unenacted behavior. She will obsess over if/then scenarios. Such as: If James stays out all night with Tanner (again), then she will divorce him. If James flirts (pitifully, desperately) with the actresses in the film (again), then she will lock him out of the house. If James drinks too much and throws up out the cab window (again), then she will throw all his clothes out the window. (James does not understand that he is skating on thin ice. Very thin ice.)

His black marks are mounting: She's known him for ten years and still can't trust him. He doesn't do exactly what he's supposed to do. He can't be relied upon (even to get the right groceries at the supermarket). He acts like a baby (he is a big

189

grown-up baby). He's turning out not to be important. (And he doesn't pay the bills.)

She might (actually) be better off without him: It would mean one less person to take care of.

Winnie hits a button on her computer and goes to her e-mails.

Her assistant comes into her office. Winnie looks up. The assistant's dark hair is messy. She is wearing sloppily applied red lipstick; a short black skirt with no stockings; a rumbled black V-neck sweater (at least she is wearing a bra); clunky black shoes. She looks like (pardon the expression) someone rode her hard and put her away wet.

The assistant flops down on the couch. "What's up?" she says. (What's up? Like Winnie is the assistant and has just plopped into *her* office.)

Winnie is never sure how to respond to this greeting.

"How are you?" she says. Briskly. Reminding the assistant that this is an office. And she is her boss.

The assistant picks at her manicure. Fingernails painted a mud brown. "I've got a urinary tract infection. I'm wondering if I can take the rest of the day off."

Someone did ride her hard and put her away wet.

"No," Winnie says. "I've got that big Internet conference this afternoon and I need you here. To cover the office." (The magazine is expanding their Web site, and they want Winnie to be involved. Very involved. It could mean more money.)

"It hurts," the assistant says.

(Winnie wants to tell her — scream at her — to stop having so much sex, but she can't.) "Buy some cranberry juice. And take five thousand milligrams of vitamin C."

The assistant just sits there.

"Is that it?" she asks.

"Is what it?" Winnie says.

"What you just said."

"About what?"

"About you know."

(No, I don't know, Winnie wants to scream.) "I don't understand."

"Neither do I."

"About what?"

"Whatever," the assistant says. She stands up. She goes back to her cubicle. (Like a dog.)

Winnie tries to concentrate on her e-mails. Her shrink tells her not to envision if/then scenarios.

What if Tanner kept James out for two nights and James slept with prostitutes? What then?

She can't help herself. She can never help herself.

JAMES HAS A THEORY

In the week before Tanner comes, Winnie is concerned and James is excited. They both know something bad could happen, and they're going to have to talk about it.

James and Winnie know when Tanner comes to town, James can get away with doing bad things. Tanner is bad. (He's a bad influence.) Tanner is so bad, in fact, that when James does bad things with him, Winnie always blames Tanner. Winnie thinks (knows?) that James would never do these bad things if it weren't for Tanner. And she's right. James wouldn't. He doesn't have the guts to defy Winnie.

But Tanner does. Tanner doesn't care what Winnie thinks. (He probably thinks she's boring. Which James is beginning to think himself. He wishes Winnie would do something interesting, like go away. Then maybe he could fall in love with her again. Or find somebody else. Like a six-foot-tall Swedish woman with large breasts.) Winnie would like to control Tanner (the way she controls James), but she can't. Winnie can't do anything to Tanner.

Tanner is a big movie star and Winnie is not.

Tanner is a celebrity. Compared to Tanner, Winnie is an insignificant journalist. Compared to Tanner, Winnie is a woman. Women don't mean anything to Tanner, except as something to have sex with. (James wishes he could feel the same way. If he did, maybe then he would feel like a man. But he can't. Winnie is the mother of his child. She grew their son inside her body. Green stuff came out right after his son emerged, and he wished someone had warned him it was coming. It was like the green stuff in the body of a lobster. Sometimes, when he is performing oral sex on Winnie, he thinks about the green stuff. He can't help it. He feels guilty. And sometimes he thinks about that time he had sex in college. With the crazy girl. Who asked him to fuck her up the butt and then gave him a blow job afterward. He felt guilty about that too.)

But more than anything, Tanner is a man. When James and Tanner were roommates at Harvard, Tanner had one or two different women every weekend. (And once five. He fucked every one of them, too.) Women chased him. They sent him notes. They called. They threatened suicide and Tanner had no respect for them. He didn't have to. "Let the bitch kill herself," he once said. James laughed, but later, he couldn't help himself, he called the girl and took her out for a coffee. He listened to her talk about Tanner for three hours, and then he tried to fuck her. (She would only let him put his fingers in her vagina. "I want Tanner," she sobbed through the whole pitiful, aborted encounter.)

James thinks (and Winnie thinks too) that someday, something bad is going to happen to Tanner. It has to. He'll get arrested or (Winnie hopes) he'll fall in love and the woman won't fall in love back, or (James hopes) he'll do three bad movies in a row and his career will be over. But it never does happen. Instead, Tanner keeps getting richer and more successful. He makes bad blockbuster movies, and the critics are beginning to take him seriously. He dates female movie stars and has affairs on the side. He plays golf and skis. He smokes cigars (and does drugs whenever he wants). He supports the Democratic Party. He makes at least twenty million dollars a year (and maybe more). For doing (James thinks) nothing.

James would like to hate Tanner, but he can't. He would, however, hate him if he were not his friend. He would probably agree with Winnie — that Tanner is the product of a misguided, badly educated, shallow society that elevates people solely on the basis of their looks, and if the public really knew what Tanner Hart was like, they wouldn't shell out seven or eight or nine dollars to see him in a movie.

On the other hand, they probably would.

And if they didn't, they would probably want Tanner to do something worse. Much worse. Like lead an army and rape and pillage.

This is, James thinks, the thing that Winnie doesn't understand about men. And never will understand. It is, James thinks happily, the thing that will prevent Winnie from ever really becoming a threat to his masculinity. It is what allows him to stay home and visit porn sites on the Internet or play chess against his computer, or even hang around with his boy, playing violent computer games (James does feel a little guilty about this, but he tells himself he's preparing his boy for the real world, and besides, the boy is so good at them, quick and clever) while Winnie goes to work in a high-rise office building. (She thinks she's a man, but she's not, James thinks, even if she does wear suits, and, when he met her, shirts with straps that tied around the neck like a bow tie.)

This is the thing that James knows and Winnie doesn't: Men can't be tamed.

Men are by nature violent.

Men always want to have sex with lots of different females.

James has always known this (don't all men know this, and haven't they been telling women for the past thirty years, but the women haven't been listening?). But now, he thinks, he knows it in a different way.

James has been reading up on chimpanzees.

He's been studying everything he can about chimps.

Chimps are violent. They sneak off in the middle of the night and raid other chimp tribes. The big chimps (the alpha males) pick out a small chimp (a beta male) and kill him mercilessly while the small chimp screams in pain and terror. Then the alpha chimps steal a few female chimps and have sex with them.

At first, James began looking into this chimp business (as he's begun to think of it) to get even with Winnie. (He can't remember what he was planning to get even with her for.) But then he got into it. Lately, he's been looking up scientific articles on the Internet. E-mailing researchers. He isn't sure how all this information adds up, but he knows there's a piece in there somewhere. An important piece.

James has a theory: Tanner is an alpha male.

This is why Tanner can get away with whatever he wants, and James can applaud him. (Hell, James can be bad with him and get away with it.)

"Winnie," James says, when she gets home from work and has taken off her shoes (she always takes off her shoes as soon as she gets home. She says they hurt, even though her shoes tend to be sensible one-inch loafers). "I think I've got an idea for a new piece."

"Hold on," Winnie says.

"Winnie," James says. He follows her. She has gone into their son's tiny bedroom, where he is trying to read a book about dinosaurs to the Jamaican nanny.

"Pur . . . pur . . ." the boy says.

"Purple," Winnie says. (Impatiently, James thinks. Winnie has no patience for their son, has no patience for children in general.)

"You should let him figure it out for himself," James says. Knowing by the expression on Winnie's face that he has said the wrong thing. Again.

"James," Winnie says. "If I waited for everyone around me to figure it out on their own, I'd be waiting for the rest of my life."

"I suppose you're talking about me," James says.

"I don't know what I'm talking about anymore," Winnie says. Lying. She just wants to avoid a fight.

James follows Winnie into the kitchen. Winnie takes off her earrings and puts them on the kitchen counter. She opens the refrigerator door and takes out three carrot sticks.

"I think I'm going to do a piece on chimpanzees," James says.

Winnie says nothing. She raises her eyebrows and bites a carrot stick in half.

"There are all these new theories," James says. "Theories than can apply to humans. For instance, Tanner is an alpha male."

"Did you talk to Tanner?" Winnie says.

"No," James says. "But I'm going to talk to him. About this theory. I could even write about him. Use him as an example."

Winnie gives a short, mean laugh. "You know his publicists would never let you do that."

"I could change his name."

"Did you talk to Clay?" Winnie says. (Ignoring him again. She used to suck up to him when he talked to her about his work.)

"I told you I did. How else would I know Tanner was coming to town?"

"How are . . . Clay and Veronica?"

"I don't know," James says. Helplessly. Once again, he's losing control of the conversation.

"Is Veronica still threatening to divorce Clay?"

"*Was* she threatening to divorce him?"

"That's what she said. The last time we saw her. When Tanner was in town."

"Oh yeah. I remember," James says. He has to be conciliatory. It's his only chance now. Somehow Winnie has managed to turn the conversation around to a slippery, potentially unpleasant, topic. In which he is about to lose.

"I wish Clay would wise up," Winnie says. "She's going to walk if Clay behaves the way he did the last time Tanner was in town."

"Have you talked to Veronica?" James asks.

"I only talk to her when Tanner is in town. Really, James, I don't have time."

"I know."

"And she's not that interesting. At the end

of the day, she's just a housewife."

"You're right."

"Do you mind?" Winnie says. "I've still got some calls to make. We had that big Internet meeting today, and they might want me to run it."

"That's great," James says. He goes back to the tiny room he calls his office. He feels relieved. Like he has barely escaped something bad. He sits down in front of his computer.

No matter what happens, he reminds himself that he and Winnie have a better marriage than Clay and Veronica. Veronica is Tanner's sister, and she's an even worse bitch than Winnie. (She was once beautiful, but she let herself get fat.) Clay and Veronica have two children. Clay is a sculptor. He's becoming famous now. He has affairs. (Veronica must be like a millstone around his neck. She doesn't work and never has. At least if something happened between him and Winnie, Winnie would be able to take care of herself.)

An hour later, Winnie comes into his office.

"I've been thinking," she says. "About that idea of yours."

"Yes?" James says.

"It has an inherent flaw. If Tanner is an alpha male, what are you, James?"

She smiles and leaves the room.

III

SOMETHING BAD HAPPENS

Tanner Hart is on. Sitting in the back corner of the VIP room at Chaos (a room that can only be reached by private elevator, which can only be accessed by a separate entrance, guarded by two bouncers and a young lady with a list), Tanner Hart is chain-smoking Marlboro reds and drinking martinis. Tanner Hart is laughing. Tanner Hart is frowning. Tanner Hart is nodding, his eyes wide with surprise, mouth open. "Uh-huh, uh-huh, yes I do remember meeting you on the set of *Switchblade* how have you been since then? You had a dog right and something happened to the dog, something with an elephant? Oh, a cat a cat." And then to somebody else: "Hey that night that was pretty hot, huh, stick around you going someplace let's talk later after all this but you're doing well, right? You *look* great."

Tanner Hart looks at his watch. Soon he'll be bored. (It's just another movie premiere.) In an hour, he'll be able to pick up a chick and go back to his hotel room. Then he'll be bored again. (And he'll have to do it all over again, which in itself will be boring.)

"Jimmy!" Tanner shouts. James and Winnie Dieke are squeezing through the crowd. They're still wearing their coats. James looks pained. Winnie looks annoyed. (James has been going downhill, Tanner thinks, ever since he married Winnie and had a child. He looks like a prisoner. Tanner has to free him. Winnie looks like she needs a good fuck. Tanner has to free her too.)

Winnie spots Tanner. She waves.

"We're going to say hi and then we're going home," she says to James.

James says nothing. He's waiting for a moment when he can escape.

"Jimmy my boy. Jimmy baby." Tanner grabs James around the neck, swaying him from side to side. Then he pushes James away and puts his hands on either side of Winnie's face. He pulls her toward him and kisses her on the lips. "I love you guys," he says.

"Everybody loves us," Winnie says.

"Yeah, but I especially love you," Tanner says. "Did you have any trouble getting in?

"Those people at the door are such assholes. I keep telling the publicity people, but it doesn't make any difference. Jimmy, where's your drink? Somebody get this man a cocktail," Tanner screams. He sits down and leans back. He pulls Winnie onto his lap. "Watch out, Jimmy boy," he says. "I'm going to steal her from you one of these days."

I wish you would, James thinks.

Winnie giggles, plucks the martini glass out of Tanner's hand, and takes a large gulp. (Winnie is a different person in front of Tanner. She flirts. Disgustingly, James thinks. Does she think Tanner would ever be interested in *her?*)

"Whoa. Go easy, baby, easy," Tanner says, taking his glass back and patting her on the butt. He slides his hand underneath the back of her coat. Winnie doesn't object. (She hates Tanner until she sees him. And then she can't help herself. She loves him.)

"How are you?" Winnie asks. "I mean, really?"

"I'll be right back," James says.

"Hold on, bro," Tanner says. He passes James a vial of cocaine. Turns back to Winnie. "So where's my future wife?" he asks.

James is elated. He feels like a naughty schoolboy who has just run off with the teacher's chalk. (He did run off once with the teacher's chalk, when he was very young. It felt good for three minutes, until he got caught. Then he was sent home from school. It was embarrassing. It was unfair. It was only a tiny piece of chalk.) James runs into Clay Ryan in the bathroom. "Christ," Clay says. "I'm trying to get away from my wife."

"So am I," James says. He hands Clay the vial of cocaine. Clay sticks in the tip of a key and holds it up to his nose. "So what about Winnie's sister, Evie?" he asks.

"She's hot," James says.

Evie wants to fuck Tanner and she's excited about it.

She's met Tanner three times before, and every time, he made a point of putting his hands on her. It's his way of saying that if she wanted to fuck him, he would.

She tells herself that nothing will come of it (she tells herself that something might come of it, that she might, through some fluke of nature, be "the one"), but she doesn't care. She just wants to fuck him once. To see what it would be like. (She wants to fuck a movie star. She'd like to fuck lots of movie stars. Who wouldn't?)

Evie runs into James and Clay outside the bathroom.

They look like they've been up to something. James is wiping his nose. (He is so uncool, Evie thinks. Pathetic, really. How can Winnie sleep with him? He has no hair.)

"Have you seen Winnie?" she asks.

James and Clay take Evie into the bathroom. "I never do this," James says.

Evie says, "Oh James, shut up."

"Don't tell Winnie," James says.

"I'm going to tell Winnie," Clay says. "I'm going to tell the whole fucking world. Including my wife. Fuck her."

They run into Tanner outside the bathroom. Tanner, Clay, and Evie go into the bathroom. James goes to the bar to get a drink. In the stall, Tanner presses up against Evie. Like Clay isn't even there. Evie thinks she might swoon. Tanner is better in person than he is on the screen.

"How come you weren't at the wedding?" he asks.

"Which one?" Evie says.

"James and Winnie."

"Rehab," Evie says.

Veronica and Winnie are sitting at a table. "I'd just like some appreciation sometimes," Veronica says. "When I met Clay, he was living in an apartment with no bathroom."

"James is either working or on the Internet or watching TV," Winnie says. Why does she always get stuck with Veronica?

"I mean, could he listen? To me? His latest thing is bad investments."

"They have time for everything except you," Winnie says. "Well, now I don't have time for him."

"And does he even notice? And now they're all on coke," Veronica says. "Look at them all jabbering away like monkeys. It's disgusting."

James and Evie and Clay sit down with Veronica and Winnie.

"James is doing a piece on chimpanzees," Evie says.

"Oh James, don't talk about it. It's so dull," Winnie says.

"I just found out that the government is illegally importing chimpanzees for secret medical research. They're stashing them in a warehouse in lower Manhattan," James says.

"Why would anybody bring monkeys into Manhattan," Winnie says.

"Did you know that in some chimp tribes, the females are lesbians? And they let the male chimps watch?" Clay asks, leaning over to Evie.

"Clay, we're going," Veronica says.

"Hold on," Clay says. "I haven't finished my drink."

"Who wants another drink?" James says.

"That's enough," Winnie says.

"Tanner's ordering another drink," James says.

"Tanner's leaving," Veronica says. And, in fact, Tanner is leaving, moving toward the elevator, kissing and squeezing people along the way.

"We'll give you a ride uptown, Evie," Winnie says, standing up.

"That's okay. I don't have to be up in the morning," Evie says. She has one eye on Tanner. She can't let him get away. "I'll be back," she says.

"Sure," Clay says.

Veronica gives him a dirty look.

Evie hurries after Tanner. Winnie and James and Veronica and Clay are so boring. Why is Winnie always trying to control her? Doesn't she understand that Evie and Tanner are one kind of person and Winnie and James are another? (They are partiers. Fun people.) She manages to squeeze herself into the elevator with Tanner just before the doors shut.

"Good girl," Tanner says. He looks at Evie appraisingly and thinks, She'll do. (He's had hundreds of girls like Evie. Sexy and available. Too available. After a certain age they can't find husbands. Or even boyfriends. He'd rather fuck Winnie. At least she isn't available.) "Just promise me one thing," Tanner whispers. "Don't give me any of that marriage shit." He starts singing, "It ain't me, babe. It ain't me you're looking for. Babe."

"Don't be so sure." Evie giggles.

The elevator doors open on the ground floor. Tanner grabs Evie's hand. They hurry out to the street. The limo driver is holding open the door. There's a crowd, held back by police barricades. "Maestro!" Tanner screams.

He pulls Evie into the limo.

Clay and Veronica and Winnie and James are standing on the street corner. Trying to get a cab. (Or trying not to get a cab, James thinks.)

"If you want to kill yourself, go right ahead," Veronica says to Clay. "I really don't give a flying fuck anymore."

"What *are* you talking about?" Clay asks.

"Oh, for Christ's sake, Clay. How stupid do you think I am?"

"Let's get a drink," James says.

"You've both been doing coke," Winnie says.

"I haven't been doing coke," James says.

"Can you believe this, man?" Clay says to James. "I mean, how much more of this do we have to take?"

"You are such a loser, James," Winnie says. "Let's get in a cab and go home."

"I'm not getting in a cab," James says. "I'm getting a drink."

"James!"

"No!" James says. "Tanner sits there snorting up a gram of coke and no one gets on his case."

"Tanner is a famous movie star who makes fifteen million dollars a picture," Winnie says.

"Tanner is an alcoholic, a drug addict, and a sex addict. He's a complete sicko degenerate," Veronica says.

"So it's all about money," Clay says.

"What *are* you talking about?" Veronica says.

"She," Clay says, pointing at Winnie, "just said that Tanner makes fifteen million a year. So that makes it okay."

"Picture. Fifteen million a picture. And no, it's not okay."

"I've had enough," Clay says to James. "What about you?"

"I just want a drink," James says.

Tanner's limo pulls up to the corner. Tanner rolls down the window. "Anybody need a lift?"

"I'm with you, Tanner," Clay says.

"Me too," James says. He doesn't look at Winnie.

"Don't you get in that limo, Clay."

"Hey sis, lighten up," Tanner says. "Me and the boys are going to have a few pops."

Clay and James get into the limo, climbing over Evie, who's lying on the floor, laughing. "Hello, boys," she says. As the limo pulls away, James sneaks a look back at Winnie. Her mouth is open, but for once, nothing is coming out.

JAMES FEELS ILL

Four A.M.

James doesn't feel so good. He stole the chalk. He's being punished. He thinks (but he's not sure) he hears voices. "What have you done now, James?" his mother says. "At the rate you're going, we'll have to send you to reform school. Do you want to be a failure? Like your father?"

Was his father a failure? His suits were always rumpled. He owned three dry-cleaning stores. Was he having an affair with Betty, the woman who did his books? "Pull down your pants, James," his father says, taking off his belt.

It was only a tiny piece of chalk. A sliver, really.

"Hey, let me in," James says. His voice is a croak. It seems to be coming from somewhere to his left. (Somehow he's at his building. Somehow he got into a cab and obviously gave the cab driver his address. But it seems like ages ago. Maybe yesterday.)

"Yes?" the doorman says. James has never seen him before.

"I'm James Dieke. I live here," he says, holding up his keys.

The doorman lets him in. "Are you new?" James says. It feels better to talk. If he can just keep talking, maybe he can get through this. "Are you married? I'm married. I'm not sure if I like being married, but what can you do?"

"Good night," the doorman says.

James rides the elevator to his floor. Does it take a minute or forever? He grew up on Long Island in a row house. Every house was the same. His had rattan furniture from Sears.

(His grandmother ate red-and-white-striped candies. Peppermints, she said. She wore flowered housedresses.)

Winnie's house had a pool and a tennis court. Her father was a judge. Winnie had a black Prince tennis racket.

This is very, very important.

Someone brought a monkey to school once. Its tail was worn.

211

Birds are chirping. It's a terrible noise. Who knew New York City had so many birds? He enters his apartment. He's going to show them all. He's going to write this book. It's earth-shattering. People have to know about this.

"Winnie," he says.

She's lying in bed. She opens her eyes and glares at him. Turns over.

Someone's got to know about this.

James shakes her. "It's this giant government plot, Winnie. Winnie, are you awake? It's the overcrowding of the niche structures but instead of using rats they're using monkeys and they're finding that the same behavior occurs in primates which means that it goes all the way to the heart of the inner-city housing crisis. Of course, Stephen Jay Gould discovered the same construct in his snail studies . . ."

"Go . . . to . . . the . . . couch."

". . . which he then applied to primates, and Darwin never read Mendel. Do you know what that means? Darwin never read Mendel?"

"What the hell are you talking about, James?" She looks at him. Then she must really look at him because she says, "Holy shit. You're a mess. You look like a bum. And you smell."

"I'm sorry I woke you up," James says. He isn't sorry. Suddenly, he feels an over-whelming (and inexplicable) affection for her. He wants to make love. He wants to have sex. He's got to have sex.

He sits on the edge of the bed. "You're so wonderful. You're such a wonderful wife. I always want to tell you how much I love you, but you never give me a chance."

"You're disgusting," Winnie says. "I'd ask you to move out right now, but it's too late. You can go to a hotel in the morning." She pulls the covers over her head.

"Everybody admires you so much. Tanner is crazy about you."

"I can't have this," Winnie says. She's going to explode. She has work in the morning. (Why is it that everybody else thinks that their shit is so much more im-portant than her shit? She'd like someone else to acknowledge the importance of her shit. For once.)

James puts his arms around her. He tries to kiss her.

"James," she says.

"You're so . . . pretty," James says, trying to stroke her hair.

"James, go to sleep. . . . James, stop it. . . . I'm going to have you arrested for conjugal rape. . . . James, get off me."

Winnie screams. James rolls to the side. He moans.

"Go to the couch!" Winnie says.

"I can't."

Winnie throws off the covers. "We're going to have a long talk tomorrow. About your behavior. We're going to start making some big changes around here."

"Winnie . . ."

"I mean it, James. We have a child. You have responsibilities. Where the hell, and I really want to know this, where the hell do you and Clay get the idea that you can run around and act like six-year-olds? Do you see Veronica and me going out and drinking and doing drugs and staying up until four in the morning? How would you like it? How would you like it if I went out and stuck my hand down guys' pants and did drugs with them in the bathroom and God knows what else? Maybe I'm going to do that some night. Because you know what, James, I don't care anymore. I've had it."

"Winnie?"

"And this business about chimpanzees and alpha males. I'm beginning to think you've lost it. Wake up, James. It's the millennium. Men and women are equal. Get it? So why don't you think about how I feel? Do you think I like taking care of you all the time? What about me? I'd like to be taken care of. I'd like to have a husband who could at least pay . . . all the rent. You're a burden, James. I'm tired of doing eighty percent of the work and reaping twenty percent of the profits. I'm tired of —"

"Winnie?"

"Shut up, James. It's my turn. I've had to listen to your bullshit all evening. I've been sitting here for the last five hours wondering where you were and what you were up to. I'm so sick of you, James. You're no better than Evie. Does she think we didn't see her hiding in the limo? Hiding! She's thirty-five! She's obviously trying to sleep with Clay. And God knows what she's trying to do with Tanner."

"Clay?" James says.

"Yes. Clay. A married man."

"Winnie, I —"

"What?"

"I . . . I . . ."

"Spit it out."

"Winnie, I think I'm having a heart attack. I'm going to die. Winnie. I think I'm dying."

"Oh James. You're *such* a loser." Winnie puts her head in her hands. "You can't even do coke right."

IV

JAMES SAYS NO

James wants to be nursed and coddled. (Like when he was a little boy. Like when he was sick. His mother would make a bed for him on the couch and let him watch TV all day. His father would call him on the phone. "Hey sport," he'd say. "How's the sport?") He wants Winnie to say, "Oh James, you poor sweet baby." (He wants Winnie to be like his mother. Or at least mother*ly*.)

Instead she says, "They said you're fine."

I'm not fine, he wants to scream. He wishes Winnie would go away. He wishes he could tell her to go away. He can't now. He can't ever. "I know," he says.

"You can leave now."

"I know," he says. He pushes the buttons on the remote control, changing the channels on the TV above his head.

"So. Can we go?" she says. "James. I've got to get back to my office."

"I need my clothes."

"They're right here," Winnie says. She picks up his clothes from the chair and dumps them on the hospital bed.

James looks at his shirt, his sweatshirt (with the logo of Winnie's magazine on it), his jeans, socks, and white briefs. His clothes look tainted. "I need clean clothes," he says.

"Haven't you embarrassed yourself enough?" Winnie says in a stage whisper. (She doesn't want to be overheard by the old man in the next bed, who is practically dead. Who has a scab-covered leg sticking out from under the covers.)

"I'm not going home," James says. "I'm going to a press conference." He paws through his clothes. He still doesn't feel quite . . . normal. (He feels high. Probably from all the cocaine he consumed the night before, combined with the shot of Demerol they gave him in the hospital last night. Or rather, early this morning. When he thought he was having the heart attack. From cocaine. Other people have done worse. They've shot up heroin. But they aren't married to Winnie.)

"Do you have a notebook I can borrow?" he says.

"I want you to go home."

"No," he says. If he gives in now, he's finished.

"What do you mean, 'No'?"

"No," he says. "What do you think it means?"

"You must still be high," she says.

"Probably," he says. He looks up at the TV. He doesn't feel unpleasant. The world has an interesting intensity that is, for once in his life, non-anxiety producing.

"Where are you going?"

"To a press conference." (He has something important to do, too.)

"A press conference!"

"Monkeys," he says. "Chimpanzees."

"Which, James?" Winnie says (cleverly, he thinks. If she is back to her old tricks of trying to trick him, maybe she's not that angry).

"I need a pen, too," he says. "I can't find my watch. I can't leave without my watch."

"Oh, for Christ's sake!" she says. She marches (and she's the only person he knows who does march) the few feet to the head of the bed and presses the buzzer with her thumb. "I am praying that none of our friends get wind of this incident. This could ruin your career."

"Could," he says.

"Do you even care?"

"No," he says.

A nurse comes into the room. "Yes?" she says.

"My husband can't find his watch," Winnie says. "Can you find it for him, please?"

"It's on his wrist."

"Well, how about that," James says. He leans back on the pillows and looks at his silver Rolex with fresh appreciation. "It's ten-thirty."

"I know what time it is. I had to leave my office. Now get up and put your clothes on."

The doctor walks in. "How are we doing this morning, Mr. Dieke?" he says.

"Richard?" Winnie says.

"Winnie?"

"How are you?" Winnie says, smiling pleasantly, as if James weren't lying in a hospital bed, high, smelly, and partly naked. "I didn't know you worked at Lenox Hill."

"Why should you?" Richard says. "We haven't seen each other since college."

"We went to college together," Winnie says. "What a coincidence. Richard Feble, my husband, James Dieke."

"Well, I'm happy to say that your husband is doing just fine," Richard says. "His EKG and his chest X rays came back normal, so all I can say is since you never know what's in this stuff, stay away. If you have to indulge in illegal substances, smoke a joint. Okay? I don't want to see you guys in here again."

"Believe me, Richard, this was a complete fluke," Winnie says. "James and I *never* —"

"I'm not your mother," Richard says. "By the way, we found this in Mr. Dieke's pocket. You might want to keep this." He hands Winnie a small brown vial. It's half full of white powder. He winks.

"Oh," Winnie says. "Thank you." She puts it in her purse. Glares at James. Now she's a drug addict too. What if she gets caught with this stuff?

Richard pats James on the leg. "I've read your stuff in *Esquire*. You must lead a wild life."

"Untamed," James says. He doesn't look at Winnie.

"I've got a column in *X*," Winnie says, naming the magazine she works for.

"Oh, we always knew *you* would succeed," Richard says.

"Let's get together sometime," Winnie says, cocking her head to the side and smiling. "Are you married?"

"Me? Nah. Listen guys, I've got rounds. Nice to see you, Winnie," Richard says. He points at James. "Can't wait to read your next piece. Stay alive, huh, big guy?"

Richard walks out of the room. Winnie

turns to James. "Untamed?" she says. "Oh James, now I've heard everything."

James looks at her. He feels like sticking his tongue out. But he doesn't. Instead, he smiles.

SOMETHING GOOD HAPPENS

James slips into the back of the grand ball-room in the Hilton Hotel just in time for the commotion in the front of the room.

An attractive (on second thought, make that very attractive) dark-haired girl in a tight-fitting purple top (her breasts look like they could spill out at any second) is waving her arm frantically. "Hey, Danny. Danny!" she says in a raspy voice. "Where were the customs agents in all this?"

Danny Pico, the head of customs, a greasy-haired balding guy in a cheap navy blazer, glares at her. "Not today, Amber," he says. *"Not today."*

Amber! James can imagine what her breasts would look like. Full and soft. And quivering. He hasn't had breasts like that in a long time.

"Please, Danny," Amber says. "Why are taxpayer dollars being wasted on completely irrelevant scientific experiments?"

"Next," Danny says.

"Hello. The fourth amendment," Amber says, waving a hand with blue fingernail polish.

(The fourth amendment?)

"This press conference is over!" Danny Pico says. The room erupts. Amber turns and clomps towards the door on a pair of four-inch platform sandals. She's wearing a short skirt. Leather. White. She's headed straight for James.

"Excuse me," he says, touching her arm as she passes.

She stops and turns. "Huh?" she says. "Do I know you?"

"I'm James Dieke."

Her face lights up. "James Dieke. Ohmigod," she says. "You're one of my heroes."

"I am?" (He is?)

"Sure. I loved your piece on satellites. You're the only writer who could make magnesium sulfide interesting. Important. You know?"

"Really," James says. (Magnesium sulfide?)

She switches some papers from one arm to another. She holds out her hand. "Amber Anders."

"Wow," James says.

"Wow?" she says.

"Your name. It's great." (It sounds like a porno star's.)

"You think so? I always thought it was a good name for a byline. I write for *X*," she says, naming the same magazine Winnie works for. "I'm a staffer. But I hope not a lifer." She leans closer. "Some people never get out of there, you know? I swear, there are dead editors in obscure offices hidden behind piles of back issues."

"I'll tell you something," James says. "There are always dead editors. Lurking in obscure little offices. Torturing writers."

"Hey, you're funny, you know that. No-body ever said you were funny."

"Maybe they don't know me," James says. He wonders if she knows Winnie. (He wonders if she knows he has a hard-on.)

"Who are you covering this for?" she asks.

"The Sunday *Times Magazine*," he says.

"Cool," she says. She sticks her finger in her mouth and nibbles at her nail. She looks up at him. Her eyes are large and brown. Uncreased. "These guys aren't talking. But it doesn't matter. I've got the address of the warehouse in Brooklyn where they're hiding these monkey fuckers."

"Monkey fuckers?" James says.

"The monkeys. The chimps. The chimps

223

they're doing the secret government experiments on. Get it?"

James can't help it (how could he help it?), he follows her right out of the hotel and onto Fifty-sixth Street. "And you'll never believe where I got the address," she says. "Danny Pico's driver. Can you believe that?" They're on the sidewalk, walking toward Fifth. "Got a cigarette? No? Well, never mind. I didn't figure you for a smoker. Hey, why don't you come with me?"

"Come with you?" James says.

"To the warehouse, dummy. The warehouse in Brooklyn. I've got the address, remember?"

"Oh, right. The address," James says. "But how are we going to get to Brooklyn?"

Amber stops and looks at him. "Company car service. How else?"

"Car service?" James says.

"Well, I'm not taking the IRT in this outfit."

Fifteen minutes later, she says, "Hey, James. I have an idea. Why don't we cover the story together? Like Woodward and Bernstein. Only I don't want to be the short one. What's his name again?"

"Who?" James says, looking at her breasts. "Woodward? Bernstein?"

"Yeah," Amber says. "That's the one."

They're sitting in the back of a Big Apple town car. Crossing the Brooklyn Bridge. Amber leans across the seat and puts her hand over his. "Isn't this a *blast?*"

"Have I told you my theory about alpha males?" James asks.

WINNIE MAKES A DECISION

Winnie wants to be loved.

She wants to be cherished. She wants to be valued. (She doesn't really know what "cherished" means. Does anyone?) She wants a man to say, "I love you, Winnie. You're so beautiful."

She wants him to give her a nice piece of jewelry.

Is that asking too much?

Was she ever really loved? Her mother loved her. (She would rush home from school to see her mother. They would go to the supermarket together. And to Ann Taylor. Her mother bought her sweaters and skirts in bright colors. Kneesocks. She wore kneesocks even in college. Headbands too.)

Her father criticized her. A lot. About everything she did. (If she got straight As, and she did get straight As most of the time, he said, "That's what I expect. That's what I expect from a child of mine.")

Her father made her feel like she wasn't good enough. Like she was missing something (maybe some brain cells). That was his favorite trick.

"Winnie," he would say. "What's your address?"

"One, one, one . . ."

"You're so stupid."

She was three and a half. And she could read. How can you be stupid when you're three and a half?

"Winnie? Which is bigger? The sun or the moon?"

It was a trick question, and she had known it was a trick question. (She knew that she wasn't good at trick questions. She always overtricked herself). "The moon?"

"You're so stupid." (She was four.)

Her father didn't understand her. (Neither does James.) She couldn't understand him (her father. And James). Couldn't understand why everything she did was wrong. (What did he want? What did men want? Nothing. Maybe to be left alone.) Couldn't understand why whatever her father said was law, even if he was wrong. (Why did she have to listen to him? Why couldn't he listen to her?) And he often was wrong. He let their French poodle run without a leash, and he got attacked by a German shepherd.

("I knew he would," Winnie sobbed. "Shut up," he said.)

"I'm tough on you, Winnie," he said. "I have to be. You're lazy. If I'm not hard on you, I don't know how you'll turn out."

She certainly is smart enough (she's achieved a lot). Why does she have to fight for every ounce of respect? James doesn't.

Why does everyone make her feel like a bitch? For standing up for herself. "You've got to learn to stand up for yourself, Winnie," her father said. "Because nobody else will."

He was right. Nobody else has ever stood up for her. Especially men.

What a useless gender. Ever since she was four and had to go to school with them and then her mother actually had one, she's believed they should just be eliminated. Aborted. Okay, a few could be allowed to live. But only for their sperm. And they'd have to be excellent specimens.

What was all that crap about men that she grew up with? That one day, one of these (pitiful) specimens was going to fall in love with her (and actually love her — hah — whoever dreamed that one up should be worth a kazillion dollars), and make her whole. Give her something she couldn't live without. (She can live without most of the penises she's met so far, so it's all a lie.)

Take James.

She had to get him. (It was supposed to be the other way around. But if she had waited, let him "make all the moves" the way men are always telling you to let them, she'd still be waiting.)

She had to pursue James the way she's had to pursue everything else in her life. With straightforward determination. (She didn't know how to play the boy-girl game. No one ever taught her. And besides, it seemed disgusting and dishonest.) "Listen, James," she said at the beginning, after she and James had had six dates (and slept together on the fourth). "Listen, James. I'm not going to play games." This was one week after their sixth date, and James suddenly wasn't calling. She had to call him. (How dare he? And why? Why was he treating her this way?)

"I've been on deadline," he said.

"You could have called me," she said. (No one is too busy to pick up the phone, to make a one-minute phone call. No matter how busy they say they are. Sorry.)

"I forgot," James said.

"You . . . forgot?" Winnie said. (Was it possible for a human being to be so stupid?)

"I've been on deadline," James said. (As if

this were an excuse. She should have known then. She should have run in the other direction.)

She didn't know how to play games.

"You forgot," she said. Again. (And he was an award-winning journalist.) "How dare you forget," she said. "I slept with you, James. I had sex with you. We have a relationship. How dare you?" She hung up the phone. (She was shaking.) She called back.

"And you're fucking lucky to be going out with me."

Ten minutes later, he called. "Do you want to go to a book party with me on Monday?"

She accepted.

She should have run in the other direction.

She didn't.

(A man once described his love for a former girlfriend to her: "She was like my lover, my mother, my sister, and my child," he said. To James, she is only his mother.)

James needed her. (He still does nothing.)

When she met him, he was living in a tiny studio apartment with a loft bed. He had a bureau and a desk under the loft. He had one old couch and bookshelves made of cinder blocks and two-by-fours. He was thirty-two and his sink was full of dirty dishes.

Winnie washed his dishes.

"Listen, James," she said. "You're fucking lucky to be going out with me." (She was an editor at a women's magazine. A full editor. She got a free ride home in the company car if she worked past seven. She assigned pieces and had lunches with writers; sometimes she had to kill pieces too. Then she'd call the writer and say, "I'm sorry, this piece just isn't working for us. Maybe you can try to sell it someplace else." Sometimes the writers would cry. Everyone said that Winnie was going to go far.)

"Listen, James," Winnie said. "I think you have a fear of success. You have a fear of change. You're afraid that if you commit to me, you'll have to change. You'll have to acknowledge your success."

"Do you think so?" James said. "I never thought about it that way. You could be right."

All James does is agree. He agrees and then he does nothing.

"It's too much, James," she says now. "It's too much for me."

"I know," he says. (He can't even plan a vacation. She plans it, and then he goes along for the ride.)

He does nothing.

Winnie knows what she has to do. She has

230

to stop taking care of James. And start taking care of herself. Isn't that what all the shrinks tell you to do in relationships? Stop focusing on the man? And focus on yourself? (Of course, if you stop focusing on the man, he'll probably leave. That's what they forget to tell you.)

She has to focus on her needs.

Winnie is going to sleep with Tanner and she's excited.

She calls her office. Speaks to her assistant. "What's up?" the assistant says.

"I'm still in this emergency situation. I won't be back this afternoon. I'll call at the end of the day."

"Someone named Jess Fukees called," her assistant says.

"He's not important. He's only the CEO of the company."

"Okay," the assistant says. (Sarcasm is beyond her.)

"It's not okay," Winnie says. "Call his secretary and tell her that I'm out of the office . . . no, out of town, and I'll call him first thing tomorrow."

"You go girl," the assistant says, and hangs up.

Winnie goes home. "Hello," she says to the Jamaican nanny, who jumps up and quickly turns off the TV. Winnie ignores this.

231

"Mrs. Dieke. You're home early."

"I'm not home at all," Winnie says. "I'm just stopping by. On my way to a meeting."

She goes into the bedroom and opens her closet. Rifles through her shoes. Unopened, and still in their box, are the strappy sandals James gave her for her birthday.

She puts them on.

"Good-bye," she says to the Jamaican nanny.

She hails a cab. "Morgans Hotel on Madison Avenue," she says. At the desk, she says, "I'd like you to ring Mr. Paul Bunyan, please."

"Is he expecting you?"

"Yes," Winnie says. She looks around the lobby. It's so small, it's claustrophobic. She drums her nails on the white linoleum.

The desk clerk turns away and whispers into the phone. "Mr. Hart? There's a woman here to see you?"

"Winnie," Winnie says.

"Winnie," the clerk says. He puts down the phone. "You can go up. It's Suite A. Top floor."

"Thank you," Winnie says.

She takes the elevator. Gets out in a narrow, gray-carpeted hallway. She presses the buzzer for Suite A.

"Just a minute . . . coming," Tanner says.

"Coming . . . uh . . . uh . . . ohmigod . . . co-o-o-o-ming." He flings open the door.

"Hello," Winnie says.

"This is an unexpected surprise."

"I hope I'm not . . . interrupting anything."

"If you were, I would throw her out."

The bedroom is on the first floor. Winnie passes the open door. The sheets are rumpled. The suite is a duplex, two floors with terraces. She goes up the steps. Tanner follows her. He's freshly showered. She can smell his cologne. (Cologne! The last time she was with a man who wore cologne was probably fifteen years ago. She can still remember it. Paco Rabanne. It was that one-night stand, and she probably wouldn't have had sex with him if it hadn't been for the cologne.)

"I'm just having tea," Tanner says. "Want some?"

"Sure," Winnie says. She sits down in front of a glass coffee table containing a tray with two teacups, a pot of tea, and lemon slices. "Were you expecting someone?"

"No. Someone just left. Unexpectedly," Tanner says.

They both laugh.

"Evie?" Winnie says.

"I don't kiss and tell," he says. He pours the tea.

"I've got something of yours," she says.

"I like your shoes."

"James gave them to me for my birthday."

"Old Jimmy's got better taste than I expected." He pauses. Takes a sip of tea. Looks at her over his teacup. "How is old Jimmy, anyway? He wasn't in very good shape when he left here last night."

"I think he's going to live. Unfortunately," Winnie says.

"Have you come here to force me to make amends?"

"You could say that," Winnie says.

"I think I know what you've come here for, Winnie."

"I think you do," Winnie says. (She isn't sure what to say next. She's never been good at flirting. Even with James, at the beginning, she flirted by being interested in his work. Her loss of interest in him sexually has decreased at the same rate as her loss of interest in his work.)

"I think this belongs to you," she says. She opens her purse and hands him the small vial of cocaine.

"Aha," he says. "What would I do without this?"

"I thought you might need it," Winnie says.

"Thank you very much," he says.

He stands up. He comes around behind her.

Winnie doesn't breathe.

"Winnie," he says. "How long have we known each other."

"Fifteen years."

"I always said James was a lucky bastard."

The Big Apple town car pulls up in front of a corrugated metal warehouse. Amber and James get out of the car.

"What if we get caught?" James says. (God, Winnie's right. He sounds like a girl. He should be in charge here. But he isn't.)

"So? They'll arrest us. I've got a great lawyer. We'll be out in twenty-four hours," Amber says.

"I don't think my wife is going to like it if I end up in jail," James says.

"Who gives a fuck about your *wife?*" she says.

Do you know her? James wants to say. Instead, he says, "It's just that the last twenty-four hours have been a bit . . . trying for her."

"By the way, exactly what *has* happened to you in the last twenty-four hours? You haven't explained this to me yet," Amber says.

"I've already been in the hospital," James says, picking his way over the broken sidewalk.

"Ambulatory surgery? Liposuction? That stuff?"

"No, not exactly."

Amber pulls open the door to the warehouse.

"Are you just going to walk right in?" James asks.

Amber turns. "Excuse me, James, but I think that's what doors are for?"

The warehouse is empty.

Was he really expecting anything else?

(Why is he here? He hopes he knows.)

"Christ. We're too late," Amber says. She lights up a cigarette. "They moved the fuckers. I should have known I couldn't trust Danny Pico's driver."

She throws down the cigarette and stomps out.

"What do we do now?" James says.

"We go back. To Manhattan. What else?" she says over her shoulder.

They get back into the town car. "My house, please," Amber says. She looks out the window. Bites her lower lip. "Fuck it," she says. "Now I'm just going to have to make it up. Pretend I saw monkeys."

"Make it up?" James says.

"Everybody makes shit up. Who's going to know?" Her expression changes. She looks like a scared little girl. "James," she says. "You don't think . . . I'm a liar, do you? I'm the most honest person you'll ever meet in your life. This was the address Danny Pico's driver gave me. It's not my fault they moved the monkeys."

"No, of course not," James says.

"People always think I'm lying. It's because I'm beautiful and smart. And I actually go out and get these stories. They sit around in their offices, you know. They're jealous. I can't help it if they're jealous. It's not my fault."

Holy shit, James thinks. She's going to cry.

"Hey," he says. "It's not that bad."

"I know you can understand, because I'm sure people are jealous of you, too." She moves closer. "You're just like me, James," she says, in that sexy, raspy voice. (Is he just like her? Who cares.) "I'm just like you, James," she says. "We're like twins."

Suddenly she's kissing him. She's so easy. She's so great. (Of course she's not a liar. How could a girl like this be a liar?) Does she know he wants her as much as she wants him? He puts his hand down the front of her shirt, squeezing great soft handfuls of breast. He wants to pull down his pants and give it to her right then (the way he did once when he was seventeen with the ugly, fat girl who would do it with anyone, only he couldn't get it in and came between the wet, moist crack in her ass). Amber puts her hand on his penis. She moans.

The car pulls up to a shabby walk-up building on the Lower East Side. He follows her up two flights of steps. Is it his imagination, or is she pushing her ass out at him? Or is it the shoes, the clunky platform sandals? He pushes her up against the wall of the landing. Puts his hand under her skirt. (She's not wearing any underwear, and she's hairy.) She pulls his hand away and puts her fingers in his mouth.

"I'm a really good fuck," she says. "You're not going to be disappointed."

"I know I'm not," he says.

It's like a porno movie. Since when did girls become this easy? Why didn't anyone tell him? (Why is she so easy?) They go into her apartment. It's dark and dingy. Small. Messy. (Horribly messy.) There's a mattress on the floor. She lies down and puts her legs up. "Fuck me, big boy," she says. He unzips his pants and pulls them down. He crawls towards her. There's a faint odor of garbage. He can't tell if it's coming from her apartment or the street below. He puts two fingers inside her. Then he puts himself inside her. She's wet, but big. Enormous. It's like an empty space in there. She's bigger than Winnie, and Winnie's had a baby.

What is he doing? What if Winnie finds out?

He comes.

He falls on top of her.

After a minute, he looks at her face. She isn't looking at him. She's looking up at the ceiling. Her face is blank. What is she thinking? Did she come?

"I should call my office," she says.

James sits. He pulls up his pants. "That was great," he says.

"Yeah. I know," she says. She crawls off the bed and opens the tiny refrigerator. "I hope you don't mind. I need a drink." She pours herself half a glass of straight vodka. "Don't look so shocked, James. I never judge anyone. Because it's your problem, not mine. Right? If you have a problem with this, don't give me a hard time about it. I don't deserve it."

"I know," James says. Suddenly he feels horrible. The drugs have worn off. He's exhausted. He feels dirty. (He is dirty.) He wishes he were back in his apartment, in his own bed, sleeping. If he could just go to sleep, maybe when he woke up it would be like none of this ever happened.

"If you're worried about my telling your

wife, don't," Amber says. "I'm not that kind of girl. I don't ever want you to think that I'm that kind of girl, because I'm not."

"Okay," James says cautiously.

She moves toward him and puts her hands on either side of his face. She kisses him on the lips. "You've never met anyone like me before in your life. You don't have to worry about me. I'm your best friend."

"I feel a little . . . anxious," he says.

"Why didn't you say so? I've got tons of pills. Xanax? Clonopin? Dexedrine?"

Dexedrine?

"Do you really know Winnie?" he says. Trying to sound casual.

"What do you think, James?" she says. "Duh."

Winnie and Tanner are lying naked in his bed in his suite at Morgans Hotel. Winnie has her eyes closed. She's smiling.

Tanner leans over and brushes her hair away from her face. He kisses her cheek. "Did you like that?" he asks softly.

"Oh yes," she says.

(What she really wants to say is, That was the most mind-blowing fuck I've ever had in my life thank you very much and now I finally understand what a mind-blowing fuck is, but she isn't that kind of girl.)

He cups her bottom and pulls her closer. She runs her hand over his back. (She wants to remember his body for the rest of her life. She will remember his body for the rest of her life. It's perfect. Slightly tanned and hairless. Muscular but not overly built. Whoever said that men's bodies don't matter to women was wrong. She never knew that sex could be so clean. And beautiful. Tanner is so clean. She's never seen such a clean man in her life. James has white skin and nobbly moles. And black pores where the blond hair springs out. Sometimes he has blackheads on his back.)

"Wanna do it again?" Tanner says.

"Can you?"

"What do you think?"

She can already feel his erection.

"Just a minute," she says.

She leans over and picks up the phone. He strokes her bottom. So gently, she feels excited again. She opens her legs just a little bit. "Hello," she says.

"What's up," her assistant says.

"Just checking in. Tell Amber I need her copy first thing tomorrow morning."

"I can't," her assistant says. "She's still at that press conference."

"Just tell her, okay?" Winnie says. Thinking, Typical. Amber Anders was the girl who plagiarized her piece.

She hangs up the phone.

"Everything okay?" Tanner asks.

"Perfect," she says.

JAMES AND WINNIE AT HOME

James can't get home fast enough. For once. If he can get home before Winnie, he can take a shower. He can pretend everything is normal.

From now on, everything is going to be normal. He's going to concentrate. He's going to write that book. (He feels like shit. He can't take it, this feeling like shit anymore. Is this how Tanner feels after he takes drugs and fucks some random chick he doesn't care about? Mixed up and confused?)

He opens the door to his apartment. Closes it. "James?" Winnie calls out. "I'm glad you're home."

Winnie is in their boy's room. Playing with their child. Helping him string beads on a cord. She's sitting on the floor with her shoes off. She looks happy.

"Look, Daddy," his boy says.

"Hello, Sport," James says.

"Daddy. Bang bang," the boy says.

"No," Winnie says. "Don't shoot Daddy."

She smiles. "Isn't he such a boy?" she says.

"Bang bang," James says to his boy. "Bang bang back."

"Clay's here," Winnie says in a stage whisper. "Veronica kicked him out of the house. I'm thinking I should kick both of you out and let you go to a hotel. But on second thought, maybe I should go to a hotel and let you pay for it."

"Do you want to go to a hotel?" James asks.

"What do you think?" Winnie says.

"How was your day?"

"Great," Winnie says, looking up. "I fucked Tanner all afternoon in his hotel room."

I wish you had, James thinks. Then they'd be even. Then he wouldn't have to worry about anything. (But he would have to worry about Tanner. He wouldn't be able to be friends with him anymore. And every time he looked at Winnie, he'd have to think about Tanner fucking her. And all the other girls Tanner had fucked. Maybe he'd have to divorce Winnie.)

"Uncle Clay threw up in the sink," his boy says.

"Sssssh," Winnie says. "How was *your* day?"

"I went to that press conference. It was useless."

"I told you," Winnie says.

(Should he tell her? Should he tell her he met Amber Anders at the press conference? If he's going to tell her, now is the time. What if Amber tells Winnie she met James? What if she tells her she fucked James? If she tells Winnie she met James, Winnie will wonder why James didn't tell her first.) "I met someone who works in your office," he says.

"Who?"

"Andy . . . Amber something . . . ?"

"Amber Anders," Winnie says.

"I think that's it."

"What did she say?"

"Nothing," James says. "She said she read my piece on satellites."

"She'll probably plagiarize it. She was the one who plagiarized my piece. I'm trying to get rid of her, but I can't."

"You should," James says. "She seems kind of crazy."

"She's worse than Evie."

"Do you think Evie slept with Tanner?"

"I have no idea," Winnie says. She picks up a few beads and threads them onto the cord. (She thinks about Tanner. How he was so strong; he kept gently picking her up and moving her into different positions. He knelt over her like a god. He overwhelmed her. He kissed her neck until she thought she was going to swoon. She did swoon. She slid off the chair onto the floor, and that's when he picked her up and carried her into the bedroom. She was incapable of protest.)

"I bet he didn't," James says. "Evie's a little too close to home. Even for Tanner. She's your sister."

"You think so?" Winnie says.

(She's not even yelling, he thinks. Maybe he is going to get away with this after all.)

"I'm going to take a shower," he says.

"I think that's a good idea."

He passes the living room. Clay is sleeping on the couch. Did he fuck Evie? When James had left Tanner's hotel room last night, Clay and Evie were still there. Would they (Clay and Evie) really do that?

Christ. He'd wanted to fuck Evie. For about two seconds. But then he'd started talking to Tanner about that monkey shit. And alpha males. What the hell was he talking about?

(What if he had slept with Evie? Winnie's sister. It would be like Tanner sleeping with Winnie.)

He goes into the bedroom. It's clean. And neat. His glasses are on the night table next to the bed, along with his black Braun traveling alarm clock and three old business magazines he keeps meaning to get through. Winnie's shoes are on the floor. The strappy sandals he gave her for her birthday.

Suddenly he feels okay. Maybe he didn't fuck up after all.

When he comes out of the bathroom, he can hear Winnie on the phone. "I'll send him home as soon as he wakes up," she's saying. "Oh God, Veronica. I don't know. I don't give a shit anymore. . . . I know, but maybe you should try to have the same attitude. Maybe you should go out and fuck someone else."

"Veronica," Winnie says as James passes by on his way to his little office. He nods. "I don't think we should get involved."

"Neither do I," Winnie says. "I don't give a shit."

James sits down at his desk. He turns on his computer. The phone rings again. Shit, he thinks. What if it's Amber? He didn't give her his number. But she might have Winnie's number.

They work in the same office.

He's just being paranoid. Amber isn't going to say anything. She's not that kind of girl.

He can hear Winnie giggling softly into the kitchen phone. "We definitely have to do it again," she says seductively. He's never heard her use that tone of voice before. "The next time you're in town.

"It's Tanner!" she shouts.

Oh.

He picks up the phone. "Hey, man."

"Hey, man. How you feeling?"

"Rough." (He wants to tell Tanner he got laid. Because he did. He did get laid. But he definitely wouldn't tell Tanner about the girl's vagina. It was enormous. And a little stinky.

He definitely can't do that again.)

"I hear you, man," Tanner says.

"Clay's here," James says. "Veronica kicked him out of the house."

"She'll be begging him to come back in about two hours."

"She already has," James says.

They laugh.

"You heading back to L.A.?" James asks.

"Tomorrow morning. I'll see you next time I'm in town."

James hangs up.

He checks his e-mails. The top one, sent at 5:03 P.M., says, "From Amber 69696969. Re: Alpha Males."

This can't be happening. Should he delete it or read it?

He'd better read it. Find out how bad the damage is.

Dear James,

"It was great to meet you. It's so hard to find decent guys. (Don't worry about your wife. I told you, I'm not that kind of girl, and I NEVER go back on my promises. Unlike other people we know.) I really want to talk to you about this idea I have about alpha males. (I think there are alpha females, too, and I'm one of them.) This would be a terrific piece for the magazine. And, I think you should know this, I'm going to proceed with it. Let's meet on Monday at six at the Café Grill. My friend Jerry is the bartender and he always gives me free drinks.

Big Kiss.

Oh fuck.

Should he respond? What if he does respond and his e-mail goes to the wrong address? What if, somehow, Winnie sees it? (Amber and Winnie work in the same office. E-mails are always getting passed around in offices.) What if he doesn't respond? She might keep sending him e-mails. She might get mad. She might tell Winnie.

He has to be very, very careful here. He has to cover his tracks. (She's crazy, this girl. She's trying to steal his idea. And he's going to have to let her.)

"Dear Amber," he writes. (No, he can't write "Dear Amber." It sounds too intimate.) Amber:

It was nice to meet you today. However, I believe I led you astray. There is no such thing as an alpha male. At least not in human beings.

Good luck with your story on monkeys.

He hits the send button.

The phone rings. Again. "Jess!" Winnie says. "What a privilege." (She's such a suck-up, James thinks.) "It was an emergency situation, but I can promise you, it won't happen again. . . . Oh yes. I love the project. . . . With the right management, it can be a huge success. . . . Thank you. Thank you so much, Jess. . . . My goodness. I promise you, I'll be worth every penny." She hangs up.

"James," Winnie says.

He jumps. (Is this how he's going to be from now on? Jumping in terror every time Winnie comes into his office? In terror of what she might find out?)

"That was Jess Fukees. The CEO. He's just offered me the job as head of their new Internet site. It pays five hundred thousand a year. With stock options."

James says nothing. He's shocked.

"Can't you sound a little more excited? I'm a really big deal now."

"I am excited," James says. "Can't you tell?"

And then Winnie does something she's never done before. She walks over. Puts her hand on his hair. Ruffles it.

"I'm proud of you, too," she says. "You've been working really hard. I'm sure this piece on monkeys is going to be great. Maybe you're right. Maybe it could be a book."

Winnie yawns. "I'm kind of tired. I'm ordering sushi and then I'm going to bed. Should I order you the usual? California roll?"

"Sure," James says.

PLATINUM

I

MY DIARY

Smile.

You have everything.

Oh God.

No names.

There are spies everywhere.

Hate everyone and everything, including my husband.

Why?

I'm so vicious.

This morning, I totally got even with him for coming in at one-twenty-three A.M. When he PROMISED, PROMISED, PROMISED he'd be home by midnight. At the LATEST. It was a test, and he failed. Again. But instead of screaming at him when he got home, I ignored the whole thing but lay awake all night again, feeling like my head was going to explode, which I'm sure it is, one of these days very soon. But if I tell him that, he'll just say, Why don't you take some more pills? Well, why doesn't he stop being such an asshole, and then I wouldn't have to take any more pills. As it is, some days I feel like my legs are made of rubber. It's no wonder I can barely walk across the room to answer the phone.

So this morning, when he got up, I pretended to be asleep. As soon as I heard the water running in the bathroom, I went to my secret stash and snorted a large line of that shitty cocaine that N. got from the bartender at M. Sure enough, in about one minute I felt a huge puke coming on and I ran into the bathroom and vomited several times while *he* stood there in horror with shaving cream on his face. And when I stood up, I was trembling, and I sort of stumbled back against the wall, wiping my eyes.

"Are you okay?" he asked.

I smiled mysteriously and said, "Oh, I'm okay now, I guess. I don't know what came over me."

"Maybe you should see a doctor," he said.

All he wants is for me to be pregnant. That's what they all want. They think, once I'm pregnant, that all the trouble will end and I'll settle down.

I'm like Mia Farrow in *Rosemary's Baby.*

"I'm so sorry I was asleep when you came home. Did you have fun?" I asked. Then I got back into bed, and he came in before he left for that STUPID office, and sure enough he said, "Do you think you're pregnant?"

"Oh, probably not."

"But you're sick. Do you think you should see Dr. K. again?"

"ALL I DO ALL DAY IS GO TO DOCTORS," I started to shout, but then I saw that closed-up expression on his face again, so I switched into my sexy voice and said, "It's nothing. Don't worry about me. I'll be fine."

"But I *am* worried about you," he said.

"Then why don't you stay home and keep me company?" I asked.

Well, fuck him. That was obviously the wrong thing to say as well because he just shook his head, patted me on the leg, and went away.

I HATE HIM. What does he want me to do? Who does he want me to be? Who am I supposed to be, here, please? Will somebody PLEASE tell me?

Went to see Dr. Q. at one-thirty. He kept me waiting for three minutes and forty-two seconds, which is almost four minutes and completely unacceptable. Two and a half minutes is the cutoff for ANYONE. I always tell everyone I won't be kept waiting for more than two and a half minutes unless I'm the one who's keeping them waiting. That's one of the reasons why I refused to be on the cover of that stupid *Vogue* magazine, because that idiotic woman said, I'll have someone call you right back and I said, What do you mean by right back and she said, In five minutes and she called back in eighteen and I said, Sorry, I'm not interested. Plus, I have my other reasons, which are that I hate that woman (I hate her so much I won't even say her name), but more about that later.

So, this is typical, the person who was before me eating into my appointment time with Dr. Q. is some forty-year-old woman wearing sweatpants. They're not even Calvin Klein. And she's holding a tissue.

Why do women always cry in shrinks' offices?

"Well," Dr. Q. says. I think he notices I'm being extremely cold and standoffish. "How are you today? Do you still think that someone in the family is secretly poisoning you?"

"What on earth makes you say that?"

"That," he says, flipping through his notebook, "is what you said yesterday."

"I did throw up this morning."

"I see."

Then I don't say anything. I just sit in the chair, drumming my fingernails on the metal arm.

"I see," Dr. Q. says again.

"And what exactly is it that you see, Dr. Q.?"

"I see that you're wearing a head scarf again."

"Your point?"

"You've been wearing a head scarf and black sunglasses for the last two weeks."

I give him a withering smile.

"So . . . How does it make you feel when you wear a head scarf and dark sunglasses?"

"How do you think it makes me feel, Dr. Q.?"

"Why don't you tell me?"

"NO," I say. "Why don't you tell me?"

"That would, ah, defeat the purpose of our . . . visits."

Ugh. Dr. Q. is so THICK.

"It makes me feel safe," I say.

"From the family poisoner?"

Sometimes I want to kill Dr. Q. I really do.

D.W. called. I haven't talked to him for three months. I've been avoiding him.

HELP.

I used to write that on all my books when I was a kid. I used to wrap my books in brown paper bags and then write my name on the front in different colored Magic Markers. I used to dot my Is with circles.

D.W. knows too much.

Of course, he calls at the most inconvenient time. Right in the middle of *The Karen Carpenter Story*, which I'm watching for something like the fifty-seventh time. The phone rings just at the part when Karen finally moves into her own apartment and her mother finds the box of laxatives. D.W. has on that sugary voice I hate sooooo much. "Hello, my darling," he says. "What are you doing?"

"Shhhhh," I say. "Karen is just about to lie to her mother and tell her that she won't take laxatives anymore, and her mother is actually going to believe her. Can you believe how dumb that woman is?"

"And then . . . ?"

"And then Karen is going to get down to seventy-eight pounds and have a heart attack after she eats Thanksgiving dinner. In other words, she is basically killed by turkey meat."

"How fabulously . . . charming," D.W. says.

"I'm really in the middle of something, so what do you want, D.W.," I say, which I know is horribly rude, but if I am rude, maybe he'll get the message and go away for another three months.

"What are you doing later?"

"Oh, later?" I say carelessly. "I think I'll snort a few lines of cocaine and take a few Xanaxes and make crank phone calls to my husband's office. And then I'll walk the dog for the tenth time and scream at a couple of photographers. What do you think I'm doing?"

"You know, you're really a funny, charming girl. That's what no one realizes about you, and it's a shame. If only people could see the real you . . ."

There is no real me anymore, but who cares?

"Do you think my husband is having an affair?" I ask.

"Oh, come on, my dear. Why would he have an affair when he's married to one of the most beautiful women in the world?" Pause. "Do you think he's having an affair?"

"Not right now," I say. "But I'm just checking to make sure I'm not crazy."

"You see?" D.W. says gleefully. "This is what happens when you lose touch with your old friends."

"We haven't lost touch —"

"And that's why I absolutely insist on seeing you for dinner tonight."

"Don't you have some fabulous gala to attend?"

"Only a small soiree in a store. For a very worthy cause. But I'm free after eight."

"I have to see," I say. I put the phone down and walk slowly through the living room, up the stairs to the master bath. I take off all my clothes and step on the scale: Weight, 117.5 pounds. Percentage fat, 13. GOOD. I've lost a quarter of a pound from the morning. I put my clothes back on and go downstairs. I pick up the phone.

"D.W.?"

"Thank God. I thought you'd died."

"I'm saving that for next week. I'll meet you at eight-thirty. At the R. But only you. And DON'T TELL ANYBODY."

I wear Dolce & Gabbana workout pants and a Ralph Lauren Polo sweatshirt, no bra, and when I walk into the restaurant, I remember that I haven't brushed my hair for three days.

D.W. is sitting at the wrong table.

"Oooooh. You look so . . . American. So . . . gorgeous. I always said you were the quintessential American girl. The American girl begins and ends with you," he says.

"You're at the wrong table, D.W. I never sit here."

"Of course not. But those pants, darling. Dolce & Gabbana."

I walk to the back of the restaurant and sit down. D.W. follows. "You should only wear American, dear. It's soooo important. I was thinking about putting you in some Bentley."

"Bentley hasn't had a client under sixty in fifty years."

"But I'm making him hot. He's going to be hot, hot, hot again. Those young S. sisters are wearing him."

I roll my eyes. "I want a martini," I say. "You don't have any pills, do you?"

"What kind of pills? Allergy pills? I don't know . . ."

"Can I get off on them?"

"Oh my dear, what has happened to you. You're turning into a little Courtney Love. I soooo wish you'd become friends with those lovely, lovely S. sisters. They adore you. And think of the parties you could throw together. Toute New York would be abuzz. It would be just like the old days."

Why can't I be like those darling S. sisters?

They are perfect. They never give anyone trouble. Not even their husbands. They're twins, and one of them (I always get them mixed up, and so does everyone else) got

married when she was something like eighteen. She invited me over for tea once, and I
went because my husband said I had to go.
"My husband married me because of my
hips," she said, even though I hadn't asked
her. "I have childbearing hips," she said.
"What can I do?" I wanted to ask her where
she'd gone for brainwashing, but I couldn't.
She seemed so sad. And so lost. And so tiny
in a large checkered dress from Valentino.

"How is it that you've never lost your hair,
D.W.?" I ask, lighting a cigarette.

"Oh. You're such a card. My grandfather
had a full head of hair when he died."

"But don't you think . . . that you had less
hair three months ago?"

D.W. looks around the restaurant and
slaps my hand. "You naughty. I did have a
tiny bit of work done. But everybody does
these days. You know, times have really
changed. Everybody is photographed. I
mean, the awful people whose photographs
appear in magazines . . . but I don't have to
tell *you* about *that*. Now P., she does it the
right way. Do you know that nobody's, I
mean *nobody's*, picture appears in the society pages without her approval? And, of
course, they have to be the right sort of
person. She has the highest standards. She
can spot quality a mile away."

P. is that editor at *Vogue*.

I yawn loudly.

"Did you see that featurette they did on you last month? The one where they analyzed your hemline lengths? That's why the long skirt is so big this season."

"That was only because," I say, tapping my ash on the floor, "the hem on that skirt came unraveled and I was too lazy to have it sewn back up."

"Oh, but my dear," D.W. says. "Don't you see? That attitude, that insouciance, it's genius. It's like when Sharon Stone wore the Gap turtleneck to the Oscars."

I fix D.W. with an evil eye. I've been trying to get rid of him for two years, but every now and again I have this AWFUL feeling that D.W. is never going to go away, that people like D.W. don't go away, especially not when you know them the way D.W. and I know each other.

"I threw up today. And I still think someone is trying to poison me."

D.W. lowers his martini glass. "We know you're not pregnant," he says, with this cosy intimacy that gives me the creeps.

"And how do we know that?"

"Come on, my dear. You're not pregnant. You never have been and you never will be. Not with your body fat hovering at thirteen percent. Your husband may be stupid enough to buy that crap, but I'm not."

"Fuck you."

D.W. looks around the restaurant. "Keep your voice down. Unless you want to see yet another item in *Star* magazine — Princess Cecelia engaged in a lover's spat with the older man with whom she's secretly having an affair."

I start laughing. "Everyone knows you're gay."

"I was married. Twice."

"So?"

"So as far as the press is concerned, my dear, I might be anything."

"You're a psychopath, D.W. And people are starting to figure it out."

"And you don't think they haven't figured out the same thing about you?" D.W. motions for another round of martinis. "Princess Cecelia. Maybe the most hated woman in America."

"Hillary Clinton liked me."

"Take a deep breath, my dear." D.W. pats my hand. He has horrible fingers that narrow to little points. "Maybe not the most hated. I believe that at one time, people hated Hillary Clinton more than they hate you. But certainly, it must have occurred to you by now that all those horrendous photographs are not a mistake."

I light another cigarette. "So?"

"So there's a little game played in the offices of photo editors across the country: Let's publish the worst possible photograph of Cecelia. I believe they have a pool going and the photographers are in on it too. The pot may be up to ten thousand dollars now."

"Shut up. Just shut up." I close my eyes. And then I do what I'd trained myself to do years ago, when I was a kid. I start to cry.

My life sucks.

It's always sucked, if you want to know the truth.

D.W. laughs harshly. "I've seen that act before. And you don't deserve an ounce of sympathy. I've never seen anyone who's been given so much fuck up so spectacularly. Get yourself together. Go do a line of cocaine or something."

"I'm going home now. And I'm going to forget we ever had this conversation."

"I wouldn't do that, my dear," D.W. says, gripping my hand. Ah yes. I'd forgotten how strong D.W. can be, even though he's a faggot.

"You're hurting me," I say.

"That's absolutely nothing, my dear, compared to the amount of pain I can inflict upon you and am perfectly prepared to do so."

I sit back down. Light ANOTHER cigarette. GOD. I have to quit smoking one of these days. When I get pregnant. "What do you want, D.W.?" I ask, although I have a pretty good idea. "You know I don't have any money."

"Money?" D.W. sits back in his chair and starts laughing. He's laughing so hard tears came out of the corners of his eyes.

"Don't insult me," he says.

"You're like that character in *All About Eve*. Addison DeWitt, The Evil Queen," I say.

"Why don't you order something to eat?"

"I'm not hungry. You know that."

"I'll order something for you."

Why is he torturing me? "I'll throw up. I swear to God, D.W. I'll vomit."

"Waitress," he says.

He moves his chair closer to the table. I move mine back. "All I want," he says, "is to be very, very close to my very, very good friend Cecelia. Who is now about to re-launch herself as the queen of society. Backed, aided, and abetted, of course, by her very, very good friend D.W."

I sit back in my chair. Cross my legs. Swing my foot. "I'll do nothing of the sort," I say, mashing my cigarette on the floor.

"Oh . . . yes . . . you . . . will," D.W. says calmly.

"Oh . . . no . . . I . . . won't."

"Are you aware," D.W. says, "that there's a Princess Cecelia tell-all book in the works? The writer is a very, very good friend of mine, but I have to say he's quite an excellent investigative journalist. The book would be — well, let's just say that 'embarrassing' would be the least of it."

"Are you aware," I say, "that I have now been married for over one year, so therefore whatever you want to say about me makes absolutely no difference?"

"Are you aware," D.W. says, "that your marriage sucks and your husband is constantly considering filing for divorce?"

"My husband is madly in love with me. He won't let me out of his sight."

"And where is he tonight?"

"You know my philosophy, D.W. I always bite the hand that feeds me."

"Is that so? Well, take a good look at yourself, dear. You're a mess," D.W. says. "You can hardly afford to have your name raked through the mud. Think about it. The photographers camped outside your door again, people going through your garbage, your face on the cover of the tabloids. You barely escaped last time. Just think of the . . . schadenfreude."

"I think . . . I need . . . a Xanax," I whisper.

"Oh, you'll need much more than a Xanax by the time they're through with you. I should think you'll be on Librium by then. Which, incidentally, is what they give to schizophrenics. Just in case you're not up on your pharmaceuticals."

I slump in my chair.

"It's not that bad," D.W. says. "All I'm asking is for you to attend a few parties and a tea every now and then. Chair a couple of committees. Wear some designer dresses. Maybe a fur. You're not against fur, are you? And then maybe host a trip to India, but by the time we arrange it, India might be passé, so maybe someplace like Ethiopia. We'll do some photo shoots, get you signed on as a contributing editor at *Vogue*. It's only the sort of life that every woman in America dreams of."

"D.W.," I say. "Society is . . . dead."

"Nonsense, my dear," he says. "You and I are going to revive it. We'll both have our place in the annals of history."

I wish I were in Massachusetts, riding around in the back of someone's car.

Smoking a joint.

Listening to Tom Petty.

"Come, come," D.W. says. "It's not like I'm asking you to be a homeless person. No one's asking you to urinate in subway stations. You've had a nice long rest, and now it's time to go back to work. Because that's what women in your position do. They work. Or did someone forget to tell you that?" He picks up his knife and smiles into the distorted reflection of his mouth. "People are relying on you, Cecelia. They're relying on you not to fuck up."

"Why?" I ask.

"Here's what I want you to do," he says. "Number one. Start putting on a happy face. Happy, happy, happy. Weren't you voted Most Popular in your high school class?"

"No."

"But you were voted something," he says.

"No," I say definitely. "I wasn't."

"You showed me your yearbook, Cecelia. Years ago. I remember the evening. It was right after Tanner dumped you."

"Tanner never dumped me. I dumped him. Remember? For my husband."

"Rewrite history with other people, my dear. I was there. Now what was it?"

"Most Likely to Succeed," I whisper.

But there were only forty people in my high school class. And ten of them barely graduated.

"And you have," he says.

"You can't use it."

269

"You have to stop being so afraid of every-thing. Really. It's embarrassing."

"I'm just so . . . tired."

"So go to bed. Number Two. We have to find you a charity. Something with children, I think; maybe encephalitic babies. And then maybe some lessons — cooking or Italian, because everyone's going to be sum-mering in Tuscany next year, and we should hook you up with some new spiritual trend thing . . . like druids. Druids could be very, very big, and you look like someone who could worship trees and get away with it."

D.W. holds up his martini glass. "To you, my dear. We're going to turn you into . . . into America's very own Princess Di. What do you think?"

"I think," I say, not even sarcastically, "Princess Di is dead."

"That's irrelevant," he says. "Her spirit lives on."

"And so is Princess Ava. Dead."

"So is Marilyn Monroe. And Frank Si-natra. Who cares? They're all dead. You've got to stop being so negative. Don't you wake up some mornings and think, 'By God, we did it.' We accomplished our goal. You're a princess. A real princess."

"No," I say glumly. "I always knew it would happen."

Along with a lot of other things, I suppose.

"You're never to say that. Ever again. To anyone," D.W. says. "Good God, Cecelia. That's why you're so bad at this. You've got to stop telling the truth. When someone asks — and they *are* going to ask, you've managed to avoid doing interviews so far, but you're going to have to start very soon — you're to say that you had no idea who he was when you just happened to sell him that painting in a gallery —"

"But I did sell him that painting in a gallery."

"That's not the point. Destiny only works in Arab countries. In America, destiny makes you sound . . . calculating. Which," he says, finishing his martini, "we know you are. But nobody else has to know that. Now about those S. sisters . . ."

"No," I say. "They freak me out."

"Why? They're young, beautiful, rich, and married. Everyone wants to be their friend."

I glare at him. I want to put my head in my hands, but I'm too tired. I can't explain anything. What it was like sitting there in that big empty room — it had two Regency couches and a coffee table and a fireplace with a marble mantle — with that S. sister.

The one who was married off at eighteen.

"Cecelia," she had said. "Have you had a lot of lovers? You look like someone who has."

"What's a lot?" I said cautiously. I didn't understand. What did she want from me? I hadn't gone to private school in Europe.

"I'm one of those women who must be in love to have sex. If I'm in love with a man, I can have an orgasm from him touching my toe."

I didn't know what to say.

A baby started crying from somewhere in that vast, cavernous Tribeca loft she shared with her husband, an aspiring American politician, and four in help.

"I'm going to let him cry," she said, not ashamed.

I got out of there as fast as I could. "I have childbearing hips. What can I do?" she asked and I felt soiled.

She'd told me a dirty little secret I didn't want to hear.

The waitress comes over with two plates. She puts one of them down in front of me. On it is chicken with green beans and mashed potatoes.

"You need to eat," D.W. says.

I pick up one of the green beans with my fingers. I put it into my mouth. Chew. I manage to swallow it.

I immediately feel full.

"The chicken," D.W. says, "is delicious."

It has some kind of brownish glaze on it. It's shiny.

It's a dead piece of meat.

I cut into it. It's a little pink inside. Like a pink little baby.

"Oh GOD," I say. I put down my utensils, pick up my napkin, and throw up into it.

II

LA LA LA LA LA LA

Every day, in every way, I'm getting better and better.

Not.

I'm getting worse and worse.

And who can blame me?

Everyone.

Everyone blames me.

I can't handle fame. I'm really, really bad at it.

My husband knows this. Isn't that one of the reasons he married me in the first place? I don't care about fame. Or money. I don't want to be famous. I only want to be with him.

He is *everything* to me.

And I am nothing.

Without him.

"Leave my wife alone!" Hubert had shouted at the photographers during our honeymoon in Paris and Rome and then on a remote island off Tunisia. *"Quittez ma femme. Quittez ma femme,"* he had said over and over, with his arm wrapped around me protectively as I bowed my head and we walked quickly from the hotel to the car, from the car to the museum, from the museum to the boutique, until it became a sort of joke mantra. I'd be in the tub, under heaps of bubbles, and Hubert would come in, and I'd say, *"Quittez ma femme,"* and we'd both crack up.

We haven't *cracked up* in a long time now.

I think it was the food in Tunisia that first put me off my feed. You had to eat unidentifiable stews — God only knows what was in them — yak? — with soggy pieces of bread, and I couldn't do it. Not in front of Hubert. I suddenly felt like he was watching me. And secretly criticizing me. Wondering if maybe he shouldn't have married me after all.

Okay. So I'll starve.

Nobody likes me. Do you think I don't know that? Do you think I don't sit for hours and hours, partly because they're feeding me all these pills all the time (they say they're going to kick in any day now, and then I won't be depressed anymore, but I doubt it), agonizing over every slight, knowing there are people out there laughing behind my back, saying, "Why doesn't she get a clue . . . what a tragedy . . . what a bummer for him having married her it sure didn't turn out the way he expected I bet and I bet he's miserable," when I'm the one who's miserable, but you can't tell people that, can you?

Especially if you're a woman. Because marriage is supposed to make you happy, not make you feel like a rat trapped in a very glamorous cage with twenty-thousand-dollar silk draperies.

And this is the *best* there is. It doesn't get any better than *this,* does it?

Because this is it. The crown. The dream. The brass ring. No more worries. Not a care in the world. Your mother will never starve in her old age. Your sister will have her new car. Your children will go to private school, have nannies, and all the toys they want, including a pony. Honor will be restored to your family name. Your mother will be proud of you. Your father, wherever he is, the bastard, will realize he made a terrible mistake.

And you will have: 1) A castle. 2) Houses around the world. 3) A chauffeur. 4) Lots of clothes with matching shoes and handbags. 5) Jewelry. 6) A horse. 7) A saddle(s) from Hermès. And 8) No friends.

Now here's what really pisses me off: Everybody thinks they could live my life so much better than me. They think, if they had my life, they'd be so happy to be me that they'd do everything perfectly. But they just don't get it. They don't have a clue. They couldn't *get* this life unless they had my personality and looked the way I do. If you changed one thing, the destiny part wouldn't work at all.

For instance, Hubert would only be with a woman who was tall, blond, thin, and had large breasts. And was younger. And had a certain kind of face. Classy. He never wanted to be with a model, because he doesn't want to be with a woman other guys might masturbate to.

And personality. You have to really know how to work guys. You have to be able to manipulate them, except "manipulate" isn't really the right word, because it has negative connotations. What you have to do is you always have to be different. You have to be unpredictable. Some days, you're really really nice and sweet and loving, and other days, you're a total bitch and steely. They keep coming back because they never know what they're going to get. You have to be able to be aloof, and you have to be willing to make a man jealous. But you can't do any of this unless you have the right physique, because otherwise the guy will just say you're a bitch and who needs it and dump you.

Of course, there are women without the physique who do marry well, but they don't marry men like Hubert.

In fact, right up until I married him, Hubert wasn't totally sure that I was going to marry him. You've seen his face in the wedding photographs. How happy he looked when we came out of the church.

Oh. And one other thing. You can never think that your husband, or anyone he introduces you to, is better than you. Just because your husband is a prince does not mean he's better than you are. You could meet a guy who's just won the Nobel Prize, and you have to know that he isn't any better than you are or more accomplished. I've always thought that I was just as good as anyone, no matter what they've done or how many hit songs they've had or how hard they say they've worked. One day, Tanner told me I had no sense of proportion because I wasn't fawning all over his acting career, and I broke up with him on the spot. Life just isn't like that, you know?

I feel better now. I think I can go to sleep.

III

I am confused.

About a small point, really.

Going back to last year, right after Hubert and I were married.

I asked him for money to buy clothes.

"I don't understand," he said.

"Hubert," I said. "I don't have any clothes."

"What's all that in your closet?"

"I need *new* clothes," I said, as tears began forming in the outer corners of my eyes. It was the first time my husband had openly refused me, proof that he didn't love me anymore.

"I never saw my father give my mother money for clothes."

"She had an allowance," I said, not knowing whether this was true, and also knowing that this statement was very brave indeed, as Hubert would probably take it as a criticism against his mother, which he did.

"What are you saying about my mother?"

"Nothing," I said.

"Then why did you bring her up?"

"I didn't. You did."

"You brought her up. You said, 'she had an allowance.' Didn't you say that?"

"Ye-e-e-e-s," I said. "But — oh, fuck you," I said mildly, and ran into the bedroom crying. He didn't come in right away the way he usually did, and when he did, he pretended to be getting a tie out of the closet.

"Hubert," I said patiently. "I need clothes."

"I don't want a bunch of reporters following my wife around and writing stories on how much my wife spends on dresses. Do you want that?" he said. "Do you want to be the laughingstock of the papers?"

"No-o-o-o-o," I sobbed, not wanting to point out that I was already beginning to be the laughingstock of the papers, so what difference did it make? I rocked back and forth on the bed, crying and crying like my heart was breaking, (which it was) thinking, "What am I going to do now? What am I supposed to do now?"

And *now* — ha ha — I am sitting here surrounded by strange *new* clothes. So in other words, everything that I was doing in the last year has finally resulted in getting my way.

Which was wearing the same old simple black-and-white pieces I always wore before my marriage, until some fashion reporter wrote: "Can't someone get this princess a new frock?" Which I didn't have to point out to Hubert, because it was in the Styles section of *The New York Times*, and that's the section he reads first on Sundays. Believe it or not. (I didn't believe it myself, when I first met him: that and the way he secretly reads all the gossip columns, scanning the items for his name. No matter what is written, he never says anything about it; and his face always remains impassive, like he's reading about somebody else, someone whom he doesn't know.)

And yet, there is something insulting about all this. As if Hubert didn't want to spend money on me for the first year of our marriage because he wasn't sure he was going to keep me around.

(I so wish that we could talk about these things openly. I really did believe, when we first got married, that we would talk about everything honestly, but the opposite has occurred: We're like two people on separate islands, with only tin cans and string as a means of communication.)

And so I must act slightly displeased by it all. Especially since it's really D.W.'s doing.

Including the short hair. I have short white hair, and when I look in the mirror, I don't recognize myself. It's part of their plan to wipe me out and start over.

And my husband is all for it.

"I'm on board," he said. (Ugh. I hate that expression. It's so corporate America, which Hubert is not but likes to pretend he is.) "I'm on board. It's good for you."

"I suppose you'll be wanting me to EXERCISE next," I said.

"Exercise is good for you," he said. At which point I told him that it's very difficult to exercise when you're so doped up you can barely lift your hand to your mouth.

When I said this, he said (suspiciously, I thought), "There is no reason to lift your hand to your mouth unless you're putting food in it." To which I smartly replied, "Actually, you have to lift your hand to your mouth to apply lipstick," and that shut him up for a minute.

We were having this conversation yesterday morning while I was still in bed, and in the middle of it the apartment buzzer began ringing incessantly. I put several pillows over my head, but it's no use. Hubert goes downstairs, then comes back up and says, "Get up. D.W. is here." Instead of staying to comfort me, he goes back downstairs and makes another pot of coffee, like he's some kind of real person (he actually takes pride in this), which I can never help but believe is a total act.

I hear some kind of commotion downstairs, and voices, and Hubert calling, "Come on, sleepyhead, come downstairs." And then D.W.'s voice: "Get up! Get up, you lazy thing!" I therefore have no choice but to wrench my drugged, and tired bones from the comfort of my bed. I go immediately (do not pass bathroom) downstairs with my hair in a mess, still wearing my silk spaghetti-strap negligee, which is all wrinkled and has tiny stains on it because I've basically been wearing it for four days.

Just as I enter the kitchen, I hear D.W. say, "I declare, Hubert, you get more handsome every time I see you," which nearly sets me off, because who does D.W. think he is, acting like Scarlett O'Hara in *Gone With the Wind*?

Hubert is dressed in a gray suit with a white oxford-cloth shirt and a yellow tie, and unless you're actually married to him, I suppose he does look pretty amazing, pouring coffee into large mugs, smiling and making light conversation about a movie he's seen called *The Seventh Sense*.

"Why didn't I see this movie?" I ask.

He pulls me to him and puts his arm around me. "Because you were sick. Remember?"

"I wasn't sick," I say. "I was only pretending to be sick because I hate movie theaters."

"That's right," he says, to me and not to D.W., which actually makes me feel a tiny bit good, "because you think movie theaters are filled with germs."

"Germs and sick people," I say.

"She's such a princess," D.W. says. "I always told her that if she didn't marry you, the only other person she could have married would have been Prince Charles."

"I'd be dead then," I say.

"That would be a terrible tragedy. Not just for Hubert, but for the world," D.W. says unctuously.

"I'd like to be dead. I don't think it would be bad at all," I say, and I can see Hubert and D.W. exchange glances.

"Besides," I say, pouring myself a cup of coffee even though coffee is yet another one of the FORTY MILLION things in the world that makes me VOMIT, "if I hadn't married Hubert, I would have married a movie star."

I hand my cup of coffee cup to D.W. "Try it."

"Why?" he asks.

"Just try it."

D.W. and Hubert exchange glances.

"It's coffee," he says, and hands it back to me.

"Thank you," I say. I cautiously take a sip. "I just wanted to make sure it wasn't poisoned."

My poor, poor husband. He ditched the European girl and got something much worse. Something crazy. Which he has to ignore.

"But you wouldn't be happy," Hubert says, again trading glances with D.W., "because a movie star wouldn't love you as much as I do."

"Well," I say, "since you love me zero, what difference would it make?"

"Oh, come, come," D.W. says.

"What do you know?" I ask hatefully. And I look over at Hubert and see that closed-down look has come over his face. Again. For the millionth time.

He empties the rest of his coffee in the sink and rinses his mug. "I've got to be going."

"He's always going to that stupid office," I say casually.

"Studio," D.W. says. "When a man is the executive producer of a hit TV show on a major network, he goes to a studio."

Hubert kisses me on the forehead. "Bye, kiddo," he says. "You two have fun today."

I look at D.W. balefully.

"Don't," he says. "Don't say anything stupid. Especially after that completely pointless display."

My poor husband.

I run into the living room and grab Mr. Smith, who is sniffling around the couch, and run for the door, passing the kitchen where D.W. spots me and shouts out, "Keep that beagle away from me!" And I run down the stairs, still clutching Mr. Smith, who has absolutely no idea what is going on, and I run onto Prince Street, where Hubert has just gotten into the limo (he supposedly told them he didn't want a limo, but The Network insisted). I knock on the window and Hubert lowers the glass. He looks at me like "Oh God, here's my crazy wife standing on the street barefoot in a wrinkled old negligee holding a beagle in her arms," and he says (pleasantly enough), "Yes?" And I say, "You forgot to say good-bye to Mr. Smith."

He says, "Good-bye, Mr. Smith," and leans out and kisses Mr. Smith on the nose. It's all so cute, and I actually think I might be okay for the next couple of hours, but then I hear that telltale click, click, click behind me, and I turn, and there's that photographer in full combat fatigues, snapping away and yelling, "Smile!" and the limo takes off, and I hold Mr. Smith (who is struggling viciously now) over my face and run crazily down Prince Street, finally taking refuge in a news shop.

At which point the proprietor of this dirty shop with its overpriced cigarettes has the nerve to say, "No dogs. No dogs in the store." And begins waving his arms like he's just been attacked by an infestation of fleas.

I'm about to hurl a string of invectives at him (and, in fact, have opened my mouth to do so), when I see IT: the cover of *Star* magazine, which features photographs of a couple of actresses and ME, with my mouth open, wearing baggy shorts and a tank top, arms and legs akimbo. The photograph was taken a few months ago at a celebrity basketball game that Hubert not only made me attend but insisted I participate in (which ended up working in my favor, because I was such a horrendous basketball player and yet so high strung under the stress of competition that Hubert said I never had to do anything like it again), and underneath the photograph the caption reads: *Princess Cecelia, 5'10" 117 lbs*. And this raft of falsehoods is topped off with the headline:

STARVING TO DEATH?, which really pisses me off because I'd actually eaten two hot dogs that day. I grab Mr. Smith and the *Star*, and I run down the street and back up the stairs and throw open the door to the loft. D.W. is sitting in the living room, calmly sipping a cup of coffee and perusing the photographs in *New York* magazine. I collapse onto a chair, hyperventilating madly.

"Really, Cecelia," he says. He looks at his watch. "It's eight-forty-three. Don't you think you ought to get dressed?"

I really do not know what to say to this, so I fall to the floor, shaking and clawing at my throat, until D.W. throws a glass of water on my face.

Riding uptown, wearing sunglasses and a head scarf and clutching Mr. Smith to my chest, I felt the sinking weight of depression, like someone has placed a board piled with cement blocks on top of my body. When I'm in this state I find it hard to move, difficult to make even the slightest gesture — like lighting a cigarette — and sometimes, since I spend so much time alone in the apartment, I end up sitting for hours and hours, occasionally on the stairs or on the kitchen floor, staring into space. I don't want anyone to know how bad it is, so I lie and say, Oh, I've been reading magazines all day or running errands, like picking up a spool of thread at the dry cleaner, but quite often I find myself scratching "help me help me" on the palm of my hand with an old ball-point pen, but by the end of the day, I have invariably washed it off. My thoughts always run along the same lines, like a small electric train going back and forth, back and forth: Everyone hates me and may or may not be laughing at me behind my back, waiting for me to fuck up, to say something stupid (or anything at all, because when people are judging you that closely, almost anything you say sounds stupid) or give them an evil eye, so they can run to their friends and colleagues and say, "I met Princess Cecelia and it's true what they say. She's a bitch."

And then everywhere you go, people look at you like they expect to hate you, and their reactions are like stones, hitting you again and again until finally you shut down, you stop, you put your arms over your head and then you begin to slowly disappear.

D.W. is drumming his nails on the armrest. "I've been married . . ." he says. "Twice."

"Yes," I say blandly. "I know," in a small voice, truly upset now by that photograph in

Star and the accompanying article that accuses me of being an anorexic, which I'm NOT, but what I am is so complicated that I can't begin to explain it to myself.

"I've been married," D.W. says again, "and the one thing I've found is that the superficialities of marriage are the most important. In other words, pleasant conversation at breakfast, amusing banter at parties, and a compliment once or twice during the day matter more than whatever one is actually *feeling*, which, frankly, no one really cares about anyway."

I nod mutely, wondering why it is that D.W. and I have the same conversations over and over again, so that I don't even have to point out that D.W.'s last marriage ended so horrendously (in a war on Page Six) that his wife, who is at least eighty now but has had a dozen or so face-lifts and always wears rose-colored sunglasses, will leave a party if his name is mentioned.

"In fact," D.W. continues, oblivious, "I would say that the superficialities are the most important thing in every aspect of life. I mean, who cares that you're really a piece of shit if you're sitting at a dinner with lovely flowers and a fabulous person on your left and a fabulous person on your right, and the photographers are taking your picture, and your socks, for God's sake, are cashmere, and you're smiling just so, and the photograph ends up in the society pages of *Vogue*. That's what really counts, isn't it? Of course, you probably wouldn't understand that because, like all people with mental problems, you're completely obsessed with yourself. You don't really care anything about me, or the fact that that dog of yours is liable to dribble on my Prada suit at any moment."

"Mr. Smith doesn't dribble," I say, unable to even get angry because of the aforementioned state I'm in.

"Oh. I'm sorry. I meant you," D.W. says.

I allow myself (still clutching Mr. Smith) to be led from the town car out onto Madison Avenue, where someone is jackhammering the sidewalk, and a Mercedes sportutility vehicle passes blaring rap music, and people walk by all emitting high-frequency vibrations of "Look at me, look at me, look at me," so that even in this brief moment the noise of the city is crushing and I feel like everything is collapsing in on me. We walk up narrow terra-cotta stairs and enter the beauty salon, which is all skylights and marble columns with a fountain in the middle (meant, I believe, to be some kind of imitation Roman baths), around which women in white robes with turbans on their heads lounge reading magazines. I'm whisked off to the private area, where they minister to "celebrities," and someone dressed in a sari keeps trying to give me coffee, tea, or water (when I ask for a Bloody Mary, they all look shocked) and keeps shoving bowls of water with lemon slices floating on top under Mr. Smith's nose, which he sensibly refuses.

And then they begin cutting. Cutting away my long hair which I've had all my life (which is my life — long hair, men love it), and which has gone through various and sundry colors of blond, depending on whether or not I actually had money at the time to pay someone to color it or if I had to do it myself with Sun-In or if one of my gay friends took pity on me and arranged for someone to do it for free (that was easy, as soon as it came out in the gossip columns that I was dating the prince of Luxenstein), and D.W. comes over and says, "So many people have worked so hard to get you here, Cecelia," blowing smoke out of his nostrils. I say, "So I am supposed to feel guilty?"

"Just grateful," he says, and walks away.

And I swear, as they're cutting, I keep hearing people talking about me. Whispering my name. Until finally, it's too much and I scream, "Will everybody please shut up?" And they all do, except for one unfortunate soul who goes on and on, speaking into his cell phone in a high-pitched nasally voice, ". . . that's right, Dick. She's here now. Complete makeover. And completely loony. She won't let go of that dog. Won't speak to anyone. She's got the worst energy of anyone I've ever met. Maybe she should try crystals. . . ." Finally, he looks up, and after that, nobody says anything at all.

"What did I ever do to you?" I whisper hoarsely.

I stare at myself in the mirror. My eyes are very wide and blue. Very wide because I KNOW this isn't a good time to start crying, not with all these PEOPLE (if you can even call them that) standing around in various forms of emotional attitude, ranging from disdain to shocked horror to pity, reminding me of the first time I had to go to that school in Massachusetts when I was ten years old and taller than all of them and they stood around in the playground and called me —

"Miss . . . Cecelia," the colorist says. She has a long face and large teeth and she looks like a talking horse, but a kindly one. "I hope you don't think that was a reflection of . . . our salon. He's new. I'm going to fire him immediately."

I could have someone fired?

"Oh," I say softly, nodding over the top of Mr. Smith's head.

"That was very, very wrong of him," she says, pumping the back of my chair so it goes up and down. "David," she snaps. "Pack your things and don't come back."

This David person, who is lurking around the edges, is thin and dark-haired and sloe-eyed with dark circles, and he reeks of anonymous sex.

"Whatever," he says haughtily. Our eyes meet for one second in the mirror and I see his whole pitiful story: fresh off the bus from some lousy town in the Midwest, ambitious and a born hustler, will do anyone for a piggyback to the next rung (for fun or profit), anything to erase his dirty origins and make believe he is someone else. Mostly, though, he'll talk about how I got him fired, and talk and talk, and he'll spread this topic of conversation among his acquaintances like a virus.

I know. I used to hang out with people like that.

I used to be like people like that.

I can deny it. Even to myself.

"I'm really very . . . normal," I say softly.

And isn't this one of my problems? I'm normal?

"Oh yes. I can see that," the colorist says.

I'm just like a million other girls in New York.

"Aren't you from . . . ?"

"Massachusetts," I say.

"My grandmother was from Massachusetts."

"That's nice," I say. Realizing that for the first time in — what? weeks? — I'm having a normal conversation.

She paints white goop on my hair.

"What's your doggie's name?" she asks.

IV

Dr. Q. licks the tip of his pencil.

"You think that . . . ," he says, consulting his notebook, "your husband and this, this *friend* of yours, D.W., the publicity man, have formed a conspiracy against you and are forcing you to become . . . let me see here . . . the American version of Princess Di. Who, you so adroitly pointed out, is dead. Meaning . . . you believe that, consciously or subconsciously, your husband secretly wants . . . *you* dead." Pause. "Well?"

"I heard them discussing it on the phone."

"Your death."

"NOOOO," I scream. "The conspiracy."

"Oh. The conspiracy."

"D.W. told me there was that tell-all book."

"Cecelia," Dr. Q. says. "Why would anyone want to write a book — an 'unauthorized biography' — about you?"

"Because the press . . . they're always after

me . . . and there's that girl, Amanda. The one who . . . died."

"You call someone who was, according to you, your best friend 'that girl'?"

"She wasn't my best friend by then."

"That girl?"

"Okay. That woman." Pause. "My photograph was in all the newspapers this morning. From last night. At the ballet . . . ," I whisper.

"Was that you, Cecelia? That girl with the short white hair, running down the stairs, looking over her shoulder, laughing, holding the hand of an unknown boy?"

"Yes! YES. Didn't you see my NAME . . . Princess Cecelia. . . ." I'm breaking down, crying, covering my face with tissues. "There are photographers outside the window!"

Dr. Q. stands up and pulls back the blind. "There's no one there. Except the doorman and old Mrs. Blooberstein and that disgusting Chihuahua."

"M-m-maybe the doorman sent them away."

"Cecelia," Dr. Q. says, returning to his chair. "Where were you in August 1969?"

"You know where I was."

"Where were you?"

"Yazgur's Farm," I say defiantly.

"And what were you doing there? *Gonna join in a rock 'n' roll band?*"

"Dr. Q., I was three years old. My mother dragged me there. No one paid attention to me. I had shit in my pants for hours. My mother was on an acid trip."

"*And everywhere was a song and a celebration.*"

"It wasn't a celebration . . . the hippies made me dance . . . I was lost . . . my mother was on an acid trip. . . ."

Dr. Q. turns into Mrs. Spickel, the guidance counselor. "Hello, Cecelia. Your mother is dead. Aren't you lucky it happened now, when you're seventeen, and not when you were a little girl. I hear your mother was very wild. . . ."

I'm crying. I'm crying hysterically like I'm going to break in two. I wake up.

Of course, it's Hubert's mother who is dead, not mine.

She died in a freak skiing accident when Hubert was seventeen.

Poor little lost prince, standing on the deck of his twenty-two-foot racing sloop, one hand on the rudder, staring out at the sea, wistful and a little bit fierce (like someone training himself to hold back tears), a forelock of dark hair falling over his forehead. He is a teenage girl's dream: hurt, in need of rescue, a prince, a teen idol.

"I can save him," I think, staring at the black-and-white photograph on the cover of *Time* magazine, sitting on the cheap, Scandinavian-wood coffee table in the living room with the nubbly green polyester couch in the house in Lawrenceville, Massachusetts, where my mother has decided to settle with the man who works in the fish business.

"I can save you, little prince," I think, although he is not little (six-two) and just on the edge of manhood, and forever away, staying at the home of rich society people in the Caribbean and planning to attend Harvard in the fall. I stare at the photograph and fantasize that he is in the hospital, felled by an accident, with bandages on his head, and he says, "I want Cecelia. I must have Cecelia," and I rush into the hospital room and he kisses my face.

I am ten years old.

What has happened to me?

I used to be so strong. And determined. And aggressive, people said. They were scared of me. It was obvious that I wanted something, but no one knew what.

I knew.

I wanted the prince.

Ever since I was ten, I worked at putting myself in the path of the oncoming train of destiny. How did I know that I should major in art history in college? (I just knew.) And that I should finagle a job at a famous SoHo art gallery where I would meet rich and glamorous men and women (mostly men), who would embrace a beautiful young girl with attitude and a sense of humor and take her up and show her off on the town, so that, even without the approbation of family money or name, her picture would appear in the newspapers and magazines as having attended this or that event? And how did I know, when Tanner walked into the gallery that day, that I must do everything in my power to become his girlfriend, so that when my real object of desire walked in, which I knew he would eventually, given the laws of consequence, those being that he lived in SoHo and bought art, I would already be taken by a worthy opponent and this would make me more valuable in his eyes?

You just know these things. They're instinctual. I was all instinct then. Raw, aggressive instinct, and I lived my life like an alien thing was driving me.

But now that thing is gone. It has failed me.

(Where did it go? Can I get it back?)

And I am FRIGHTENED nearly all the time now. By EVERYONE — doctors, lawyers, politicians, photographers, gossip columnists, anyone who might use words I don't know or talk about events that I should know about but don't, all actors and journalists, women who go through natural childbirth, women who speak three languages (especially Italian or French), and anyone that other people say is talented or merely cool or simply English. As you can imagine, this encompasses pretty much everyone in Hubert's life, and that is why, if we have to go out, I tend to become deathly ill beforehand (in which case I can usually get out of going); or, if I cannot muster a life-threatening illness, I sit in a corner with my hands folded in my lap, my head tilted and a blank expression on my face, which seems to prevent people from attempting to converse with me.

But on this particular evening, no amount of vapors can prevent the inevitable: attending the fiftieth anniversary of the ballet.

Without my husband.

Who is actually having a CARD GAME instead.

He's sitting in the living room in a red-and-white-striped shirt, suspenders still looped over his shoulders, drinking a beer with his buddies from the network whose names I still can't be bothered to remember, when I come down the stairs, wearing a white brocade dress with gray mink trim and long gray gloves. My mother is married to a fishmonger. My father is gay and lives in Paris. I am going to the ballet.

Doesn't anyone understand how TERRIBLE life is?

I used to beg to go to these events. I used to connive and cadge an extra ticket, suck up to gay men who wanted to help me, buy a dress and tuck the tags in and arrogantly return it the next day, all with the specific ambition of landing myself in the position I'm in tonight.

"Hello," Hubert says nervously, putting down his beer as he stands. "I . . . I wouldn't have recognized you."

I smile mournfully.

"Is D.W. here yet?"

I shake my head.

He looks at his buddies. "I guess we'd know it if he were. D.W. He's Cecelia's friend. He's —"

"An escort," I say quickly.

The buddies nod uncomfortably.

"Listen," he says, approaching to take my arm, leading me a little bit out of the room, "I really appreciate this, you know?"

I stand with my head bowed. "I don't know why you're making me do this."

"Because," he says. "We've been over this before, and it's a good thing."

"It's not a good thing for me."

"Listen," he says, nodding at his buddies over his shoulder while pulling me deeper into the library, "you've always said you wanted to be an actress. Just pretend you're an actress and you're in a movie. That's what I always do."

I look at him pityingly.

"Hey," he says, touching my shoulder, "it's not like you don't know how to do this. When I met you . . ."

What?

He stops, seeing that he has said the wrong thing.

When he met me, I had crashed the event. Looking for him. He found out six months later, over pillow talk, and thought it was funny; but then he realized the story would make me look bad, so it's one of the many awful truths about my past that we have to keep hidden.

I am standing stiffly, my eyes wide, staring into space.

"Oh no," he says. "Oh no, Cecelia, I'm sorry, I love you." He grabs for me, but it is too late. I gather up my skirts and run out the door, run down the stairs and out onto the sidewalk, panting for a second, looking around, wondering what I should do, and then I see a cab, run to the street and hail it, and as I get in and slam the door and look back I see the photographer in the camouflage outfit, who stares at me with a sort of muted curiosity on his face and then shrugs.

"Where to?" the cab driver says.

I sit back on the seat. I touch my hair. "Lincoln Center," I say.

"Are you an actress?" he says.

I say yes, and he lets me smoke.

I consciously think of nothing as my heels click briskly across the plaza at Lincoln Center. I hurry slightly because of the February drizzle and flow into the crowd that gathers at the door, laughing, stomping their feet, shaking umbrellas. I somehow manage to blend in, passing the photographers, who look at me and then turn away to take someone else's picture, and I am relieved until a short young woman, dressed in black and wearing a black headset, approaches and says, "Can I help you?"

I look around in confusion and open my mouth and then close it and look at the girl again (who is smiling at me, not unkindly), and I narrow my eyes, not believing that she doesn't know who I am. "I'm . . ."

"Yes?" she says, and I suddenly realize that she doesn't recognize me. It's the short white hair. I look around, lower my voice. "I'm Cecelia Kelly's cousin. Rebecca Kelly. Cecelia wanted to come, but she's . . . sick . . . and she felt so bad about it, she insisted I go in her place. I know it's an inconvenience and all, but I've been in Paris for the past five years and —"

"Don't worry about it," she says cozily, reaching across a table and picking up a card that reads PRINCESS CECELIA LUXENSTEIN. "No one ever objected to a beautiful woman, you know, and you're sitting at a table with Nevil Mouse, who has been bugging and bugging and *bugging* me to set him up with some 'eligible woman' even though he's here with that model, Nandy, and, well, I hope Cecelia feels better, you know?" She hands me the card. "She seems to be sick a lot. Which is really too bad, because" — the girl leans in conspiratorially — "she's kind of our secret hero in the office. I mean, our boss is such an asshole, but the thing about Cecelia is that you can tell she thinks it's all such a bunch of . . . crap . . . and after you've done this for a couple of years, I can tell you that it is."

"Well, um, thank you. Thank you very much," I say.

"Oh. And watch out for Maurice Tristam. That actor? He's at your table too. He's married, but he cheats on his wife. Constantly."

I nod and move away, making my way into the theater, passing more photographers (one of whom lamely lifts his camera and takes one picture, in case I might be someone important they don't know about), and I cross over knees and ankles to my place, Row C, seat 125, in the middle of the third row. The seat next to me is empty, and a man nearby smiles at me as the lights dim and I nod imperceptibly, and the music starts.

I begin to drift away.

I'm thinking.

About days and days of lying on a dirty sleeping bag on a dirty mattress on the floor, staring out the window at the bare branches of trees turned black from the endless drip, drip, drip of rain. It was Maine and the sky was always steel gray and the temperature was always 33 degrees with 100 percent chance of precipitation and the insulation was coming out of the walls. There were too many people in the house or too few, there was no food or too much — bags of potato chips and cans of chicken soup and ice cream in paper cartons — and I had a rotten tooth that someone pulled out by tying one end of a string around the tooth and the other end around a door handle and then slamming the door. I was six years old, and we were making an important political statement. We were rejecting society, we were rejecting Mother's family and Mother's husband's family and the kind of person they expected Mother to be. We were rejecting false values and the evils of capitalism (although we didn't reject the tiny bits of money when they came), and we were running, running, running, but all we were running away from was clean linens and blue water in the toilet bowl and Sunkist oranges in winter.

But Mother never did figure that out. Not even after she "reformed" and we went to live in Lawrenceville. Where we tried to act "normal."

The ballet ends.

I sit.

Long after the audience has leaped cheering to their feet, the champagne has been poured, and the cloud of balloons has descended on the crowd, I remain seated in the theater. Row C, seat 125. The crowd swells then falls back, thins out, and eventually disappears for dinner. Ushers shift through the theater, picking up discarded programs.

"Are you all right, Miss? They'll be starting dinner soon. Lobster quadrilles. You don't want to miss that."

"Thank you," I say. But I remain, thinking about my dirty Barbie doll, stained and naked with matted hair, which I took everywhere, crying once when someone's dog tried to take it away. "She's a little princess, isn't she," people had said as they picked me up in my worn flowered skirt, and I howled even louder, tears streaking my face.

Even back then I couldn't believe that I'd never have a pony.

I look up and am not astonished to see the beautiful boy from my dream threading his way through the rows until he stands above me, smiles, and sits down.

"Memory is just an alternate version of reality," he says.

We stare at the empty stage.

They are serving the foie gras with mango slices on the mezzanine level of Lincoln Center as we stand at the top of the stairs. It could be my imagination, but it seems there is a tiny, perceptible hush, and people swivel their heads to look at us as the boy takes my arm and we make our way slowly down the steps and across the floor to my table. The photographer, Patrice, is squatting next to

Nevil Mouse, the Australian media wunderkind who once tried to hire me but then rejected me when I wouldn't go on a date with him. As the boy pulls out my chair, he whispers, "Your table looks as bad as mine," and winks just as Patrice whispers to Nevil, "Who's that girl?"

Nevil, who is nervous and high-strung, stands up awkwardly and says, "Excuse me, but I think that seat is reserved for Princess Cecelia Luxenstein."

"It is," I say calmly, adjusting the shoulders of my dress. "But I'm afraid Cecelia couldn't make it. She's sick. I'm her cousin, Rebecca Kelly."

"Well, I suppose . . . it's all right then," Nevil says.

I put one elbow on the table and lean toward him. "Are you in charge of this event?" I ask demurely.

"No. Why should you ask that? It's just that . . . the committee works so hard to get the tables . . . just right."

"I see," I say. "So it wouldn't be unfair to assume that your greatest preoccupation is . . . being seen at the right table with the right people."

Nevil looks for help from Patrice, who kicks Nevil under the table and slides toward me, taking the seat that I suddenly realize is reserved for D.W.

"I didn't realize Cecelia had such a beautiful cousin. Do you mind if I take your picture?"

"Not at all," I say, smiling as Patrice leans back and fires off several shots. "You look so much like Cecelia, you know. But Cecelia hates to have her picture taken. I can't figure out what's wrong with her."

"She's . . . shy," I say.

"With me? I'm one of her oldest friends," Patrice says.

"Are you? I've never heard her mention you, but that must be because I've been in Paris for the last five years."

"I've known her forever. I remember when she first came to New York. She had big hair. Used to hang out at Au Bar. She was wild. I can't figure out what happened to her. I mean, she got the guy that everybody wanted, right? Champagne?"

"Yes, I'd love some."

"Ooooh, Mrs. Sneet," Patrice says to an elegant woman in her early fifties who is passing by, "Mrs. Sneet, I'd like you to meet Rebecca Kelly. She's Cecelia Luxenstein's cousin. She's been in Paris for the last five years, studying . . . art. This is Arlene Sneet, the head of the ballet committee."

I hold up my hand. "So lovely to meet

you," I say. "The ballet . . . I don't think I've ever seen anything so beautiful. I was so transfixed I had to remain in my seat, digesting it all, and I'm afraid that I kept my dinner partners waiting as a result."

"My dear, I completely understand," Mrs. Sneet said. "It's so lovely to see new faces at the ballet. And I must say, you're making quite a stir. Everyone is wondering who you are. You must allow me to introduce you to some eligible young men."

"Did I hear you say you studied art at the Louvre?" came a voice from my right.

I turn. "Why yes. Yes, that's right, Mr. Tristam."

"I always wanted to be a painter, but then I got caught up in this acting business," Maurice Tristam says.

"Oh yes," I say. "It's so difficult, the way one often has to sacrifice art for commerce."

"You should see some of the parts I've had to take just for the filthy lucre."

"And you're so talented."

"You think so? I ought to bring you in to talk to some of my producers. What did you say your name was again?"

"Rebecca Kelly."

"Rebecca Kelly. That sounds like a movie star. Well, Rebecca Kelly, I must say I'm an admirer of yours already."

"Oh, Mr. Tristam —"

"Call me Maurice."

"You're too kind. And who is your lovely date? Why, you naughty man. You've brought your *daughter*."

"I'm *not* his daughter!" says the lovely date, who, at no older than eighteen, already has obvious breast implants and a hardened expression.

"This is Willie," Maurice says with obvious embarrassment. He leans toward me and whispers in my ear. "And she's not my date. She's my, er, costar in this movie we just shot."

Willie leans across Maurice. "Are you friends with Miles?"

"Miles?" I ask.

"Miles Hanson. That guy you're with."

"Oh. You mean that pretty blond boy. Is his name Miles?"

Willie looks at me like I must be an idiot. "He just finished that movie. *Gigantic*. Everyone says he's going to be a huge star. He's the next Brad Pitt. I'm trying to get Maurice to introduce me —"

"I told you, I don't know him," Maurice says.

"But he won't. And I think he'd be a great boyfriend for me," Willie says.

"Champagne?" I ask, pouring myself another glass as the lobster quadrilles arrive.

Forty-five minutes later they're playing that song "I Just Wanna Fly," and I'm quite drunk, dancing wildly with Miles, when I look over and there is D.W., in a damp tuxedo, smoothing his wet hair and trying to look calm although I can see that he's fuming, and he spots me and marches over and shouts, "Cecelia! What are you doing? Hubert and I have been searching half of Manhattan for you."

Miles stops and I stop and the whole room seems to stop, expanding away from me, and I can hear Patrice shouting, "I knew it! I knew it was Cecelia all along!" And suddenly a black swarm of photographers descends and I am caught, with one hand in Miles' and the other clutching a bottle of champagne, and Miles jerks my arm and we start running through the crowd.

We run down the stairs with the photographers following us and run outside where it's really pouring now, across the plaza, down more steps, dodging limousines and four traffic cops, right onto Broadway, where a Number 12 bus is just pulling up.

We run up to the bus, waving and shouting, and we get on and Miles has two tokens and we're laughing, walking to the back of the bus where we sit down and look at each other and crack up, then we look up and everyone on the bus is staring. I hiccup and Miles takes a swig from the bottle of champagne. Then our clasped hands fall apart as we stare out opposite windows, watching the thick streaks of rain against the glass.

"Good morning."

"Good morning."

Hubert is sitting at the kitchen table, drinking coffee and reading *The Wall Street Journal*.

"Is there, ah, coffee?" I ask.

"In the coffeemaker," he says, not looking up.

I wander over to the counter and bang some cabinet doors, looking for a coffee cup.

"Try the dishwasher," he says.

"Thanks," I say.

I pour the coffee, sit down. "You're up early," he says.

"Mmmmm-hmmm," I say. He slides the *Post* toward me.

I take a sip of coffee. I open the paper to Page Six.

The headline reads PRINCESS BRIDE LIFE OF THE PARTY.

And then the copy: "It seems it's Prince Hubert Luxenstein who is keeping back his glamorous wife, Cecelia, and not the other way around. Cecelia Kelly, the former art dealer, has been laying low ever since her nuptials two summers ago in Lake Cuomo, Italy, at the 200-acre family castle owned by the groom's father, Prince Heinrich Luxenstein. But last night at the fiftieth anniversary of the ballet, the beautiful new princess, sporting a new gamine hairstyle and wearing a gown by Bentley, arrived solo and charmed dinner guests who included . . . before making a dramatic exit with new screen heartthrob Miles Hanson."

I fold the paper.

"Cecelia . . . ," he says.

"Do you still love me?"

"Cecelia . . ."

I hold up my hand. "Don't. Just don't," I say.

V

Dear Diary:

I think I'm getting better.

Today I get up and put clothes on and have a cup of coffee and read Hubert's leftover papers, and I look at my watch and it is nine o'clock and I suddenly realize that I could do something today. This is such a strange feeling that, for a moment, I consider taking a couple of Xanaxes, but then I realize that, for the first time in — what? years? — I don't want to be high. I am actually thinking about going uptown and — HA — making a surprise visit to my husband's office.

And the horrible thing about it is that the more I think about it, the more compelled I am to do it. After all, Hubert is my husband, and what could be more natural than a wife's going to visit her husband at lunchtime? Especially if she thinks he might be having an affair (which he might be), and especially if she thinks that he probably has other plans for lunch (which he most likely does). This conundrum will force him to choose his wife or the previous lunch plans. His choice will tell the wife just about all she needs to know about her husband, which is a) if he chooses work over his wife, he's a shit and he doesn't love her, or b) if he chooses his wife over his work, he's probably still a shit but he may love her. Either way, I have a feeling that Hubert is going to lose today, and I want to be there to witness it.

For some reason, I am wearing a navy-blue hat and navy-blue-and-white-striped gloves when I tap on the receptionist's desk with a gold Dunhill lighter. I also have a cell phone that doesn't seem to work in my bag, along with two old tampons and a crumbly dog biscuit. "H.L., please," I say to the receptionist, who doesn't do anything at first and then says in a cold, bored voice, "Whom shall I say is here?" and I say, "His wife," and she looks me up and down and says, "Just a minute," and all I can think about is that she hasn't recognized me, for some reason, and this infuriates me and makes me want to KILL her, so I bang annoyingly with the lighter again.

Then I remind myself that I am getting better.

She picks up the phone and says to

someone, "Is H. there?" and then, as if there's some question about it, she says, "Well his wife is here?" Then she puts down the phone and says, "Someone will be out to see you."

"What do you mean, someone will be out to see me? Where's my husband?" I say. "I didn't come here to see someone, I came to see my husband."

"He's not in his office."

"Is anybody ever in their office these days?"

"Does he know you're coming to see him?"

"Of course he does," I say, realizing that this is beginning to go badly.

"Well, he's probably on the set. Dianna Moon is on the show today."

"And am I supposed to *care* about Dianna Moon?"

The receptionist seems to look at me for the first time. Her nails are fake, lacquered in red, white, and blue stripes. They appear to be her only distinguishing feature.

"A lot of people . . . care . . . about Dianna Moon."

I remove my gloves, pulling at each of the fingers. "Is that because she . . . murdered her husband?"

The receptionist looks around nervously.

"He died of a drug overdose. And besides, Dianna Moon is a . . . hero. The ratings are going to be huge."

I yawn loudly. "But what has she ever done?" I ask, realizing this is a totally arrogant question on my part, as it could be argued that I've never done anything myself, except for marrying Hubert, supposedly one of the world's most eligible bachelors.

The receptionist glares at me. "I'll just see if I can find H. for you."

At that moment, Constance DeWall walks through the gray armored door that leads to the secretive maze of studios belonging to The Network.

"Cecelia," she says, holding out her hand. "So nice to see you again. Unfortunately, this isn't a good day for a surprise visit. We've got Dianna Moon on the set and she's . . . well, she's Dianna Moon."

"And I'm Princess Cecelia Kelly Luxenstein," I say, somewhat casually, cringing about the princess bit, knowing that it's the kind of thing that sets people off and makes them ring up gossip columns. "And I'd like to see my husband."

"Is this urgent, Princess Luxenstein?" Constance says with extreme sarcasm, which I will make her pay for later, perhaps by trying to get her fired. She is, I've heard, a "younger, nicer, smarter" version of me. What I know is that she's madly in love with my husband (just like all those other dummy Harvard graduates), has been trying to get him into bed since she first started as his line producer two years ago, and truly believes he would be better off with her instead of me.

"Does the situation have to be urgent for me to see my husband?" I ask, with equal sarcasm.

"It's just that . . . we've got a lot of security around."

"To protect Slater London from Dianna Moon, I assume."

Constance and the receptionist exchange a quick look. The receptionist looks down, pretending to rearrange phone messages.

"I can put you in the green room," Constance says finally. "But I can't guarantee anything."

Minutes later, illegally smoking cigarettes in the green room, I'm half watching the TV monitor as Dianna Moon, wearing a satin evening gown (one strap carelessly fallen off her shoulder) leans toward Slater London and, with complete earnestness, says, "I never look back at the past. I've been lucky and" — staring directly into the camera — "I thank Jesus every day." Then she sits back triumphantly, crossing her legs and throwing her arm over the back of the chair so that her cleavage is exposed. She giggles.

Slater London, who is half English and half American, former teenage screen heart-throb whose own career ended (briefly) when he was discovered wearing women's clothing, leans across his desk and says, "Dianna. Have you become a Jesus freak?"

Dianna Moon's face goes blank, and without seeming to be able to help herself, she says, "Slater. Do frilly pink underpants mean anything to you?"

Slater, who is caught off guard but covers it up by running his hand across his blond crew cut, says, "Wasn't Alice in Wonderland wearing them when she went down the rabbit hole?"

"Hole," Dianna says flirtatiously. "Is that a word you like?"

Slater looks at the camera. "Okay, folks. That's all the time we have. Dianna, thank you so much for being on the show, and good luck with your new movie. . . ." Then he smiles at the camera for a few seconds before ripping off his mike and screaming, "I hope we can cut out that last bit." The sound goes off as technicians walk onto the set with Hubert following. Dianna throws her arms around him as she looks over her shoulder at Slater, then they all walk off and the screen goes blank.

I suddenly feel sorry for my husband.

Does he know he's being USED? What IS his job, really? Booking guests and making sure that Slater isn't convicted for statutory rape? Who would choose to do this?

Hubert. EUROPEAN CROWN PRINCE IS NOT ONLY GORGEOUS, HE'S A REGULAR GUY, a headline screamed three years ago when Hubert first took the job. On his first day, he was photographed buying a sandwich from the corner deli, and when he came out, brown bag in hand, he actually waved the bag at the photographers and smiled. PRINCE'S FIRST DAY OF SCHOOL was the cover of *The New York Post* the next day, and I actually did not, at the time, think it was strange.

"I just want to do something normal. Like a regular person," Hubert had said. And I had agreed. "I just want us to be able to walk down the street and buy an ice cream cone," I had said, pouting, even though I HATE ice cream because it makes you fat, and Hubert had said, "So would I baby, so would I." Mournfully.

I encouraged him to take the job. Show biz. How difficult could it be? Hubert had already had a spate of jobs in banking, all of which, strangely, had turned out to be disasters. He had no head for numbers; in fact, he left generous tips because he couldn't calculate 20 percent. I ignored this back then.

But now I suddenly realize: My husband is charming, convivial, and beautifully mannered. But also kind of . . . dumb.

They're USING him for his connections.

I light a cigarette in disgust, and as I do, the door to the green room opens (that damn Constance probably locked me in), and Hubert comes in with Dianna Moon, who for some strange reason rushes over to me and throws her arms around me like a two-year-old, nearly knocking the cigarette out of my hand.

"I've always wanted to meet you," she gushes. Then she stands back and says, "You are as pretty as everyone says." She takes my hand and says, "I hope we can be really good friends."

I want to hate her but I can't, at least not right then.

"Constance told me you were here," Hubert says lamely. "And Dianna said she wanted to meet you."

"I was hoping you might be able to have lunch," I say. Wondering, is it me or is his Dianna comment subtly hostile?

"Let's all have lunch together. At one of

those Ladies Who Lunch places," Dianna says. "I'm feeling very, very ladyish today."

"Can't," Hubert says casually. "Bob and I have a standing invitation for lunch every Wednesday."

"Oh really," I say.

"Of course, there's no way you would have known that," Hubert says. "If you'd called before you came. . . ."

"Oh, who's this damn Bob person? Blow him off," Dianna says. "Tell him you're having lunch with me. I'm sure Bob will understand."

"He'll understand, but he's the head of The Network," Hubert says.

"But don't you want to have lunch with your wife?" Dianna asks, in what seems to be genuine confusion. "She's so pretty. . . ."

"We hardly ever see each other," I say in a completely neutral tone, pulling on my gloves.

"Norman and I used to spend every minute together," Dianna says. "Every minute. We couldn't get enough of each other. We were obsessed. We'd spend days and days together in bed. . . ." She screws her face up. "I miss him. I miss him so much. No one really understands." And then she begins to cry.

Hubert and I look at each other in alarm.

Hubert does nothing. I cough politely into my glove.

"He was the greatest love of my life. My only love. I don't think I'll ever be able to date anyone, even," she says, although it's a well-known fact that she is at the moment not only dating someone (the head of a movie studio) but, according to *Star* magazine, living with him (or at least leaving all her stuff at his house), but it's clear the tears are just part of her little performance, because she suddenly grabs my hand again and says, "Well, at least you'll have lunch with me. I just can't be alone right now."

Hubert looks relieved. "Why don't you go to Cipriani's? The Network will pick up the tab, of course," he says, adding, "Cecelia, just be sure to bring me the receipt, okay?"

And I just stare at him in horror, not believing that he is saddling me with this woman and treating me like some kind of . . . EMPLOYEE, for God's sake.

"I'll have Constance make the arrangements," he says. And just at that moment, Constance walks into the room and appears to "immediately sum up the situation."

"I'll call Giuseppe," she says, nodding at Hubert. "I'll tell them to be expecting you. That way you won't have to wait."

"I never have to wait. Anywhere," I say to

Constance, not believing her insubordination. I look at Hubert for confirmation, or at least some kind of support, but all he can do is smile uncomfortably.

"Well. Good-bye then," I say coldly.

"I'll see you later. At home," he says, like I'm annoying him or something.

"Right. I'll make that phone call," Constance says, looking at Hubert but not actually going anywhere. "Slater was a real comedian today, wasn't he?" she says, like she and Hubert are the only ones in the room. "It's all because of that damn Monique. That's what you get for dating a child. Except now it's our problem." And then she actually touches Hubert's arm. Specifically, his bicep.

I was right. He is having an affair with Constance.

"Who was that fucking bitch?" Dianna demands as she falls into the limo. "Christ. If I were you I would have smacked her. Listen, honey, rule number one: Never let any other bitch mess with your man. Because, guaranteed, that bitch is after your man. If you knew how many women I had to beat up, I mean, literally beat the FUCK off Norman, you wouldn't believe it."

I want to say that I would believe it, since

Dianna Moon's barroom brawls are legendary, but I am either too afraid or too polite or too pissed off at Hubert right now to say anything, so I just nod and light a cigarette, which Dianna grabs out of my hand and begins smoking rapidly with large gestures. "I nearly cut a bitch's tit off once, did you know that?"

"Actually, I didn't," I say, lighting another cigarette, figuring that surely even she can't smoke two cigarettes at the same time. "It's true," she says. "Bitch wanted to sue, but Norman and me, we had the biggest most powerful lawyers you could get in show business."

She sits back against the gray leather seat. I stare at her, unable to help myself. Her face is at once beautiful and ugly, the ugly part being original and the beauty the result of skilled plastic surgeons. "Yep," she says. "Everybody loved Norman. I mean everyone. The first time I saw him on that movie set — it was in the desert — I knew I'd seen Jesus. And everybody else knew it too." She turns to me and takes my hand. "That's why I love Jesus so much right now, Cecelia. I love Jesus because I've *seen* Jesus. Right here on earth. He was only here for a short period of time, just enough to make three movies that grossed over a hundred million dollars. But he touched everyone, and once he'd touched everyone, he knew it was time to go back up to heaven. So he went."

"But — didn't Jesus consider suicide a *sin?*" I say, wondering how much more of this I can take and if Hubert and Constance are having lunch and whether or not it's some secret love-nest lunch place that they go to practically every day where Hubert says things like "I love you, but my wife is crazy."

Dianna stares into my eyes. "He didn't commit suicide, Cecelia. Norman's death, as you may have suspected, was a complete mystery. No one knows exactly how he died. They don't even know what *time* he died. . . ."

"But surely," I say, "modern medicine . . ."

"Oh no," Dianna says. "Modern medicine is not as modern as everyone thinks. There are some things even the doctors can't figure out. . . ."

Yes, I can't help thinking, *and you are one of them.*

"Like the fact that his body wasn't found for four days."

"And," I say, unable to help myself, "weren't parts of it missing? Eaten by wild animals?"

Dianna looks out the window. "That's what everyone thinks," she says finally. "But the truth is . . . the body parts may have been carried off by . . . special disciples."

Oh dear.

"I'm almost certain my husband is having an affair," I say.

"And these special disciples, they're really . . ."

"With Constance. That bitch."

". . . they're like angels, sort of. Sent down to kind of watch over him but . . ."

"And I really don't know what to do about it," I say.

". . . the fact is that several people, I mean *several* people, think these special disciples are some kind of . . ."

"I suppose I have to think about divorce."

"Aliens," Dianna says.

I just stare at her.

She leans toward me. "You do believe Norman was Jesus, don't you, Cecelia? Please say yes. Please. Because I really want us to be best friends. I could use a best friend in this town, you know?"

Luckily, at this moment the limo pulls up in front of Cipriani's.

After a more-than-usual amount of fuss, we're shown to a table in the front of the restaurant by the window. There are whispers all around us: "That princess . . . Cecelia . . . who's that woman? . . . Oh, Dianna Moon . . . Norman Childs . . . Dianna Moon and . . . Luxenstein . . . Prince Hubert Luxenstein . . . dead, you know. . . ." And I know this will be an item in Page Six tomorrow, especially when I look up and see D.W. staring at me from five tables away, waiting for me to catch his eye so he can come over. He's sitting with Juliette Morganz, the "little girl from Vermont" who's marrying Richard Ally of the giant Ally cosmetics family at the end of the summer, at the Ally estate in the Hamptons.

The waiter comes over, and Dianna nearly slugs him when he attempts to place her napkin on her lap, but the brawl is averted by the appearance of D.W. He leans over and, in what is commonly called "syrupy tones," says, "My dear. What an absolute delight to see you. I can't imagine anyone I'd rather see more. You've made my day."

"Dianna Moon, D.W."

Dianna lifts her face to be kissed, and D.W. complies, kissing her on both cheeks. "Yeah," she says. "What do the initials stand for?"

"Dwight Wainous," I say.

"I was Cecelia's first boss," D.W. says. "Years ago. Since then Cecelia and I have been great, great friends."

I just look at him.

"And I hear congratulations are in order," he says to Dianna.

"Yeah," Dianna says, completely unimpressed.

"On your Ally cosmetics contract."

"Can you believe that?" Dianna says. "Me, selling blue eyeshadow."

"The Allys are great, great friends of mine. In fact, I'm lunching with Juliette Morganz, Richard Ally's fiancée, right now."

"Yeah?" Dianna says, squinting across the room. "You mean that little dark-haired thing?"

Juliette waves eagerly.

"I think I'm supposed to go to their wedding," Dianna says.

"She's a very, very good friend of mine as well," D.W. says.

"Sounds like everyone in this town is a very, very good friend of yours. Maybe I should get to know you better," Dianna says.

"That," says D.W., "would be a delight."

"Sweet Jesus," Dianna says as D.W. walks

away from the table. "That guy looks like something someone dug up from under a rock in Palm Beach," and I start laughing, even though Palm Beach reminds me of the two-week holiday Hubert and I took after we first got engaged, during which it became apparent to me that we may have had different expectations for our future together. Mine were: Louis Vuitton luggage, my hair always perfectly straight, jeeps in Africa, khaki jodhpurs, white columns set against the blue Caribbean Sea, dry-yellow Tuscan fields, a masked ball in Paris, emerald jewelry, the president, Lear jets, hotel suites, huge beds with white sheets and down pillows, an open roadster, my husband always kissing me, notes in my luggage that said "I love you," and the wind always blowing through our hair. This is what I got instead: an "exciting" tour of America. Which began in Palm Beach. Where "the glamorous, just-engaged couple" stayed at the home of Mr. and Mrs. Brian Masters. Brian Masters (Hubert's uncle) was a fat old man with moles all over the top of his head, whom I was seated next to at every meal, and who, on the first evening, leaned toward me and whispered, "This family was actually okay until Wesley went out to Hollywood and made all that damn money," as a black man wearing white cotton gloves served lamb chops. His wife, Lucinda, who spoke with a slight English accent but was actually from, I think, Minnesota, had an odd sort of vagueness about her, and I discovered the reason why after a particularly frustrating game of mixed doubles in which I swore at Hubert and threw down my tennis racket.

"Come with me, Cecelia," she said quietly, with an odd sort of half smile, and I followed her, still stomping mad, through the house and up to her bathroom, where she closed the door and directed me to sit on a yellow silk-covered stool. "There's only one way to survive as the wife of a Masters man."

"But Hubert —"

"His mother was a Masters. And so is he," she whispered. And I saw with alarm that she was really quite beautiful, and much younger, maybe forty, than she had appeared at first, surrounded by this grand house and faux servants, and I thought, What's going to happen to me?

"Dolls," she said, revealing the inside of the medicine cabinet, which contained such an array of prescription bottles I was sure it could rival that of any pharmacist. She removed a brown bottle and handed it to me.

"Try these," she said. "They're completely harmless. Just like candy. Makes you feel sweet."

"I don't need pills," I said. Which was really rather strange, since I was always a little bit on coke back then and, in fact, had a small vial in my bag which no one knew about and never would, and I said, "My marriage is going to be fine. It's going to be great."

"Oh Cecelia," Lucinda said, handing me the bottle. "Don't you understand? It isn't, and it's never going to be."

But it wasn't until the end of our holiday, when we went on that "fishing expedition" in Montana and I was dirty and my hair was frizzy and I was sleeping in a cabin with a scratchy army blanket and getting up at five in the morning and not having any decent place to take a shit, much less a shower, and Hubert and I had hardly anything to say to each other, that I opened the bottle of pills and shook one into my hand. It was small, white, and oval. I took one, then another.

I immediately felt better.

And I continued to feel good; even after we drove twenty miles in the rain to that honky-tonk bar Hubert had found in the guidebook and he danced with that waitress with the frizzy hair and saggy tits (she was only twenty-five) and I consumed six margaritas, I continued to maintain an aura of laissez-faire.

And Hubert was convinced he'd made the right decision in asking me to marry him.

Isn't that what it's all about?

"White or yellow?" Dianna asks, and I snap back and say, "What?" and we break out laughing because it seems we are on something like our tenth bellini.

"Xanax," she says.

"Blue," I say. "Yellow is for homosexuals."

"I didn't even know there was a blue," she says, putting her hand over her face and laughing at me through her fingers. "Hey, guess what? I ate dog food too. I made Norman eat dog food. Come to think of it, I made Norman do a lot of things."

"Don't start crying again," I say.

"Oh sweet Jesus. Norman. Norman," she wails. "Why did you have to go and die and leave me a hundred and twenty-three million dollars?"

"Why Norman?" I ask.

Then we have to pee, so we stumble upstairs, and sure enough, Juliette "that little girl from Vermont" follows us into the bathroom. Dianna takes one look at herself and stumbles back, screaming, "I need makeup," and Juliette slips in and whispers, "Hi," and before anything else can happen, Dianna grabs Juliette's Prada handbag and shakes it upside down, and sure enough, a pile of MAC cosmetics spills out, along with a junior Tampax, a brush containing a tangle of hair, and a condom.

"Oh Juliette," I say. "Don't you even use Ally cosmetics?"

"I use Ally cosmetics," Dianna says, carelessly smearing lipstick all over her lips, "and look at me. I've gone from crack addict to society lady. And guess what? You can too."

"Cecelia," Juliette says meekly, "you're coming to my wedding, aren't you?"

"I wouldn't miss it," I say. "Even though I hardly know you."

"But isn't that the great thing about New York? It doesn't matter," Juliette says. "I mean, everyone is —"

"I'm gonna conquer this town. Just the way I conquered Los Angeles," Dianna says.

"You're coming too, aren't you?" Juliette says to Dianna.

"Ask my publicist," Dianna says.

"Oh. Well, I've got a publicist too," Juliette says. "D.W."

"So get your publicist to call my publicist. Let the publicists figure it out." And with that, we leave Juliette in the bathroom, wiping her tube of lipstick with a tissue.

The phone is ringing when I walk through the door of the loft, and sure enough, it's Dianna.

"Hi sugarpuss," she says. "That's what I used to call Norman. Sugarpuss."

"Well, hi there," I say. "Hello Norman."

"Are you lonely, Cecelia? Because I sure am. I sure am lonely," Dianna says.

"I guess I'm lonely. Yeah," I say.

"Well, we won't be lonely anymore. We're going to be best friends."

"That's right," I say, the champagne beginning to wear off.

"Hey. I was wondering if you wanted to hang out. Maybe we could go shopping tomorrow. I've still got the limo and the driver. Hell, I've always got the limo and the driver. Sometimes I forget, you know?"

My husband is having an affair. With Constance.

"Hey Dianna," I say, looking out the window as a bus from the Midwest deposits a gaggle of tourists onto Prince Street. "Is it true what they say? That you killed your husband?"

There's a pause, then Dianna gives a short, loud laugh. "Well, let me put it this way. If I didn't, it's the kind of thing I *would* do, isn't it?"

"Is it?"

"Well . . . I'd know how to get it done. If that's what you're asking. And just remember. It's a lot cheaper than divorce."

She laughs and hangs up.

VI

I'm going away.

Sitting in Dr. Q.'s office, watching the dirty gauze curtains fluttering in the breeze coming off of Fifth Avenue, I think about yachts and movie stars in satin dresses and Louis Vuitton hatboxes like the one I just bought for the trip even though I don't have a hat, and Dr. Q. interrupts this reverie with one word: "Well?"

"You can see in through those windows," I say.

Dr. Q. puts down his yellow legal pad and looks out. "Is that a problem?" he asks. "You've been here for — what? — a year and a half now, Cecelia, and you've never mentioned it before."

Like I never mentioned Hubert's affair with Constance. Until a few days ago. Right after I told Hubert I was going to the Cannes Film Festival with Dianna.

"Maybe I'm getting paranoid," I say, half attempting a joke.

"You *are* paranoid," Dr. Q. says, looking down at his legal pad. "We all know that's why you're here."

" 'We?' Who's 'we'? What is this? Some kind of conspiracy?"

"Me, your husband, the press, or should I say 'the media,' and probably this D.W. character you're talking about all the time . . . should I go on?" Dr. Q. says in kind of a bored voice, so I say no, and then add suddenly, "Maybe I use my paranoia as a sort of weapon. Did you ever think about that, Dr. Q.?"

"Do you?" he says. "Use your paranoia as a weapon?"

Shit. I don't KNOW.

Dr. Q. sits staring at me, the way Hubert stared at me when I told him I was going away. Without him. But he couldn't say anything about it, just as he couldn't say anything about the four pieces of Louis Vuitton luggage I purchased after a boozy afternoon with Dianna, not to mention the several pairs of shoes, handbags, and dresses. "I need to get away," I had said. "I have to think."

"I need to get away," I say to Dr. Q.

"What will," he says, "going away do for you?"

"Nothing," I say. "But it will get me away

340

from my husband. Did I mention that I think he's having an affair?"

"You mentioned that" — Dr. Q. flips through his legal pad — "months ago. Along with that tell-all book."

"So?"

"So the point is . . . all of this is probably in your imagination."

"I think I can distinguish between fantasy and reality."

"Can you?" he says.

"I SAW him with her."

"Were they . . ."

"WHAT? Doing it? No. But I could tell. By the way they acted."

"What does he say?"

"Nothing," I say, swinging my foot. "But he doesn't deny it."

"Why won't you at least DENY it?" I had screamed. "Cecelia," Hubert said coldly, "that kind of assertion doesn't merit a response."

He can be so cold, my husband. Underneath the beautiful manners is absolutely . . . nothing.

"He's definitely having an affair," Dianna said later. "Otherwise, he would have denied it."

Well, we ALL know that, don't we?

I can tell this session is going absolutely

nowhere, so I say, pretty much out of the blue, "I have a new . . . *friend,*" suddenly realizing how PITIFUL this sounds, just like when I was four years old and I told everyone I had a friend, but it was only an imaginary friend named Winston. I'd tell everyone I was going to play with Winston, but in reality I was going to my favorite mud puddle where I tried to float bugs on matchstick covers.

"And this friend . . ."

"Is real," I counter, realizing that this, too, sounds insane, so I quickly cover it up with, "I mean, I think we're going to be friends. We're friends now, but who knows how long it will last."

"Do your friendships with *women* . . . usually end quickly?"

"I don't know," I say, exasperated. "Who knows? That's not the point. Don't you even want to know . . . who she is?"

"Is that important? *Who she is?*"

"The point is that I haven't had a girlfriend in a long time. Okay?" I say, glaring at him.

"And why is that?"

"I don't know. Because I'm married. You tell me."

"So this girlfriend . . ."

"Dianna —"

Dr. Q. holds up his hand. "First names only."

"What is this? Some kind of AA meeting?"

"It's whatever you think it is, Cecelia. Now let's see. Dianna," Dr. Q. says, writing the name in block letters and underlining it.

"You know EXACTLY who she is," I scream. "Jesus. It's Dianna Moon. Don't you read Page Six? They've been writing about us for two weeks. How we're seen everywhere together."

Dr. Q. sucks the end of his pen. "I don't read Page Six," he says thoughtfully.

"Goddammit, Dr. Q. Everyone reads Page Six," I say, crossing my arms and swinging one foot, clad in a beige silk Manolo Blahnik shoe, four hundred and fifty dollars and completely impractical, which Dianna and I bought two days ago when we went on a "shopping spree." I picked them out, and Dianna said that we should both buy a pair because we were "sisters," and this was confirmed when it turned out that we wore the same size shoe: nine.

"I have good taste," I say suddenly. And Dr. Q., probably relieved that I'm not going to go bat shit on him after all, says mildly, "Yes, you do. That's one of the things you're

343

known for, isn't it? Good taste. It's probably one of the reasons why Hubert married you."

He looks at me. I just stare at him, so he continues, floundering, "After all, that is one of the reasons why men like Hubert get married, isn't it? They want the wife with good taste, who will wear the right things to . . . *charity benefits* . . . and decorate the house in the Hamptons . . . or no, aren't the Hamptons *over?* . . . according to you people. . . ." And I lean back in the chair and close my eyes.

I think about what Dianna would do in this situation.

"You know what, Dr. Q.?" I ask.

"What," he says.

"Fuck you," I say, and walk out.

VII

This morning I wake up and say to Hubert, "Do you think Xanaxes are illegal?" while he's in the bathroom, shaving, and he says, "Why?" and I say, "Because I don't want to have any scandal. With customs. When I go to France," just to rub it in. And he gets this sick look on his face, which he's been pretty much sporting ever since I told him, two weeks ago, that I was going away, and he says, "I don't think you have to worry about it. You know, if there's any problem, you can always call my father."

"Oh la," I say gaily, for absolutely no reason. "I just love calling the castle."

He brushes by me, lifting his chin to button his shirt and pull a tie under his collar, and I see that hurt look in his eyes, like the outer corners of his eyes are drooping downward, and for a minute I feel like a corkscrew's been thrust in my stomach, but then I remember that he SHOULD feel bad.

He's the one who's having the affair.

Which, by the way, I don't plan to mention again.

Actions speak louder than words.

I pick up Mr. Smith, who is still, naturally, sleeping on the bed, and I kiss the top of his head and say, "Do you think that Mr. Smith will miss me?" all sweet and girly.

"I think so," he says neutrally. But he does not add the natural rejoinder: I'll miss you too.

Oh GOD. What's going to happen?

"Good-bye," he says. "We're shooting two shows today, so I'll be home late."

"Whatever," I say.

He gives me the sick smile, and it suddenly hits me: He's going to divorce me.

He's going to get rid of me the same way he got rid of his first wife.

Anastasia.

I can't even bear to say the name.

She was crazy too.

BUT, I remind myself, he didn't actually divorce her. The marriage was annulled. They were both young, and everybody said she was horrible. A spoiled little spitfire from one of those aristocratic European families who probably went to the same Swiss finishing school as the S. sisters, and who still turns up regularly in the completely outdated gossip column "Suzy." Where "former wife of Prince Hubert Luxenstein," is always written after her name, even though this is not technically correct, because if their marriage was annulled, it's supposed to be like they were NEVER MARRIED — right? And when I was first married to Hubert and this offensive name with its offensive moniker would appear, I would tremblingly point to it and say, "Can't you DO anything about this?" And he would say, fearfully at first, and then after the seventh or eighth time with great annoyance, "I don't even talk to her anymore. I haven't had a conversation with her for six years." But of course, that wasn't good enough, and I would brood about that damn Anastasia for hours. And sure enough, today, having thought about her once, I have to torture myself by walking past Ralph Lauren on my way to meet D.W. at lunch.

Which is where I met Anastasia, probably seven years ago. Right there in Ralph Lauren on the third floor. I was, UGH, actually working there, a fact that I couldn't believe myself, because I was so bad at waiting on people, but at the time I felt like I had no choice. My mother had taken up painting, and my father was busy being gay in Paris.

Everyone had forgotten about me, as I had suspected that someday they would, and I had no other way to survive but to take a job as a shopgirl at Ralph Lauren. Where the pay was bad but they gave you 70 percent off on the clothes.

My job seemed to consist mostly of folding sweaters, a feat I could never master. The other girls, the girls who had already worked there for six months or a year, were always trying to give me tips on how to fold the sweaters so I wouldn't get fired. As if I cared. And one afternoon, when I was wrestling with pink cashmere, Anastasia turned up. With a girlfriend. I recognized her immediately.

She was tiny and dark-haired, with huge brown eyes, and she was stunningly, heartbreakingly beautiful, and she knew it. She actually snapped her fingers and motioned to me.

"Can you help me PLEASE," she said. It wasn't a question, it was a command, given in a heavy Spanish accent and with an attitude that made it clear she didn't enjoy dealing with peasants.

I walked over and said nothing.

"You work here? Yes?"

"Yes," I said noncommitally.

"I want the latest."

"The latest . . . what?" I said.

"Everything. Dresses, shoes, handbags . . ."

"But I don't know what you like."

She rolled her eyes and sighed like a soap opera queen. "Bring me the clothes in the ads, then."

"Very well," I said.

I returned with one pair of shoes. ONE. She was sitting in the dressing room with her friend. Discussing Hubert, even though by then their marriage had been annulled for six months. What was she still doing in New York? ". . . 's going to his aunt's house this weekend," she said to her friend, as if she were spilling state secrets. She suddenly looked up at me. I smiled and held up the shoes. Thinking, AHA. She's trying to get him back by looking American. But it won't work. It's over. And I remember thinking very clearly that I was going to get him, but also wondering how she had managed to develop that aura of arrogant confidence — was she born with it? — and whether I could get it too.

"Well?" she said.

"Yes," I said.

"What are you waiting for?"

I stared at her, slitty-eyed. I took the shoes out of the box.

"Put them on my feet, please," she said.

"I'm sorry," I said. "This is America. We don't treat people like servants here." And I stormed out of the dressing room and bumped into a tall, still good-looking middle-aged but WASPy man who said, "I'm looking for a something. For my wife." And I said, "Is that MY problem?" And he said, "If you work here it is," and I said, "It isn't because I'm about to get fired."

"Really?" he said.

And sure enough, I broke into sobs.

"I know a famous art dealer who's looking for an assistant for his new SoHo gallery," the man said.

"Will he treat me like a PROSTITUTE?" I said.

"Prostitutes are very in right now. Everyone wants to be one. No woman wants to pay for her own Christian Lacroix and shouldn't have to."

Naturally, the man turned out to be D.W.

And now he's sitting at an outside table at La Goulue, trying to work his cell phone. I slip onto the rickety white metal chair and say, "You're wearing . . . *seersucker?*"

He says, "It's Valentino. Italian WASP."

"Ooooh. The newest thing, I suppose."

"As a matter of fact, it is. What's your problem? Aren't you leaving tomorrow?"

"Can you get Bentley to lend Dianna a

dress for the film festival?"

"Dianna," D.W. says, "is from Florida."

"You go to Florida."

"I go to Palm Beach. Palm Beach is not Florida." D.W. pauses while the waiter pours fizzy water. "I've heard she's from somewhere like . . . Tallahassee? I mean, who is from Tallahassee? That we know."

"No one," I say.

"Why does Dianna Moon want to wear Bentley, anyway? She could wear something from Fredricks of Hollywood and it would look the same."

"That's right," I say.

"I don't like this friendship with Dianna Moon. You understand, don't you, that she's just like Amanda. A more successful version of Amanda, if you can call what girls like Dianna Moon do 'successful.' "

"She's a famous actress . . ."

"Her career is, most likely, going nowhere. For some bizarre reason, possibly due to magazines like *Vogue*, this little upstart wants to come to New York and become the Leader of Society. And she's going to use you to get there. She wants to *be* you. Just like Amanda."

"D.W.," I sigh. "Society is dead."

He just looks at me.

"She doesn't want to *be* me. Maybe I want to be her," I say.

"Oh please," D.W. says.

"She's enormously rich. And she doesn't have . . . a husband."

"Because she killed him."

"He was killed by . . . evil forces. And parts of his body were carried off by aliens."

"Why are you hanging out with a Jesus freak?" D.W. asks calmly, signaling to the waiter.

Good question. Because my mother is . . . strange?

"It's a very bad look for you. Very bad," D.W. says.

My mother came from a normal, upper-middle-class family, and her dad was a lawyer in Boston, but even today, years after she left the commune, she still refuses to dye her hair and wears Birkenstock sandals.

"Dianna Moon could ruin everything," D.W. says.

"Your mother is so . . . charming," Hubert said the first time he met her. But the implication was there: We don't really want the press interviewing *her*, do we, darling? We don't really want the press scratching around in *your* backyard.

And in a lot of other places as well.

"Dianna Moon is . . . fine," I say.

D.W. looks at me. "Well, just make sure you don't get rid of Dianna the way you got rid of Amanda. That might be rather . . . obvious."

For some reason, we find this hysterically funny.

VIII

I'm in a car and Dianna's driving way too fast and I know something bad is going to happen and sure enough, the car flies off the curve, launching itself over a cliff. We're airborne forever and below is a giant slab of cement and even though this is a dream and we're going to die, I can't believe I haven't woken up yet. Dianna turns to me and says, "I just want you to know that I love you. I really love you," and she grabs me and hugs me and I can't believe that I'm having a dream and I'm actually going to die in the fucking dream, which isn't supposed to happen, and I say, "I love you too," wondering what it's going to feel like when we hit the cement. We plunge down and down and I'm going to die in this dream and doesn't that mean you're supposed to die in real life? And we hit the cement but it doesn't feel as bad as I imagined it would, we just sort of squish through it and tumble out into this other place that is corridors and blue light.

Okay. Now we're dead, but we have to make a decision about whether or not we want to go back.

I don't know what to do.

"I'm going back," Dianna says.

"What about me?" I say. "Should I go back?"

"I wouldn't if I were you, darling," she says. "Your face is kind of . . . messed up."

She laughs meanly.

It's probably eleven A.M. and I do wake up, curled in the fetal position, wearing one of Dianna's silk negligees with my white Gucci jacket on top and no underwear. Dianna is on the other side of the bed, lying on her back, breathing heavily through her mouth, and in between us is a small Frenchman, whose name, I think, is Fabien, whom we picked up last night on some other yacht. There's a spilled bottle of Dom Perignon on the carpet. I roll off the bed and crawl toward the bottle. There's still some left in the bottom, and I sit up and polish it off sloppily so champagne dribbles down my chin. I look over at the small Frenchman, who might actually be Swiss, and note that he is wearing blue Ralph Lauren boxer shorts and has too much hair on his chest.

My thoughts: I hate the French, so why

should I go to Saint-Tropez?

I get up and stumble out of Dianna's cabin and into my own stateroom, which is littered with clothes (mostly tiny see-through Prada pieces with the labels prominently displayed) and Louis Vuitton luggage. I kick a small hard-sided suitcase out of the way and lurch into the bathroom, where I sit on the toilet and take what feels like an endless crap. As usual, the toilet doesn't flush, and my shit, light brown and in the shape of a large cowpat, sits there defiantly.

"Fuck you," I say to the shit. I look in the mirror and pluck some eyebrow hairs, even though there's supposedly a makeup artist on board who takes care of these things, and while I'm plucking and thinking that one of these days I'm probably going to need Botox, I'm also wondering if I did anything with the small Frenchman, but I'm quite sure I didn't because it isn't the kind of thing I WOULD do.

I've only HAD four boyfriends.

Officially.

Dianna, on the other hand, will fuck anyone.

I didn't know that about her.

And, I realize, I didn't want to.

Why am I here? For that matter, why am I anywhere?

I go upstairs, reeling from the sudden impact of relentless white light. I'd forgotten about the white light in the south of France, so blinding that you always need sunglasses, and even then, it reveals too much. The captain, Paul, a good-looking Australian who is always wearing khaki shorts and a navy blue polo shirt with the name of the boat, Juniper Berry, discreetly stitched on the pocket, is fiddling with some instruments. "Good morning," Paul says, like he's surprised to see me but is prepared to ignore whatever went on the night before. "Oh, your husband called. Hubert? He says he can't make it today, but he's going to try to get here tomorrow."

My HUSBAND is coming?

Did I KNOW about this?

I am so hungover, I can only nod numbly. After a few seconds I manage to stutter, "Are there any more cigarettes?"

"You smoked the last one an hour ago."

I just stare at him, realizing that is probably some kind of JOKE that I don't get and never will, and I say, "I think I'll just go and buy some."

"There are photographers outside."

"Paul," I say wearily. "There are always photographers outside."

I walk down the gangplank clutching my

Prada wallet, still barefoot and wearing the negligee and the Gucci jacket, which, in the bright sunlight, I see is stained with large patches of what might be wine or raspberry puree or even vomit. I suddenly remember that I have no money because I'm in France and foreign money confuses me, so I stop and ask one of the photographers, all of whom have huge telephoto lenses in hopes of getting a topless shot of Dianna Moon (and maybe me, but I'm not as famous as Dianna is in France), for *beaucoup d'argent.*

I smile fakely, and the photographers are so surprised they don't take any pictures.

"Comment?" says one, who is short with floppy gray hair and bad teeth.

"Pour fume," I say badly.

"Ah, *pour fume,"* they say, and nudge one another jocularly. One of them hands me twenty francs and winks at me and I wink back and then I set off, walking down the red carpet that lines the sidewalk of the harbor in honor of the festival, thinking: Every day this carpet gets dirtier and dirtier and I get more and more polluted, and why is Hubert coming, he's doing it on purpose. Again.

I wander into the narrow streets of Cannes, which are filled, predictably, with French people, all of whom seem to be smoking. I pass a small café filled with gay men, who, unlike gay men in New York, have long hair and are trying desperately to be women. One of them looks at me and says, *"Bonjour."*

And that's when I realize I may or may not be being followed.

I turn around.

A small girl with long blond hair, clutching three red roses wrapped in cellophane, stops and stares back at me.

I glare at her and move on.

I find a tabac and go in. More French people smoking and laughing. Near the entrance, a Frenchwoman says something to me which I automatically tune out, although I believe she's asking me if I want a croissant or maybe a ham sandwich, so I snap, *"Je ne parle pas Francais."* Then I ask the man behind the counter for Marlboro Lights, and once outside, I light up a cigarette, fumbling with the awkward French matches and I look up and there's the little girl.

Again.

"Madame . . . ," she says.

"Vous etes un enfant terrible," I say. Which is basically all the French I can remember that has anything to do with children. She says, *"Vous êtes tres jolie."*

I begin walking quickly back to the boat. "Madame, madame," she calls after me.

"What?" I say.

"You would like to buy a rose? A lovely red rose?"

"*Non,*" I say. "*Je n'aime pas les fleurs.* Got it? Get it, kid?" And I can't believe I am being so mean to a small street urchin, but I am.

"Madame. You come with me," the child says.

"No," I say.

She tries to take my hand. "You come with me, Madame. You must come with me."

I shake my head, holding the cigarette up to my lips.

"Come, Madame. Come. Follow me."

"*Non,*" I say weakly. And then for some reason, standing on the crowded street in the middle of Cannes during the film festival in the terrible heat, I begin crying, shaking my head, and the small child looks at me and runs away.

Another evening, on the — what? — third or fourth day in the south of France, and Dianna Moon and I are riding in the back of an air-conditioned Mercedes limousine with The Verve blaring as we crawl along the crowded streets of Cannes toward the Hotel du Cap, where we have been invited to have dinner with prominent movie people. Dianna won't stop talking, and I keep thinking about how, when Hubert and I first started secretly seeing each other, my phone was tapped.

"The thing about it," Dianna says, once again oblivious to anything but herself, "I mean the thing about this whole movie star business which no one gets is that you have to work so hard. You're my best friend, Cecelia, so you know I'm not being an asshole about this, because God knows, Jesus knows actually, that I was always going to be a star and I think I make a fucking *good* star, but it's never-ending. So, you know, people ought to understand why I get fucked up. Getting fucked up . . . it's like a mini-vacation. It's the only way I can ever get any fucking relaxation." And she takes a swig out of a bottle of champagne and I want to tell her to stop talking because I'm still so hungover I'm going to get sick or kill someone.

"What did you think of Fabien?" she says.

"Oh. Was that his name?" I say. I look out the window at the white tents of the festival as the Mercedes crawls to a stop.

"I thought he was adorable. I've always

wanted to sleep with a Frenchman," she says. And I do not point out that she must have already slept with four or five. Not counting the one in the bathroom at Jimmy'z in Monte Carlo.

Through the window, I see that the small girl with the flowers is standing by the side of the car.

"I wonder if I should import him. To L.A.," Dianna says, laughing loudly as the girl taps on the window with the flowers.

"Madame," she mouths. "Madame, you must come with me."

The Mercedes lurches forward. I turn to stare out the back window at the little girl, who waves sadly.

"Ohmigod," I say.

Dianna takes a moment to focus on me, and I find, sadly, that I am grateful. "I can't believe Hubert is coming," she says. "I told you my plan would work. As soon as you left, he realized he was a complete fuckwad, and now he's crawling back. Aren't you happy?"

She takes my hand and kisses it as I open the window a crack to let out some of the smoke.

In the bar of the Hotel du Cap, it's the same scene as it was the night before and the night before that and lunch the day before and lunch the day before that. Everyone is drunk on champagne and raspberry cocktails. There's the same group of twenty-five-year-old women, all tall, all good-looking, dressed in evening clothes, who spend half their time in the bathroom and half their time trying to pick up anyone famous. There are the badly dressed up-and-coming English movie directors. The perfectly dressed German distributors. Kate Moss. Elizabeth Hurley, whom I hate more than any of them because she's "overexposed." And Comstock Dibble, the five-foot-tall mega–movie producer who, even though he must be at least forty-five, still has acne. Out on the balcony, he's mopping his face with a napkin and shouting at the waiters to put two tables together and to take chairs away from other patrons. Dianna is dressed in Goth. We sweep through the lobby the same as we always do. We are someone and we will always be someone, especially when we come to places like this.

"Comstock! Caro! Darling!" Dianna screams, in case anyone hasn't noticed her. She's already too drunk, tottering on black strappy sandals, steadying herself on a stranger's shoulder who pats her arm and rolls his eyes.

"Hello, Dianna," Comstock says. "You were in the papers today."

"I'm in the papers every day. If I'm not in the papers, it's not a good day."

"You were in the papers too," Comstock says to me, sweating inexplicably, since the temperature has cooled down to about seventy. "But I know you hate being in the papers." He leans in intimately, as if we are the only two people in the place. "That's the difference between you and Dianna."

"Is it?" I say, lighting what is probably my fiftieth cigarette of the day.

Suddenly there are other people at the table, but no one introduces anyone.

"They say you're here without your husband."

"He has to work."

"You should have an affair. While you're here. In France. Everybody else is."

"Hey Comstock. I hear you've been looking for a mistress," Dianna says loudly. "I hear you've propositioned every French actress under the age of twenty-five."

"I'm casting. What can I say?" Comstock says, and I put my napkin on my lap and wonder what the hell I'm doing here.

But where else is there?

"Tanner is the one who's fighting off the girls," Comstock says.

I look up and see that it is indeed Tanner Hart, my Tanner, who is older but thanks to the wonders of plastic surgery doesn't look much different than he did five years ago when he was selected as one of *People* magazine's Fifty Most Beautiful People, and he sits down and puts his hands up and says, "Don't hassle me, baby," as I stare at him in a sort of alcoholic shock.

"Have a bellini," he says, pushing one toward me.

"When this festival is over, Tanner is going to come out the big winner. We sold *Gagged* all over the world today," Comstock says. "I'm thinking nominations. Best Actor. Best Picture."

"Hey Comstock," Dianna says. "How come you never propositioned me?"

"Because you're a Jesus freak and I'm a nice Polish boy?" Comstock says.

"I could convert you," Dianna says.

"Baby. You're a star. We all know that," Comstock says. "Right, Tanner?"

But Tanner isn't listening. He's staring at me intently and I remember why, after we split up, I climbed up a fire escape and broke into his apartment to have sex with him.

Without taking his eyes off me, Tanner says, "By the way, is anyone going to Saint-Tropez? After this?"

There's a full moon as I excuse myself, ostensibly to go to the bathroom. Instead, I hurry down the long marble staircase out to the manicured gravel walkway that leads to the pool. The summer she died, Amanda had decided to "get into the movie business," and she came here with a middle-aged character actor who sent her home after she stayed out all night with an up-and-coming young screenwriter. It was just so Amanda to get everything wrong.

I veer off to the left and into a small enclosed garden with a fountain of turtles in the middle. I sit on a bench.

Sure enough, in about a minute Tanner shows up, fingering a joint. "You look like you could use this," he says.

"Do I look that bad?"

"You just look like . . . you're not having any fun."

"I'm not."

"How are you, baby?" he says, sitting with his legs open, delicately holding the joint between his thumb and forefinger as he inhales deeply. "I told you not to marry that poofster. Didn't I? Didn't I tell you he'd make you miserable? You should have run off with me when you had the chance."

"That's right," I say miserably, thinking

about how after Tanner and I had sex, we would both be ripped and slightly bloody. He grabs my wrist now and says, "I'm still hot for you, baby. Still very, very hot," and I say, "Is this a compliment?" and he says, "It's a reality," and I say, "I have to get out of here." I run back up the path, looking over my shoulder to see if he's following and he isn't and I don't know if this is a good or bad thing, and I cross through the lobby and out the front door, where Dianna is standing in front of the hotel, shouting for the car.

And moments later we're all drunk and stoned and fucked up and in the Mercedes again, driving back to the yacht in Cannes and there are people, men mostly, in the car whom I've never seen before and never want to see again.

This guy with spiky dark hair and a black T-shirt keeps leaning over me, chanting, "Where I have gone, I would not go back," which is a line I think he read in a Bret Easton Ellis novel, but while I'm seriously wondering if he even *can* read, I respond, "I don't know why I'm here, I guess because Dianna invited me."

"I'm a big fucking STAR," Dianna screams.

And then, I don't know exactly how to describe it, I feel like the world is pulling away while at the same time becoming seriously claustrophic. I shout, "Stop the car," and everybody turns and looks at me like I'm insane, but they sort of expect me to be insane anyway, and the car does come to a stop in the middle of Cannes and I do climb over three men and fumble desperately with the door handle, which finally releases and before anyone really knows what's happened I've spilled out of the car and into a crowd of people on the sidewalk. I look back at the car and slide out of my high heels, grasping them in my hand as I begin running through the crowd toward the Majestic Hotel, where there's a swarm of photographers and kleig lights. I veer onto a side street, passing a gay bar where there's a man wearing a tutu, and I nearly run into the little girl with the red roses, who grabs my wrist and says, "Madame, come with me."

And this time, I do.

In the early morning I am walking back to the yacht, feeling even MORE hungover and wasted than I ever have in my life, except maybe when I was younger and I first met Tanner and we would spend whole weekends snorting cocaine and drinking vodka. I would very often call in sick on

Monday, but I never got in trouble because everyone knew I was seeing a big movie star and that was more important for the image of the gallery than having someone answer the phone. And it was especially useful when Tanner used to come into the gallery to pick me up. He was obsessed with me at first and would stop by the gallery quite often, just to make sure that some other man wasn't trying to seduce me, and these incidents were usually faithfully recorded by the gossip columns (although they didn't mention my name, because I wasn't "somebody" then), providing free publicity for the gallery. Everyone treated me awfully well and seemed to really like me, but did they have a choice? Even back then I was being USED by other people for my ability to attract men. And I have never wondered about this before, but I do now: Would I be ANYTHING without a man?

A taxi pulls up in front of the yacht, and a tall, handsome man wearing a polo shirt and jeans gets out and turns toward me, and I realize it's my husband.

The sun is shining; it must be later than I thought. The bustle of the harbor begins to fill my consciousness — the first mates hosing the decks, a young woman walking by with produce from the farmer's market, people scurrying by with press passes — and as Hubert approaches, holding his beat-up leather valise, I see, for the first time, his prodigious blandness. How, underneath all the fuss about his family and his looks and his background, he is still, in the end, JUST SOME GUY.

"Hey," he says. "What happened to you?"

"What do you mean?" I ask.

"You're bleeding. You've got blood on your hands." He looks down. "And on your feet. And ink stains. What happened to your shoes?"

"I don't know."

"Well, how are you, anyway? Did you get my message?"

"That you were coming?"

"About renting a speedboat. Hey, as long as I'm here, I thought it might be fun if we spent the day waterskiing."

Waterskiing?

Hubert carries his bag onto the yacht. "Marc De Belond has a house here. I thought we might hook up with him."

Hook up?

"Hey baby," he says. "What's the matter? Don't you *like* Marc De Belond?"

I turn and hold up my bloody hands.

I say, "The gay men took my shoes."

IX

Dear Diary:

You're not going to believe this, but I'm STILL on this DAMN boat floating around in the Italian Riviera.

And Hubert is still here.

Okay. Here's the problem. Number one, I think I'm going insane, but I'm not sure if it's because I'm sick to death of being stuck on this boat with Hubert and Dianna, or if maybe I really am a NUT JOB like everyone says.

Because number two: People saw me that night at that café with the little girl. And her little friends. And the strange gay men, who tried to take my dress — they kept saying the word "copier," which I supposed meant they wanted to copy the dress and then give it back — but there wasn't enough time. And all the glasses of cognac. And the broken glass on the floor. And sure enough, this "yet another embarrassing incident" was reported in *Paris Match*.

"I don't think I'm going to change much," I said to Hubert, quite threateningly, after he'd read it and, without saying anything, evinced his displeasure by raising his eyebrows. Dianna defended me: "Sweet Jesus, Hub, I've been accused of killing my husband. Aliens took away half of my husband's body. And you're upset about your wife being spotted with underage street urchins and a couple of gay guys in dresses?" And then I said, cunningly, I thought, "All I wanted was a little attention."

Which is true. That was all I wanted. Because I still don't feel like I get attention from my husband, which is really crazy because he did fly all the way here to be with me and then took an unexpected week off, but I don't just want him to BE HERE. I want him to pay a certain and specific kind of attention to me, and he just doesn't.

When I'm with him, I don't feel . . . significant. I want to be everything to him. I want to be essential. I want him to be unable to live without me, but how can I be these things if he won't let me?

And if he won't let me, what am I doing with my life?

Naturally, these thoughts put a horrible expression on my face. At least I think they do, because this morning, when I'm lying in bed and Hubert comes into our stateroom supposedly looking for sunscreen, he turns to me and says, in a tone of voice that I can only interpret as RUDE, "What's your problem?"

I know my response should be "Nothing, darling," but I'm tired of mollifying him. Instead, I say, "What do you mean, what's my problem? What's your problem?" and I turn over.

"Whoa," he says. "Maybe you should go back to sleep and try waking up again."

"Yeah," I say. "Maybe I should."

Then he leaves the room.

I HATE him.

I jump out of bed, pull on my bathing suit, and storm up to the top deck.

Dianna is there, drinking coffee and polishing her toenails, which, as we all know, is verboten on this boat because the nail polish could spill and ruin the teak decks. As we also all know, Dianna doesn't give a shit. She's already caused thousands of dollars of worth of damage to the boat by walking around in spike heels and greasing her body with tanning oil, leaving indelible footprints that the crew keeps pointlessly trying to scrub away. "Hey, I could *buy* this boat if I wanted to," she keeps reminding them. But the point is, people like Dianna Moon never do.

"Hi sugar," Dianna says, not looking up. "Want some coffee?"

"Coffee makes me vomit. In fact, everything makes me vomit."

She looks up in alarm. "I don't, do I?"

"No," I say, resignedly. I move to the railing, leaning over the side. The wind ruffles my hair slightly. This Dianna Moon business — her self-absorption, her prodigious insecurity — is getting to be too much.

"Do I look fat?" Dianna asks, and I automatically respond, "No," although the truth is, Dianna is a bit fat. She has the kind of body that will be matronly at thirty-five, no matter how much she diets or exercises.

"Are you going to Hubert's aunt's house today?"

SHIT. Princess Ursula. I'd totally forgotten about her and nod glumly, remembering that Princess Ursula hates me. Once, at a funeral, she came up to me and said, "Oh Cecelia, you're such a natural at funerals, because you always have a sour, downturned expression on your face."

And these are my relations?

"Do you think," Dianna says, examining her large toe, "that Lil'Bit Parsons will be there?"

This is such an unexpected question, so

out of left field, that I say nothing as the terrible feeling of other people knowing something I don't descends upon me like a shade blocking out the sun.

"Lil'Bit Parsons?" I croak.

"I don't want to upset you, but I read in the *Star* that she's in Europe. Vacationing with her two kids." Diana screws up her face as I begin hyperventilating and stumbling around the deck, unsure as to whether or not I'm going to throw up, and she says, "There was a picture of her in . . . Saint-Tropez?"

"That fucking BASTARD," I say, somehow getting ahold of myself and tripping down the stairs and into the galley, where Paul, the captain, is talking in whispered tones to the cook, whose name I can never remember.

"Where's my husband?" I ask.

Paul and the cook exchange looks. "I think he's on the aft deck. Getting ready to go scuba diving."

"That's what he thinks," I snap, making my way to the back of the boat, where Hubert is pulling on a dive skin.

"Hi," he says nonchalantly.

"What are you doing?" I ask coldly.

"I'm going to scuba dive into the port. I thought it'd be cool."

"That's a smart idea," I say sarcastically. "Maybe you'll get ground up by a propeller."

"Oh for Christ's sake," he says, rolling his eyes.

"You just don't give a shit about *me*, do you?"

"Leave me alone, huh?" he says, pulling the dive skin over his shoulder.

"I am so sick of your shit," I scream, running to him and hitting him until he grabs my wrists and pushes me roughly away. "What the FUCK is your problem?" he says.

I reel back, stunned. Recovering somewhat, I say, "I want to talk to you."

"Yeah? Well, I don't want to talk to you."

Has my husband ever spoken to me like this before? "I HAVE to talk to you," I say. "Right now."

"You just don't get it, do you?" he says, shoving his feet into a pair of flippers.

"Get what?" I demand.

"That I am sick and tired of you trying to control me all the time. Okay? Just let me be. Just let me do my thing for a change, okay?"

"Your thing? All you do is your thing."

For a moment, he says nothing and we stare at each other hatefully. Then he says, "What do you want from me, Cecelia?"

I want you to love me is what I want to say, but can't.

"I came on this vacation for you, okay?" he says. "You wanted to come on Dianna Moon's yacht and we're on her yacht. I'm here. You're always complaining that we never do what you want to do. And when we do it, it still isn't enough."

"Then how come we have to go to Princess Ursula's this afternoon? We always do what you want to do."

"Princess Ursula is family, okay? Do you think you can understand that concept?"

"It's not *that*. . . ."

"Oh yeah? Well, what is it? Because I'm getting pretty sick and tired of your attitude."

Oh God. Why do these arguments always go nowhere? Why can't I make myself *heard?*

"You're seeing Lil'Bit Parsons again, aren't you?" I say triumphantly.

That stops him dead. "Wha . . . ?" he says, but he looks away quickly, and I know I've got him. "Give me a break," he says lamely.

"You *are* seeing her. I know everything. She's in Europe, vacationing with her kids. She was in Saint-Tropez."

"So?"

"So you snuck out and met her," I say, even though I have no actual knowledge of this incident and can't even recall when it might have happened.

"Stop this," he says.

"You saw her. You're guilty."

"I am not going to discuss this, Cecelia."

"You're not going to discuss it because I'm right. You saw her again. Why don't you just admit it?"

"I said, I'm not going to discuss this."

"Well remember this, buddy," I say. "The last time you didn't want to discuss it, it was in . . . all . . . the . . . NEWSPAPERS," I scream. So loudly that I feel like my head is going to explode.

Hubert looks at me (sadly, I think), then jumps into the water. I turn and pass Paul and the cook, who have the fucking temerity to give me their wimpy half smiles as if nothing at all has occurred. I wonder how I can bear living like this, and I go up on the deck and thank God Dianna is there. I sit down and put my head in my hands.

"There are photographers on the dock," she says.

"There's going to be a great photo of Hubert shoving you," she says.

"Definitely cover of *Star* magazine," she says.

"I can't take this," I say.

"She's never going to give up, you know?"

Dianna says. "She's a movie star. And movie stars can't stand to be rejected. She can't believe he chose you over her. She'll be tracking him down until the day he dies, baby. And even then she'll be elbowing you out of the way at the funeral. Just like Paula Yates." She yawns and rolls over, spilling the bottle of nail polish on the deck.

One of the things you learn about being married is that you don't have to continue every fight to the death. You can take a little break. Pretend that nothing has happened. I've found this works with Hubert, who, I'm beginning to realize, gets confused easily. Which is probably why he ended up dating Lil'Bit Parsons in the first place. She completely manipulated him.

And so, when he returns to the boat, water streaming off his dive skin (which shows off all the muscles in his body, including his washboard stomach), Dianna and I are laughing and drinking champagne as if nothing in the world is wrong. I pour him a glass of champagne, and he is relieved, thinking that maybe the fight is over.

But it isn't.

I pick up the fight again when Hubert and I are in the taxi, making our way to Sir Ernie and Princess Ursula's villa in the hills of Porto Ercole.

"Why did you break up with her?" I ask innocently. Hubert is holding my hand, staring out the window at the grape arbors, and he turns and says, "Who?" but there's a tiny edge in his voice, as if he knows what's coming next.

"You know," I say. "Lil'Bit."

"Oh," he says. "You know. I met you."

This answer is, of course, not satisfying, or at least not satisfying enough, so I say, "Didn't Lil'Bit stay with Princess Ursula every September?"

"I don't remember," he says. "They're good friends. They've know each other since Lil'Bit was in high school in Switzerland."

"High school in Switzerland. What a lovely expression," I say nastily. And he says, "What's wrong with it?" And I say, in order not to divert us from the main topic, "Did you go with her? To Porto Ercole? Every September with your aunt?"

"You know I did, okay?" he says.

"It must have been so cozy," I say. "Everyone getting along. Everyone best friends."

"It wasn't bad," he says.

"It's not my fault that Ursula hates me."

"Ursula doesn't hate you. But she thinks you don't treat me well." This is an astonishing bit of information which I decide not to pursue. Instead, I yawn loudly and say, "Lil'Bit Parsons has had the easiest life of anybody I've ever known."

"She hasn't had an easy life," Hubert says. "Her boyfriend beat her up."

"Oh, big fucking deal. Her boyfriend beat her up. She had a few bruises. If he was so horrible, why didn't she leave him?"

"She's not that kind of person, okay?"

"Her daddy was rich, and when she was seventeen, she started modeling and then she got her first part at nineteen. Tough life."

"Just because she didn't grow up in a commune doesn't mean she hasn't had a hard time."

"Yes it does," I say. "Okay? Do you get that?"

"No," he says. "I don't. And I don't get you."

We ride the rest of the way in silence.

At the villa, Princess Ursula greets us by the pool, wearing her bathing suit with a sarong wrapped around her waist (she's fifty-five but still thinks she has an excellent figure and shows it off on every possible occasion), and in a casual voice which is tinged with both French and English accents, mentions "nonchalantly" that dear Lil'Bit is indeed in Porto Ercole, having taking her own villa for two weeks, and is, "ha ha," coming for lunch, and isn't this a "wonderful surprise."

Hubert looks at me, but somehow, miraculously, I don't react (much as a prisoner brought into an enemy camp knows not to react), and Hubert reaches out and takes my hand and says, "That's so funny. Cecelia and I were just talking about whether or not Lil'Bit might be here. Cecelia said she would."

Aunt Ursula looks at me as if seeing me for the first time, then says, "Well, Cecelia may be psychic. She may have hidden talents none of us could ever imagine."

This remark is soooo unbelievably cutting, but in a way that Hubert would never notice, that I decide to say absolutely nothing. I give Aunt Ursula a supercilious yet bored smile, and she says, "I hope you don't mind about Lil'Bit. You two are friends?"

"I've never met her," I say casually. "In fact, Hubert never even mentions her."

"You'll love her," Aunt Ursula says. And just at that moment, Sir Ernie Munchnot walks up in his swimming trunks, showing off his chest which, I have to admit, does look pretty good for a guy who must be sixty, and he hugs Hubert and then me. I giggle loudly when it's my turn and look over at Aunt Ursula, who is definitely watching this exchange and is not particularly pleased, and I say, "Oh Uncle Ernie. It's soooo great to see you. Gosh, you're in awfully good shape." And he says, "How's my favorite niece-in-law? I always told Hubert if he didn't marry you, I would." He puts his arm around me and we begin walking toward the patio, where lunch will be served by three small Italian women in white uniforms. "Hey," Uncle Ernie says, "I still swim five miles a day. Exercise. That's the key to life. I keep telling my kids, but they don't listen."

Princess Ursula makes a face and shakes her head. And then, she just can't help rubbing it in, "Lil'Bit's coming for lunch."

"Lil'Bit? Well . . . good," he says. "Now there's a gal who needs to get some sense in her head. I keep telling her to stop running around and get her life together, but I think she's been all mixed up ever since Hubert here broke up with her." Princess Ursula gives him a disapproving look and says, "Lil'Bit is absolutely fine. She's just not like the rest of us." She directs this at me: "I always say she's one of God's heavenly creatures."

At that moment, a car pulls into the

driveway, and we all look over to where the "heavenly creature" is extracting herself, her two illegitimate children, a nanny, a stroller, and various nappies from the car. Lil'Bit is wearing — get this — an Indian sari. She picks up one of the children and takes the other by the hand. Amid this picture of motherly bliss, she looks up and waves girlishly.

"Just look at her," Aunt Ursula exclaims. "I always say Lil'Bit is the most elegant woman I know."

"Come and see Kirby," Lil'Bit says to everyone in general, but mostly, I think, to Hubert. Her voice is soft, sweet, almost a whisper. She's all shy, with her long blond hair in front of her face. Jesus. I used to look like that. I used to do that with him. That's what he likes. That's what works on him. It makes me sick.

In fact, I'd actually like to jump on her and rip her eyes out, but I remind myself that I won. I got him and she didn't. I got him because I was smarter than she was. I played a completely different game. I was unavailable. Mysterious. While she played the victim. He got bored. But was that really the reason? Or was it because she had two illegitimate children, and Hubert couldn't, in the end, "handle it"?

384

"Hi," she says to me, holding out a long, bony hand. "You must be Cecelia."

For a moment, our eyes meet, and then she hands the "baby" — a two-year old girl — to Princess Ursula, who coos disgustingly all over it, while pushing Kirby, a sullen-faced six-year-old boy, toward Hubert.

"Hey Kirby," Hubert says, lifting the boy and shaking him slightly. "Remember me?"

"No," Kirby says (sensibly, I think), but Hubert won't have it; he laughs loudly and says, "Don't you remember playing baseball? Batter up!" He swings the boy around, which makes him start screaming, and then, as is always the case in these situations, the children are whisked away, probably to be fed some sort of gruel in the kitchen.

"Still no children of your own?" Lil'Bit says, looking up at Hubert from underneath that sheaf of hair, as if this is some private joke.

And then, for absolutely no discernible reason, Lil'Bit Parsons runs to the middle of the small, rocky yard and begins spinning around until she falls to the ground.

I want to scream, "This woman is a fucking nut-case," but as I am the only one who apparently thinks so (because the rest of them are laughing delightedly, as if they'd just witnessed a performance by Marcel

Marceau), I hold my tongue, pursing my lips in disapproval.

And after that, there is nothing to be done but to endure this long, boring lunch in which Lil'Bit dominates the conversation by talking about how she's studying with gurus (indeed, she has been told that she will become a guru herself, having been one in a past life), the importance of animal rights, the evils of caffeine, and how she's decided to start her own Internet company and (gasp) move to New York.

Throughout this, she basically ignores me, and even though it's clear this woman is an absolute idiot, I'm feeling smaller and smaller, wondering why I ever let them cut my hair and thinking maybe I need to buy new, flashier clothes, and I sit up very straight in my chair and handle my utensils formally, saying little and allowing a slight smile to play across my lips from time to time.

"Oh Cecelia . . . that's it, right? Cecelia," Lil'Bit says toward the end of the meal, "Do you work or . . . or anything?"

"Cecelia is going to start doing some charity work," Hubert says firmly, although, as far as I can remember, I have never expressed an interest in charity work, nor do I plan to do so.

"Oh really," Lil'Bit purrs. "What kind of charity?"

"Encephalitic babies," I say. "You know, those kids with big heads?"

"Really," Princess Ursula says, shaking her head. "You shouldn't joke about . . ."

"Oh, I have something for you," Lil'Bit says to Hubert, reaching into her bag and pulling out a deck of cards. "They're American Indian tarot cards." She giggles. "From when I stayed in the tepee on the reservation in Montana. Doing the Indian rights thing."

"Thank you," Hubert says.

"Really," I say. "I didn't know you were interested in the paranormal."

"Dianna Moon is with us, and she says her husband's body parts were taken away by aliens," Hubert says somewhat uneasily.

Lil'Bit shuffles the cards. "That's true, you know. I don't think they ever found his spleen."

"Am I actually having this conversation?" I say, to no one in particular.

"Dianna Moon is your best friend," Hubert says.

"After you, darling," I say, touching his arm and smiling, fakely, across the table at Lil'Bit.

"Let me read your cards," Lil'Bit says to Hubert, in what she evidently thinks is a low, sexy voice. "I want to see your future."

Will she never go away?

Lil'Bit looks at Hubert's cards. She takes his hands in hers. "Oh my darling," she says breathily. "You must be . . . careful. Don't do anything . . . dangerous."

This is quite simply too much for me. "Don't be ridiculous," I snap. Everyone looks at me. "Let me give it a try. Let me read *your* cards, Lil'Bit."

"Oh, but — you have to be . . . *trained*," she says.

"How do you know I'm *not*?" I say.

I wave Hubert out of his seat and sit down across from her.

"But I already *know* my cards," she says. "I do them every day."

"Do you?" I ask. "Are you sure?"

"You lay them out," she says.

"You know that wouldn't be right, Lil'Bit. You know *you* have to . . . *touch the cards*."

"Well," Lil'Bit says, looking up at Hubert. "This should be . . . *fun*."

She begins laying out the cards. And, just as I had a feeling they might be, they're all upside down.

"How . . . interesting," I say.

Lil'Bit sees the cards and gasps. She looks up at me. My eyes bore into hers. I can feel her squirming under my power, but she can't do anything about it.

"You know what this means, don't you?" I ask. "It means," I say, looking around the table at Hubert, who is standing there with a disturbed yet uncomprehending look on his face; at Princess Ursula, who is readjusting her sagging cleavage; and at Uncle Ernie, who is using a knife to clean under his fingernails when he thinks no one is looking, "That Lil'Bit is a complete . . . fraud."

In fact, I want to scream, you're ALL complete frauds.

But I don't.

I smile and gather up the cards. "Game *over*," I say.

X

I light a cigarette.

I'm dressed in a baby-blue Bentley gown, and I'm crunching across the gravel driveway with Hubert following behind me in black tie and we get into the Mercedes SL500 convertible to go to the wedding of Juliette Morganz, the "little girl from Vermont" and I think, Why can't we be normal? Maybe we can be normal.

Do I really care?

I can tell Hubert is in a good mood, driving the car expertly along Appogoque Lane, blaring Dire Straits, glancing over at me, and it suddenly hits me: Who is this man, really? Who *is* he? I've been married to this person for two years and with him for two years before that, and I don't really know him at all.

And he doesn't know me.

At all.

This realization is so depressing that I sit back and fold my arms, and I can feel the good vibes suddenly expire like air leaving a balloon. He looks over again, and I can feel his mood shifting downward, and it's all my fault as he says, "What's wrong?"

"Nothing," I say.

"Something is wrong," he says, in a bored and kind of disgusted voice, "again."

"It's nothing," I say, contemplating the futility of it all, how we don't really get along that well and probably never will, as I stare out the window at a big, dried-up potato field.

"Why do we have to fight all the time?" he asks.

"I have no idea," I say, fingering my dress, which is made of finely wrought mesh, artfully constructed so that it appears see-through but really isn't. "Does it matter?"

"I'm tired," he says.

"So am I," and I look away and see that we are passing the duck pond where the "incident" occurred, the incident that brought us together in mutual horror and terror. Another thing that we simply don't talk about.

We ride the rest of the way in silence.

I feel like crying out of self-pity but I can't, because we're at the church now, and there are streams of cars and people, and a valet opens my door and I slip out of the car elegantly. Hubert walks around the front of the car and our eyes meet. And then, as we have been doing for the past couple of months whenever we go out or are seen in public, we pretend that everything is perfectly . . . all right.

And as we walk toward the church, he has one hand in his pocket and one arm around my waist, and I can't help but notice how well we fit together, how we have this perfectly easy physicality, which means pretty much nothing now, and the photographers suddenly spot us and one of them shouts, "Here comes the happy couple." The flashbulbs go off like crazy as we stop on the landing and smile, our arms around each other, and then one of the photographers says, "Hubert! Mind if we get a photo of your wife alone? No offense," and everyone is laughing and snapping away as Hubert moves gallantly to the side.

I stand with my hands clasped behind my back, my head high, smiling, one leg in front of the other. When I glance toward the entrance of the church, I see Hubert standing with his hands in his pockets, looking on proudly.

D.W. is right. It is all about appearances.

And later, at the reception, walking carefully across the marble floor strewn with rose petals, I am all over Hubert and he is all over me, just like we were in the old days when it first came out that we were seeing each other but as far as the world was concerned, I might just have been another girl-friend. He is holding my hand behind my back, and my hand caresses his neck, while people look at us enviously and I wonder how long I'll be able to keep this up. Luckily, I run into Dianna almost immediately, which is a good excuse for Hubert and me to go our separate ways without arousing suspicion.

Dianna is talking to Raymond Ally, the head of Ally cosmetics. Raymond, who is at least ninety, is in a wheelchair, and Dianna is smoking a Marlboro red, seemingly oblivious to the fact that she's not really in the right kind of shape to wear the dress she's wearing, which is: pink Bentley, gossamer thin, a dress that works if you're flat-chested, which Dianna isn't because she's had breast implants. Dianna is one of those girls who looks good in photographs, but in person, there's no hiding the fact that she's a dirty girl, a fact that Raymond seems to appreciate.

"Look at our girl," Raymond says to me, talking about Dianna, who has put both arms around my neck. "She's turned out to be quite a lady." I look at him and wonder if he's being stupid or sarcastic, but realize, with a certain degree of HORROR, that he is being completely sincere.

"Yes, yes she is," I say, because it really is easier to agree with people on the surface, even if you know they're full of shit.

"And I'll bet you don't know what I know about her. You two are friends, right?"

"Best friends," Dianna says, kissing me on the cheek.

Raymond tugs at my arm. "Well, as her best friend, you ought to know this. This young lady is very, very smart. I'll betcha she's smarter than my grandsons, and they went to Harvard. This young lady didn't even go to college!"

"Thank you, Raymond. Isn't he a doll?" Dianna says.

"And I'll tell you a little secret," Raymond says, now that he has our attention. "Most people don't know this, but every woman who makes it on her own is smart. She's got to have it here," he says, pointing to Dianna's chest. "But she's got to have it up here too," touching his head.

"And you can buy that," I say, indicating his chest.

"Oh, men don't care if they're real or fake, as long as you got some. And if you got none, go out and buy them, or else you're a loser. But this," he says, tapping his head again, "this you can't buy. You've either got it or you don't. And this girl's got it."

Suddenly, his gnarled hand shoots out and grabs Dianna's hand, which he pulls to his mouth and gives a large, ferocious kiss. "There," he says. "Now you girls go and have some fun. You don't want to be hanging around with an old man like me. Go on."

I look at Dianna inquiringly as we move away. She shrugs. "Old men love me. Come to think of it, all men love me. Hey, I'd give that old guy a blow job if I thought it'd help. But I don't care about men, Cecelia. I only care about you."

"And I only care about you, too," I say, which may or may not be true but doesn't really matter as we make our way, nodding and smiling, through the crowd.

"Did I ever tell you that I'm the best in bed?" she asks, taking a glass of champagne off a tray.

"Yes," I say, laughing a bit uneasily because that is exactly what Amanda used to say about herself. I believe her exact words were: "I can get any man I want because I know exactly what to do to men in bed."

And I always wanted to scream, "Yes, but you can't keep them."

And look what happened to HER.

Dianna is probably just as crazy and fucked up as Amanda was and will probably go ape shit someday the way Amanda did and try to do something horrible to me, but for the moment, that is all in my future. And then D.W. approaches with Juliette Morganz, whose wedding dress consists of beads and lace and bows (definitely not Bentley) and Juliette gushes all over us and drags us off for photographs with her mother and about fifteen other assorted relatives.

I just smile. I don't want to make any waves.

And then I'm kind of bored, so when Sandi Sandi, the hot new singer, is playing, and everyone is dancing and drunk, I wander through the house and go into a marble bathroom on the second floor and snort some cocaine, which I remind myself is just for old time's sake, and then I go back to the party, cross the dance floor, and walk out of the tent, following a boardwalk down to the pond and onto a white dock, where I light up a cigarette.

Dianna Moon follows me.

"Hey, hey," she says. She's stumbling a bit and pretty drunk. "Let's get out of here."

There's a charmingly beat-up old rowboat which she gets in. I follow, and we almost tip over, but then we sit in the bottom of the boat and try to row a little. There's a current and the boat drifts away from the dock.

"Hey," Dianna says. "I have to tell you something."

"Not about Jesus, okay?"

"Oh Cecelia. Someone told me you killed your best friend."

"Who?" I say.

"Nevil Mouse."

"Nevil Mouse is so . . . stupid," I say.

"I think he hates you," Dianna says.

"He hates me because I wouldn't go out with him. Years ago."

"He says you're not what you appear to be. I told him to go fuck himself."

"What did he say?"

"He said you killed . . . Amanda? Your best friend? You put something in her drink?"

Oh GOD. Where do people get these lies? "It was a long time ago," I say, as if it really isn't important. And it does seem long ago, almost as if it couldn't have happened, although it was actually four years ago, to be exact. At the end of that long, crazy summer right after I'd met Hubert and was seeing him secretly. Amanda and I were sharing a house.

"She killed herself," I say.

"Jesus took her."

"No." I shake my head. "She was drunk, and she took too much coke. She got into her car and drove into the duck pond and drowned."

She had been on her way to Hubert's house. On the sly.

"Fuck. Do you think I care?" Dianna said. "People think I killed my husband."

There are lilies in the pond. I trail my fingers in the water. We both look over at the shore, where the party is in full swing.

"What I like about you," Dianna says, "is that we're both outsiders. Neither one of us fits in with this . . . society crowd."

"Society is dead," I say, for what I think is the second or third time this year.

"My mother was a prostitute. She doesn't even know who my real father is."

"Marriage is prostitution."

"But my mother . . . wasn't married."

"Oh so what," I say. "My mother was a fucking drug addict."

"I'm going swimming," Dianna says. She basically falls out of the boat, and for a moment, as she flails in the water and I realize she probably can't swim, I wonder if I'm going to have to rescue her. Luckily, the pond isn't deep, only about three feet, and she finds her footing and wades to shore.

I watch her with some degree of relief.

I sit there alone.

After a while, I begin to row back to the dock in the charmingly beat-up old row-boat. I have a cigarette between my lips and I'm aware of my short blond hair, a slight pink blush on my cheeks and my bare shoulders.

And when I'm almost at the shore, Patrice shouts, "Hey Cecelia," and I look over my shoulder and he fires off as many pictures as he can in five seconds.

The following week, this photograph is beamed all over the world. In it, the expression on my face is: frowning slightly, yet a little surprised; still young, and I'm wearing the nearly see-through baby-blue Bentley dress, the lines of my slim yet shapely figure clearly visible. The caption reads: RICH, BEAUTIFUL, AND FIERCELY INDEPENDENT, PRINCESS CECELIA KELLY LUXENSTEIN IS THE LEADER OF THE NEW MILLENNIUM SOCIETY.

And I realize: This *is* my life.

SMILE.

SINGLE PROCESS

I

We have a saying in New York: English girls who are considered beautiful in London are merely "pretty" in New York, while American girls who are called "attractive" in New York are beautiful in London. And this sums up one of the biggest differences between Life in New York and Life in London. In London, if you're an attractive, nice girl with some personality and a career, you can meet a man, date him, and — if you want to — marry him. On the other hand, in New York, you can be a beautiful woman with a body like Cindy Crawford's and a high-powered career and you cannot even get a date.

Maybe because Englishwomen can actually snag a man — and can do so with ratty hair, unpolished nails, and flabby thighs — they possess a certain sort of annoying smugness when it comes to relationships. Recently, I had an encounter with one of these women in New York. As she sat there eating a smoked salmon sandwich and interviewing me about my life (which was sounding, to my ears, more and more pitiful by the moment), my eye was inevitably drawn to her large sapphire engagement ring topped by a sapphire-studded wedding band.

It shouldn't have made me hate her, but it did.

"Let's see," she said, checking her tape recorder. "Is there any man in your life right now?"

"Noooo," I said, although I had just broken up with a man who refused to marry me after six months of dating. I believe his actual words were "I do want to get married someday, but I don't want to marry you."

Okay, maybe I did rush him a little. But on the other hand, he used to sit at home in the evenings watching *Kung Fu* movies. And when I tried to talk to him, he would say, "Shhhhh. Grasshopper is about to learn an important lesson." After this happened a few times, I realized that "Grasshopper" had indeed learned a lesson: By the time you get to Grasshopper's age, there is absolutely no reason to be with a man who watches *Kung Fu* movies unless you are married to him.

But there was no reason to tell the English journalist this.

"How . . . interesting," she said. "I've been married for six years."

"Is that so," I said. I took a sip of my Bloody Mary and wondered if I was getting drunk. "Well, if you lived in New York," I said, "you wouldn't be. In fact, if you lived in New York, you'd probably be living in a small one-bedroom apartment, agonizing over some jerky guy you slept with three times." Ah yes. Grasshopper was just getting warmed up. "You'd think that maybe you were going to have a relationship, but then the guy would call to tell you that he didn't want any obligations. He would actually say, 'I don't want to check in.' "

I ordered another Bloody Mary. "Commitment is a mystery here," I said.

"Not in London," the English journalist said. "Men in London — Englishmen — well, they're better than American men. They're rather . . ." Here her face took on a sort of disgusting look that I could only call "dreamy." Then she continued, "Steady. They're interested in relationships. They like them. Englishmen are . . . cozy."

"You mean like . . . kittens?" I asked.

The English journalist gave me a superior smile. "Now, let's see. You are . . . how old now?"

"Forty," I whispered.

"That's right. So you must be at that point where you've realized that you'll probably be alone for the rest of your life."

And so it was that a month later, Grasshopper found herself on a flight to London. In the tradition of many American heroines before her, she was off to England in search of something she hadn't been able to find in New York: a husband.

That, of course, was my secret plan.

Being one of those clever American women who are so clever that they manage to trick themselves out of having relationships, I naturally needed some kind of cover-up. And I'd found it: This big English newspaper was paying me a ridiculous amount of money to find out about sex in London. If there actually was such a thing.

It was the kind of assignment that would involve copious amounts of alcohol and quite a lot of late-night bar crawling, the kind of activities I specialized in. Which was probably the reason I didn't have a husband in the first place.

But there were two things that worried me: Sex and Death.

You see, years ago, I had actually dated a couple of Englishmen. Unfortunately, both had tried to kill me — one by "wave-jumping" ten-foot waves in Australia in a twenty-five-foot Chris Craft, which he then crashed into the dock (he was drunk); and the other by suffocating me with a pillow (he was sober). Indeed, when I called Gerald the Suffocator to tell him that I was coming to England, his response was "Good. Now I can finish the job."

My second fear was, naturally, sex. Over and over again I had heard how horrible Englishmen are in bed. The conventional wisdom was that they failed miserably on three counts: One, their willies were really small. Two, foreplay didn't exist. And three, they came in about two minutes. In other words, they were all premature ejaculators, and if they lived in New York, some sensible woman would have put desensitizing cream on the tip of their willies and then made them have sex for three hours, which would probably cause the poor man to go running to his shrink — but, hey, that's not our problem. But maybe they don't have desensitizing cream in England. Or maybe they don't really care that much about sex.

I decided to begin my "research" by staying at the home of a man known as The Fox. The Fox was one of London's most prominent theatre directors, and also one of the most notorious womanizers in London. Years earlier, The Fox's wife, whom, I was told was known in London as The Saint for putting up with him, had divorced him for something like egregious adultery and outrageous behavior. The outrageous behavior including turning up at four in the morning naked and clutching an American Express card over his privates. And so, on a Tuesday afternoon, I arrived at The Fox's house with three Louis Vuitton suitcases, stuffed, rather inexplicably, with Prada, Dolce & Gabbana, and Gucci evening clothes, plus one pair of combat pants. The Fox wasn't there, but his housekeeper, a woman who didn't speak English and was ironing towels, was. Through a series of hand motions, I began to understand that, as there were only two bedrooms and the "guest" room was, at that moment, occupied by a large man and an even larger case of wine, I was supposed to sleep in The Fox's bed.

Aha.

Luckily, as I was about to open a bottle of wine and proceed to get drunk in order to deal with the situation, The Fox's assistant, Jason, arrived. Jason was twenty-five, cute, and of some sort of indeterminate nationality, although he claimed to be English. When I quizzed him about the so-called "sleeping ar-rangements," he grabbed me and said, "Don't have sex with The Fox. Have sex with me in-stead. I'm sure I'm much better in bed."

"Jason," I said patiently. "Have you ever even had a girlfriend?"

"Well, I'm having some romantic trouble right now," he said. Then he proceeded into a long-winded story about some girl he was in love with, whom he'd had sex with once, nine months ago. He met her at a pub, and even though she was a lesbian and with her girlfriend, he had somehow convinced her to go off to a hotel room with him, where she handcuffed him to the bed and had "amazing" sex with him. The next morning he realized that he'd never felt this way about a woman before, had fallen madly in love with her, and since then, hadn't even looked at another woman although the object of his affection refused to take his phone calls and refused to see him. And then she'd changed her cell-phone number.

"So what do you think I should do?" he asked.

For a long time, I just stared at him like he was insane. Then I said patiently, "Jason. You had a one-night stand. You don't fall in love after a one-night stand with a lesbian sadist."

"You don't?" Jason said.

"No," I said.

"Why not?"

"Because," I began, but at that moment,

the door flew open and The Fox himself arrived. He ran across the room to the window and looked out fearfully.

"You're late, boss," Jason said.

"Late? Late? I'll give you late," The Fox spluttered. "My life is a fucking nightmare. Doesn't anyone understand that? Miranda's following me again. I had to run all the way around Picadilly Circus to get her off my tail."

It seemed that The Fox was being stalked by his most recent ex-girlfriend, a woman named Miranda who was an actress in one of his plays.

"Look at this!" he said, brandishing a creased piece of paper. "She faxed this to me this morning. She says if I don't comply by midnight, she's going to have me arrested."

I removed the piece of paper from his hand and examined it. It was a list of items she'd left in his apartment and wanted returned. It contained entries like "kitchen sink," "lightbulbs," and "Julia Roberts videos."

"Like I want those fucking Julia Roberts videos. Doesn't she know I can't stand Julia Roberts?"

"Lightbulbs?" I asked. "Why can't she buy her own?"

"Exactly!" The Fox said. "Finally, someone understands why I had to break up with her!"

THE CHATTY ENGLISHMAN

That night, I went to Titanic for the Fox's birthday party, where Grasshopper learned Lesson #1 about Englishmen: They won't shut up. The Titanic is a perfect London restaurant — loud, full of drunk people, and so large that you basically have to scream to have a conversation. Of course, this isn't a problem for the Englishman. Let me explain: In New York, women have to "entertain" straight men. We have to read newspapers and magazines or go to movies so we can have "conversational gambits." Otherwise, the man will a) just sit there, b) talk about his psychological problems, or more likely, c) winge on and on about his career. On the other hand, American men are great in bed, and Englishmen supposedly are not. In fact, I'm convinced there's a direct correlation between talking too much and being bad at sex.

At the bar, I met a man named Sonny Snoot, an extremely good-looking hairstylist.

"Great color," he said. When I looked at

him blankly, he said, "Your hair. You must be American. From New York. They just seem to know how to do that great ashy blond."

"I'm just happy that I have all my hair," I said. And then I laughed, "Har, har, har," and he laughed, "Har, har, har," and before you could say "blowjob," he was yapping about sex.

"This is the way it is," he said. "If sex is number one in Italy, it's number seven in London. If sex doesn't fall a man's way, he'll go off and do something else. But men *talk* about sex all the time. In fact, one of the reasons to *have* sex is to *talk* about it the next day. And we talk about it in minute detail and make the story really good.

"Sometimes," he continued, "you get the urge to talk about sex while you're actually doing it. For instance, if you're doing a weird position, you kind of want to call your mates on your cell phone and say, 'Guess what I'm doing now?' "

"Oral sex," I suggested.

"Oh no," Sonny said, shaking his head. "The Americans, they're all very horny. But we don't do that here."

At dinner, I sat next to Peter, a magazine editor. Peter's girlfriend had just moved in with him, and he couldn't stop talking about how happy he was. "We've known each other for ten years, of course," he said. "But one morning, when she was going back to her apartment, she just said, 'I think we should move in together.' And as soon as she said it, I knew she was right. So now we've bought an apartment together. Englishmen don't patently object to marriage or commitment the way American men do," he said proudly. "It's very easy to find a relationship here."

Yeah, if you've got ten years.

"Of course, I don't know what it would be like for an American woman," he continued. "You know, American women are neurotic about their careers, while Englishwomen are only neurotic about sex," he said, as if this were a good thing. "Englishwomen don't like it. Well, maybe they would like it, but they think that men are only after the one thing." Maybe it was the champagne, but Peter seemed to be getting what the English call "stroppy." "Englishwomen suffer from this half-baked feminism. They think they're really open about sex, but then — aha — they find out they have the same hang-ups their mothers did."

"Well, maybe there's a reason for that," I ventured. "Maybe if you'd stop talking —"

Peter cut me off. "Women here think that

any adventure in the bedroom is only for male pleasure!" he said triumphantly.

The chatty Englishman problem continued to plague me to the nightclub China White, where I attempted to take refuge in one of the private Moroccan-style rooms with my friend Sophie, who worked in documentaries and lived in Notting Hill. I had just settled against the cushions with a bottle of vodka when I looked up and noticed a tall, dark-haired, shockingly good-looking man. Although these kinds of things supposedly don't happen in London, the man came over and sat down next to me. And then — so much for "English reserve" — I swear to God, he immediately launched into a conversation about sex.

"Everybody thinks it's the man's fault that women don't have orgasms. Why can't they just have them like . . . like men?" he demanded.

"Actually, they can," I said, wondering if perhaps this was a come-on, and if so, what I should do about it.

"Oh yes. They're always saying they can, but then you're in bed with a woman, and she's just lying there like she's doing you a favor. . . ."

"Now, where I come from, we sort of got over that in the sixties," I was saying, when suddenly Sophie jumped in.

"Oh please," she snapped. "Don't listen to him. The first thing an Englishman does in bed is to try to flip you over. Because that's how they're used to having sex. And they all say Englishwomen can't give good blow jobs. But it's only because they're used to getting them . . . from boys!"

Sophie and the good-looking, dark-haired man sat glaring at each other. I wouldn't have minded this, but I was sitting between them, and I really wasn't in a mood to get clocked by a wayward punch. Luckily, at that moment The Fox poked his head in.

"Ooooh. Hello, Simon," he said, as his eyes narrowed. "Haven't seen you for a while."

"Right. Well, I'm . . . I'm having a baby," Simon said.

"Good for you. Then maybe you can stop chatting up my date!" The Fox grabbed my arm and pulled me out of there. "Listen," he said. "I spend most of my life with people who know fuck-all about fuck-all and deserve to be kicked to death. Most people are complete scum. Most people need someone to explain to them that their very existence is a nuisance!"

The Fox continued in this vein until we reached his house, where he insisted that I stay up with him until six in the morning, listening to obscure American cowboy music. And talking about it. At this point, I realized I needed to sleep. I also realized that the only way to get The Fox to stop talking was to drug him.

Yes, I'm very sorry to say that I actually tried to slip Xanaxes into The Fox's glass of wine. Unfortunately, it all got mixed up, and I ended up passing out instead.

When I woke up the next afternoon, there was a note at the bottom of the bed: "Darling, never mind Shakespeare, I'm in love. Still crazy after all these hours. Love, The Fox. P.S. I didn't touch you."

Englishmen are just . . . so . . . sweet!

CASUAL SEX? I DON'T THINK SO . . .

I spent the next few days going to lunches and dinners and nightclubs. The thing that's kind of weird about London is that even though people say they have jobs, no one ever seems to get any work done. I mean, how can they, when lunch begins at noon and goes until four o'clock? And usually involves several cocktails and a couple of bottles of wine?

And then that Miranda person snuck into The Fox's apartment and really did steal all the lightbulbs. So when I had to get dressed to go out at night, I had to do it by feel.

And then there was no hot water.

And then I remembered that I was actually supposed to be doing something, like working, so I called my friend Claire.

Claire is an interior decorator — has been for five years, ever since her second husband ran off with her best friend. Claire is the only truly single girl I know in London. Meaning she hasn't had a real boyfriend for three years. Which pretty much makes her an honorary New York woman in my book. But unlike most New York women, Claire has already been married twice. And she's only thirty-seven. Did she really have that much to complain about? "Let me put it this way," she said. "I haven't had sex with anyone new in over a year. I've only had sex with old boyfriends. Which everyone knows doesn't count."

We agreed to meet at Soho House, one of these private clubs where people go in lieu of restaurants and bars.

I looked around at the clumps of men and women, all of whom seemed to be in their late twenties and thirties, and all of whom seemed to be dressed in varying shades of gray or black clothes that looked like they'd been plucked out of the dirty-clothes hamper.

Right away, I realized I just wasn't getting the clothes bit right — I was wearing a Dolce & Gabbana coat with a cranberry fur collar. Everyone was drinking and laughing, but it didn't look like people were trying to pick each other up. "God," I said. "I feel like a desperate single woman."

Claire looked around wildly. "Stop it. Don't ever say that. Women in London are not desperate. People don't understand things like that here. They'll think we're serious. We don't have men because we don't want to."

"We don't?" I said.

"No." She took in what I was wearing. "And take that off," she said. "Everyone is going to think that you're a prostitute. Only prostitutes wear designer clothes. With fur."

O-kay. "Cocktail?" I asked.

"You know me," Claire said. "Oh, by the way. I've decided to become a housewife. But without the husband or kids. Did I tell you about this fabulous floor waxer I just bought? Secondhand, but it's lovely. I don't think you can get things like floor waxers anymore."

At the bar, we ran into Hamish and Giles, two Notting Hill media types whom Claire knew. Hamish had a sweet face like a baby and was in a dither over his romantic life: He was trying to decide whether or not to marry his girlfriend.

Meanwhile, Giles said that he might have to swear off casual sex because he kept running into women he'd slept with, and things were getting "complicated."

Ah. Casual sex. Now we were getting somewhere.

Or so I thought.

"The worst thing about casual sex is the cats," Giles said. "All these single women have cats!"

"Can we talk about my girlfriend?" Hamish asked. "I don't know what to do. She's threatening to leave . . ."

"Cats are the ultimate put-off," Giles said. Obviously, he'd had the girlfriend discussion a few too many times. "Once I was thinking about seeing a woman, and Hamish said, 'Giles, don't be ridiculous. She has a cat.' It's not the cats, so much, but the way they talk about the cats. 'Ooooh, look at little Poo-Poo.' It's disgusting." Giles took a sip of vodka. "I haven't mastered the relationship thing. But I'd prefer to have a girlfriend. In London, we don't have dates. We just go out together. And in London, a snog is a down payment on a shag. Once you get down to snogging, you know you're in. In New York, that isn't true."

I agreed, pointing out that in New York, it was entirely possible to kiss someone and then say, "See ya," and never see him again. And if you did see him again, it was considered good form to pretend that the snog never happened. This rule also applies if you have gone further than the snog and have actually shagged.

"Oh, here we have this fake kind of chivalry," Giles said. He seemed a little bitter about it. "The next morning, guys will say, 'Thanks very much. It was a lovely shag,' but it doesn't really mean anything."

"I'll tell you everything about sex if someone will please tell me what to do about my girlfriend afterward!" Hamish said.

We all looked at him.

"Well, British men have this bad rap for being crappy in bed," Hamish said, somewhat desperately. "But I think we're getting better at it. We try to have some foreplay and we will, you know, perform oral sex. I've tried to get better in the sack. I read my mother's women's magazines to find out what to do."

"Yeah, but they don't show you pictures of a clitoris!" Giles said.

This comment was so pitiful, I didn't know what to say.

"I can't do the casual sex thing because I fail at the post-post-coital portion," said Hamish. "Should you call? What do you say if you do call? I haven't gotten to that part of the manual."

"You pray for an answering machine," Giles said.

"Inside, I'm really a trembling mess," Hamish said. "I'm not good about being friends with women afterward, which is stupid, because if you *are* friends, you leave the door open for a shag six months later."

"The whole thing is just too fucking complicated," Giles said. "Now I'm trying to only shag girls I think I might want to have a relationship with. It's important to be choosy. Besides, I want to have kids. In fact, I'm desperate to have kids. I've wanted to have kids since I was about sixteen."

"That reminds me. I have to go home. To my girlfriend," Hamish said.

"What's with this marriage and kids bit?" I asked.

"How should I know?" Giles said. "That's the thing about Englishmen. We're not very analytical. We don't go to shrinks." He paused, then looked at Claire. "Hey. Don't you have cats?" he asked.

We left.

"See what I mean?" Claire said. "London

421

is just impossible. I would go to New York, but I'm afraid to fly. Why don't you come over for a nightcap, and I'll show you that new floor waxer?"

And then I got the phone call. From this Judy person. My supposed editor at the newspaper. That was paying me to write this stupid story. I had to have lunch with her the next day.

Judy was, to my mind, a "typical" Englishwoman. She had long, stringy brown hair and a pale face and wore no makeup. She drummed her half-bitten fingernails on the table. She was a no-nonsense kind of gal.

"Well," she said. "What have you found out about sex in London?"

"Mmmm . . . er . . . can I have a cocktail?" I asked hopefully.

She nodded to the waiter. "So?" she demanded.

"Frankly," I said, "I've never been anywhere where the sexes are so disparaging about each other. When it comes to, ah, actual sex."

"Meaning?"

"Oh, it's just that . . ." I looked at her and thought, Hang it. "It's just that Englishmen say that Englishwomen are terrible in bed and vice versa."

"Really?" she said. "Englishmen say that

422

Englishwomen are bad in bed?"

I nodded. "They also say that English-women don't know how to give blow jobs." I examined my naturally perfect nails. "What is this obsession with blow jobs, anyway?"

"Public schools," she spat.

"They also say that . . . Englishwomen are hairy and don't care about how they look."

Judy leaned back in her chair, folded her arms, and regarded me smugly. She was scaring the shit of out of me. No wonder Englishmen are a dithering mess.

"Englishwomen are not like American women. That's true," she said. "We don't care about things like coloring our hair. Or our nails. We don't have time to get our nails done here. We're too busy."

Oh, I thought. Like American women aren't?

"Men and women understand each other here." She gave a short laugh. "Englishmen understand that we're all they've got. In other words, they're stuck with us. And if they don't like it, well, they get no sex at all."

"That might be a good thing," I said. "For you, I mean."

She lit a cigarette. Smoke came out of her nose. "It seems to me that maybe you haven't been doing your research."

"Now listen," I said. "I'm perfectly willing

to be reasonable about this, but —"

"That's not good enough," she said. "You're going to have to find an Englishman, a real Englishman, and you're going to have to shag him. And don't call me until you do!"

Oh dear. All I could think about was my poor bottom.

II

There's only one thing better than being single, American, and in London over Easter weekend. And that is being single, American, in London, and in love over Easter weekend.

I wasn't planning to fall in love. Okay, I thought I was, but I didn't really think it would happen. Especially since I'd met dozens of men, and although they were all very charming and amusing and would talk about things New York men wouldn't, like novels, I hadn't found one of them appealing enough to go to bed with. To tell you the truth, they all looked a little . . . grubby. You got the feeling that if they took their clothes off, you might find something you really didn't want to know about.

Plus, this assignment was beginning to drive me crazy. I knew it was, because two days earlier, Grasshopper had apparently checked into the Halcyon Hotel in Holland Park at three in the morning. It's all pretty much a blank as to how she got there and what happened after she did, but it appeared that she had eaten a hamburger, and that somehow, in the past forty-eight hours, she had become a complimentary member of three private nightclubs. Apparently, she had also done something to the staff at the hotel, because every time one of them saw her, he or she would look at Grasshopper with a terrified expression and scuttle away.

See what I mean?

In fact, I was looking forward to the fact that everyone was going away for the weekend. I was planning to take long walks and look at the cherry blossoms and the short white buildings that were everywhere. Even without a man, London was a romantic city: unlike in New York, you could see the sky, and at night there was a full moon. When you walked down the street, the people in the coffee shops looked interesting, and at the sandwich shop on the corner, the lady behind the counter said she liked my shoes. A young man came in with flowers, and she bought some. We looked outside and a funny car was passing, a car that was half boat that you could drive into the river.

Anything can happen, I thought.

But I still had to complete that stupid assignment.

The night before, I had gone trolling at a party at the restaurant MoMo with The Fox. The Fox had promised that it would be a party crowd, as opposed to a posh crowd, which would be much better. All it really meant was that Tom Jones, the singer, was there with his bodyguards.

A pretty girl with half-closed eyes and a short flowered skirt walked by. Sonny Snoot was following her. "It's so funny to see a posh girl trying to be trendy," Sonny said. "Upper-class girls don't know what style is. They don't even know about Prada. But you know who's worse?"

"Who?" I asked.

"Upper-class guys. They don't know anything about women. They don't know how to treat a woman."

"Basically, the longer the name, the worse the person," The Fox said.

"And the worse they are in bed," Sonny said.

I had to ask the inevitable question: "Is it true that they keep their socks on?"

"Only in Chelsea," The Fox said.

Then Claire came in. "I hate the upper classes and I hate the lower classes. I only like the middle classes."

"I hate anyone who lives in Notting Hill," Sonny said. "Even though I live in Notting Hill."

All this was a bit too much for me, so I went to Notting Hill, to a tiny club called World, where there were rastafarians and a really, really dirty-looking Englishman who was dancing by himself. My old boyfriend, Gerald the Suffocator, was there with his friend Crispin. They were drinking vodka out of tiny plastic cups.

"Babes!" Gerald said. "What were you doing at a party in *Soho?* You've got to be in Notting Hill. Or even better, Shepherd's Bush. It's all happening in Shepherd's Bush. We're the new bush-geoisie!"

"I can't stand the people in Notting Hill," Crispin said sullenly. "They live wild lives, and they all say they don't want to get married, but then they do. And they all say they don't have any money, but then you see them driving a bloody Mercedes!"

"Excuse me. But aren't *you* getting married?" I said.

"He lives in Shepherd's Bush. So it's okay," Gerald said.

"Whatever you do, don't go out with one of those Chelsea types," Crispin said. "They're all upper class, and they engage in Gothic sex."

Gothic sex?

"I slept with an aristocrat once," he said. "And she could only come if she pretended I was her horse." Crispin drank my cocktail. "I didn't neigh or anything, but I had to go along with it."

"Well, I'm supposed to have sex with someone, so I might as well have sex with one of those Chelsea men."

"They've all got small willies and they're impotent," Crispin said. "It's something in the water. The entire water system in London is polluted with female hormones."

"Aha," I said. "So that's why Englishmen talk so much."

And that was why, secretly I suppose, I was walking around Chelsea on Good Friday. I was looking for one of those Chelsea Englishmen — a guy who had sex with his socks on, possessed a microscopic willy, and came in two minutes. Or less. Not that I was really looking forward to it or anything.

I was walking by Joe's Café when I bumped into Charlie, a man I'd met a couple of days before at the bar Eclipse. Which was also in Chelsea. Charlie was one of those Englishmen who was divorced but still wearing his wedding ring.

"I've been trying to reach you for days," he said. "You must come and have lunch.

I'm meeting The Dalmatian." The Dalmatian was not a dog but a person, a freckly English lord. "And this other chap might come too," he said. "Rory Saint John Cunningsnot-Bedwards."

"One of the long-names," I said.

"What's that? Oh right," Charlie said. "He's a very, very funny chap. Very, very English. I don't know him that well, really just met him last night at China White, but he's very amusing. I thought he might be good for your research. He's so very English, you see."

"How perfect," I said, for some reason picturing this obviously horrible St. John Cunningsnot-Bedwards person as being, short, fat, bald, and somewhere around the age of fifty.

I was only about half wrong.

Charlie and The Dalmatian and I were sitting, drinking Bloody Marys and smoking cigarettes when the Rory chap made his entrance. He swaggered into the restaurant with that kind of self-absorbed energy that forces people to look at you. He was in his thirties, slim, dressed in jeans and an expensive suede coat, and even though he was a little bit bald, he was beautiful in the way that Englishmen can be and Americans never are. Okay, he was damn good-looking, but also horrible.

"Right then," he said. "You must be the American."

"Yes," I said. "And you must be the Englishman."

He sat down. "And what are we talking about?" he asked, lighting his cigarette with a silver-encased Bic. He was very precise in his smoking.

"What do you think we're talking about?" I said.

"I have absolutely no idea," he said. "I have just arrived and wish to be informed as to the content of the conversation."

As it just so happened, The Dalmatian was in the middle of a story about how he once had sex with his old girlfriend in a steam room in Germany, and there were other men in the steam room, but they couldn't see who was having sex and it was driving them crazy.

"Sex," I said.

"The most overrated activity in the universe," he said. "I mean really. I find sex so boring. The repetition of it. In. Out. In. Out. You're in and then you're out. After two minutes, I want to fall asleep. Of course, I'm known for being terrible in bed. I've got a tiny willy, about half the size of my little finger, and I come almost immediately. Sometimes before I say hello."

"You're perfect," I said.

"I know that, but I have absolutely no idea why you should know that."

I smiled.

"I've heard you're doing research on Englishmen," he said. "I shall tell you everything you need to know right now. The English are a fierce warrior race . . ."

"I wasn't aware that the English were, exactly, a race," I said.

"I think you two should have dinner," Charlie said.

"YOU'RE GAY!"

The Dalmatian offered to drive me to my friend Lucinda's house after lunch. The Rory person agreed to come along. The car was a two-seater.

"I hope you don't mind," I said. "Obviously, I'm going to have to sit on your lap."

"I don't mind at all," he said. "In fact, I shall enjoy it."

I sat on his lap, and he put his arms around me. The thing about Englishmen, this type of Englishman, anyway, is that you never know where you are with them. "You can put your head on my shoulder if you want. It's more comfy," he said. He began to stroke my hair.

Then he whispered in my ear, "The thing I like about you is that you're always observing things. Like me."

Lucinda lived in Chelsea. I jumped out of the car and ran up the steps to her white house. I was shaking a little. "Darling!" I said.

"Oh *darling*," Lucinda said. She had just gotten married to a paleontologist and was decorating her house, looking at samples of fabric.

"I think I've met a man," I said.

"Darling. That's marvelous. What's his name?"

I told her.

"Oh, he's lovely. But darling," Lucinda said, looking at me. "I've heard he's really bad in bed."

"I know," I said. "That was the first thing he told me."

"Well, if he told you, then that makes it okay." She hugged me. "I'm so happy for you. And don't worry about it. All Englishmen are bad in bed."

I went to Rory's house for dinner. I couldn't decide what to wear, so I wore my combat pants. I was nervous. And who could blame me? I had never deliberately had sex with a man who had a willy the size of a little finger before.

"Calm down," he said airily. "Everything's going to be okay."

"I like your apartment," I said. It was filled with overstuffed couches and armchairs and antiques. It had a fireplace. There was quite a bit of chintz, but I didn't think that much about it, because most English people who live in Chelsea have chintz.

"Oh yes," he said. "It's terribly . . . *cozy*, isn't it?"

Then we drank champagne. American men almost never drink champagne because they think it's kind of a sissy drink. Then we put on music and danced madly. American men almost never dance. And then it hit me.

Ohmigod, I wanted to scream. You're gay!

Of course. The champagne, the dancing, the chintz . . . the only men who were like that in New York were . . . *gay*.

I turned down the music. "Listen," I said. "There's something important I have to talk to you about."

"Yes?" he said.

"You may not be aware of this . . . in fact, chances are that you've probably been wondering yourself why it is that you don't like sex with women . . . but honestly, I think you're gay," I said. "And I think you should admit it. I mean, wouldn't you be much happier if you were out of the closet?"

"I have considered that very possibility," he said slowly. "And I have come to the conclusion . . . that I am not gay."

"Gay," I said.

"Not gay," he said.

"Look here. You don't like sex," I said. "With women. You don't like sex with women. Hello? What does that tell you? Of course, I don't mind at all. You seem like a very nice man, and —"

He said, "I'm not gay." And then, "I know you're going to kiss me."

"I'm not going to kiss you," I said.

"You are going to kiss me," he said. "It's only a matter of time."

Three days later, we got out of bed.

BABY'S PUDDINGS

I went to see Sophie in Notting Hill. Sophie was getting married and was stuffing her wedding invitations in envelopes. "I'm with a man in Chelsea," I said. "I've been with him for five days. We take baths together and sing."

She sighed. "It's always like that with Englishmen in the beginning. How is he in bed?"

"Great," I said.

"Well, they can be great at the beginning. That's what they do to woo you. But then they just stop caring. One of my girlfriends says her husband goes in, out, in, out, and then he comes."

"We'll see," I said.

"Maybe you'll get lucky," she said. "But in general, men in London are not a good bet. I'm only getting married because I've known my fiancé for ten years. But other than that, the men want to get married and career women don't. It's a much better deal for the man than it is for the woman."

Sophie made us vodka tonics. "Englishmen just don't do anything. They're lazy. They make absolutely no effort. The woman has to do everything. And she has to pay for half of everything. The house, the car, the food. . . . All the man wants to do is hang around."

"Do they, uh, watch *Kung Fu* videos?"

"Oh God no. They're not that stupid. But they do want you to make them baby's puddings all the time."

"Baby's puddings? You mean . . . *baby food?*"

"No. You know. Dessert. Apple crisp."
Oh.

I went back to his house. "Do you want me to make you baby's puddings?" I asked.

"Oh Minky," he said. "What's a baby's pudding?"

"You know. Apple crisp," I said.

"Well, yes, actually. I like apple crisp. Do you want to make me apple crisp?"

"No," I said.

"Okay, well, how about an egg?"

We spent two weeks together. We rode around London on his Vespa and tried to go to bed early every night, but then we'd lie there from one to four in the morning, talking. He told stories about how he'd been caned at Eton and how he once tried to stuff his nanny in the toy closet.

"I'm confused," he said. "I have all these 'L' words swirling around in my head. 'U-S-T' and 'O-V-E.' "

I wanted to say, Well, hurry up and make up your mind, but I wasn't in New York.

"Do you want to meet my friends?" he asked.

His friends were Mary and Harold Winters, and they lived in a big house in the country. It was, I suppose, the sort of life that every single woman who's spent too many nights alone in a tiny apartment in New York City dreams of: your own house with space, dogs, children, a Mercedes, and a jolly, adorable teddy-bear husband. When we walked in, two tow-headed children were helping Mary shell peas in the kitchen. "I'm so pleased you could come," Mary said. "You've arrived at just the right time. We're having a moment of calm."

All hell broke loose after that.

The rest of the children (there were four of them altogether) came galloping in, screaming. The dog pooped on the carpet. The nanny cut her finger and had to go to the clinic.

"Do you mind giving Lucretia her bath?" Mary asked.

"Which one is that?" I asked. All the children had names like Tyrolean and Philomena, and it was hard to tell which one was which.

"The little one," she said. "With the dirty face."

"Sure," I said. "I'm great with kids."

This was a lie.

"Come along, then," I said to the little creature, who was staring at me balefully.

"Be sure to wash her hair. And put conditioner in it," Mary said.

Somehow I got the child to take my hand and follow me up the stairs and into the bathroom. She took off her clothes willingly enough, but then the trouble began.

"Don't touch hair," she screamed.

438

"I'm going to touch your hair," I said. "Hair. Nice clean hair. Shampoo. Don't you want pretty clean hair?"

"Who are you?" she asked, rather sensibly, as she was naked in front of a complete stranger.

"I'm your mommy's friend."

"How come I never saw you before?"

"Because I was never here before."

"I don't like you," she said.

"I don't like you either. But I still have to wash your hair."

"No!"

"Now listen, you little rug-rat," I said threateningly. "I'm going to wash your hair and that's it. Get it?"

I squirted the shampoo on her head, and she immediately started screaming and thrashing about like I was murdering her.

In the middle of this fracas, Rory walked in.

"Isn't this fun?" he said. "Aren't you having a lovely time?"

"Lovely," I said.

"Hello, there, tiddlewinks," he said, waving to the child.

The creature screamed louder.

"Right ho. I'll see you downstairs, then."

"Rory," I said. "Do you think maybe you could give me a hand?"

"Sorry," he said. "Bathing children is women's work. I'm going downstairs to open a bottle of champagne. He-man in the kitchen and all that."

"You know, I really admire you," Mary said after dinner, when we were washing the dishes. "You're so smart. Choosing to have a career. And not being pressured to get married. That takes guts, you know?"

"Oh Mary," I said. She was one of those lovely Englishwomen of whom the Brits are so proud, with a beautiful oval face, clear fair skin, and blue eyes. "Where I come from, what you have is an achievement. A husband, this house, and four . . . adorable . . . children. That's what every woman wants."

"You're very kind. But you're lying," she said.

"But your children. . . ."

"Of course I love my husband and children," she said. "But half the time I feel like I'm invisible. If something happened to me, I wonder if they would even miss me. I know they'd miss what I do for them. But would they actually miss *me*?"

"I'm sure they would," I said.

"I'm not," she said. "You know, it's all a big fantasy. I wanted to be a painter. But I had the big white fantasy — that dream you have about your wedding day. And then it comes true. And then, almost immediately afterward, you have the black fantasy. No one ever tells you about that one."

"The black fantasy?"

"I thought I was the only one who had it," she said, wiping her hands on a dish towel. "But then I talked to a few other married women. And they had it too. You have this vision of yourself, all in black. Still young, wearing a big black hat, and a chic black dress. And you're walking behind your husband's casket."

"Oh dear."

"Oh yes," she said. "You have a fantasy that your husband has died. You still have your children and you're still young, but you're . . . free."

"I see," I said.

Rory and Harold came into the kitchen. "Can we help?" they asked.

"It's finished," Mary said pleasantly.

Rory and I took the train back to London. The next morning, I had to leave. It was time to go back to New York.

"Now listen, Minky," he said. "Are we going to be adults about this, or are we going to have tears?"

"What do you think?" I said.

"Good-bye, Minky," he said.

"Good-bye," I said.

"I love you," he said. "Go on. You'd better go now."

The petals from the cherry blossoms had fallen off the trees and onto the sidewalks. I walked over them, crunching them into the cement.

Oh God, I thought. Now what am I going to do?

Grasshopper says: Be sensible.

What I did, of course, was get into a cab and go to the airport.

But what did I really want?

I got on the plane and sat down in my seat. I took my shoes off. I opened a magazine.

A man sat down next to me. He was tall and dark-haired and slim, and he was wearing Prada trousers. He had all his hair, and an intelligent, interesting face. He opened a magazine. *Forbes.*

Now that's my type, I thought.

God, I was so fickle. I'd left Rory only two hours ago, and already I was thinking about another man.

What was it I wanted?

The story.

I wanted the story. I wanted the big, great, inspiring story about an unmarried career

442

woman who goes to London on assignment and meets the man of her dreams and marries him. She gets the big ring and the big house and the adorable children, and she lives happily ever after. But stories are not reality, no matter how much we might wish them so.

And that's not so bad.

Somewhere over Newfoundland, about two hours from JFK, the man next to me finally spoke.

"Excuse me," he said. "Sorry for asking, but you look somewhat familiar. Do you mind my asking what it is you do?"

"I'm a writer," I said.

"Ah yes," he said. "I do know who you are. You're that famous single woman who writes about single women and, er . . ."

"Sex," I said.

"That's right," he said. He opened another magazine. He seemed kind of shy.

"Excuse *me*," I said. "But you look kind of familiar. Do you mind my asking what it is *you* do?"

"Oh," he said. "I'm a businessman."

"I knew that."

"You did? How?"

"Your choice of reading material," I said.

Well, we did get to talking after that. And we discovered that we had practically the same birthday and had grown up in towns with exactly the same name — Glastonbury — although his Glastonbury was in England, and mine was in Connecticut.

"Well," he said, "it's not enough on which to base a relationship, but it's a good beginning. Would you like to have dinner tonight?"

We did have dinner that night. And eventually, one thing did lead to another. And now all I can say is that my friends are very happy for me, and my mother has been bugging me nonstop about flower arrangements.

But that, of course, is another story.

We hope you have enjoyed this Large Print book. Other Thorndike Press or Chivers Press Large Print books are available at your library or directly from the publishers.

For more information about current and up-coming titles, please call or write, without obligation, to:

Thorndike Press
295 Kennedy Memorial Drive
Waterville, Maine 04901 USA
Tel. (800) 223-1244
Tel. (800) 223-6121

OR

Chivers Press Limited
Windsor Bridge Road
Bath BA2 3AX
England
Tel. (0225) 335336

All our Large Print titles are designed for easy reading, and all our books are made to last.